ISBN 978-1-331-47129-5
PIBN 10194702

FB &c Ltd, Dalton House, 60 Windsor Avenue, London, SW19 2RR.
Company number 08720141. Registered in England and Wales.

For support please visit www.forgottenbooks.com

DEFENDER'S TRIUMPH

EDGAR LUSTGARTEN

WINGATE

FOREWORD

This is a book about four murder trials, in each of which the prisoner was acquitted. I do not suggest that any of them should have been convicted. I do suggest that *all* of them *would* have been convicted had they not been shielded by remarkable defenders.

There are those who believe that innocence is enough. All my experience teaches me the contrary. The machinery of the law is by no means infallible, and circumstances may conspire to such evil effect that only a great advocate can hope to challenge them.

The cases that follow seem to fall into this class. If Adelaide Bartlett, Robert Wood, Elvira Barney and Tony Mancini had been defended by barristers of merely average talent, I do not believe there would have been the same result. Only the exceptional brilliance of their counsel gained for them the verdict to which they were entitled.

It is not, perhaps, a very comforting reflection. But one cannot ignore disquieting phenomena that are liable to recur in any year of our own lives.

FOR

SYDNEY CARROLL

CONTENTS

Bassano

EDWARD CLARKE

VICTORIAN TRUMPETS

Edward Clarke defends Adelaide Bartlett

1

All through that winter of 1886 London had resounded with the Bartlett case. At fashionable dinner parties, at humble public houses, at female tea fights in the remoter suburbs, at masculine strongholds in the heart of the West End; in cafés, in waiting rooms, in shops, on omnibuses—everywhere this topic commanded pride of place. Competition contemporaneously was keen. The Government fell; unemployment riots spread; on Parliament's table lay the dynamite of Home Rule. But to those attracted by a human drama—and how many in any age are not?—these became matters of secondary interest. The general public, right through from Submerged Tenth to Upper Ten, found Adelaide Bartlett a more fascinating theme.

There was much to excuse this apparent aberration. Here was no ordinary hackneyed murder case, no tedious repetition of a thousand former crimes. It was more like some baroque literary concoction—as if one had crossed the Decameron with Don Quixote and seasoned the mixture with the Book of Kings. It involved a young wife who had wed her older husband on terms that were almost exclusively platonic; a husband who 'gave' his wife (whom he loved) to his friend (whom he loved also), enjoining them to marry after his own death; a clergyman, the donee of this unusual gift, who cherished for the wife a reciprocated passion; the husband's unexpected death in circumstances that perplexed and baffled the best scientific brains; the arrest of the wife, charged with her husband's murder, and of the clergyman, charged with being accessory thereto; the ugly and painful spectacle of the latter trying to save his skin at the expense of the former. Only the most exalted—or else the least perceptive—could have failed to gaze intently on this strange panorama as it gradually unfolded before coroner and bench.

When at last the hour of the full-dress trial drew near, popular excitement rose to fever pitch. One thing only remained to raise it even higher. Just as the most enthralling play calls for the glamour lent by a great actor, so the most absorbing capital trial calls for the presence of a great defender. Artistic instinct and desire for justice are equally insistent upon this.

For Adelaide Bartlett an advocate of the needful stature was forthcoming. Her solicitors, shrewd observers of the forensic scene, offered the leading brief to Edward Clarke. He accepted it, and in so doing assured her a defence that would rise to the challenge of an unparalleled occasion.

2

Edward Clarke was a perfect period piece. It is almost impossible to imagine him in any age except his own. He possessed to a degree that has never been surpassed the highest attributes of the noblest Victorians. So deep were his roots in that distinctive generation that he cannot be fitted, like most counsel of his eminence, into the prevailing dynasties of the Bar. Russell was the forerunner of Carson and of Hastings, Coleridge of Isaacs and of Simon. But Edward Clarke was the forerunner of nobody, just as he was nobody's successor. Like Gladstone and Millais in very different contexts, he was at once the product and the symbol of his time.

His prime characteristics were not of a description popularly associated with the pleader's craft. He neither had nor wished for what is commonly called worldliness; compared with most of his great rivals he was in some respects naïve. He had none of the arrogance or haughtiness of bearing that descends so readily upon successful advocates; his demeanour reflected a true modesty of the heart. His long and great career in a disillusioning profession never infected him with the slightest taint of cynicism; at the end he remained as he had been at the beginning, inviolate in his simple piety.

The chronicle of his life would have delighted Samuel Smiles. It tells of one who was born—to quote his own words —'in somewhat humble and difficult circumstances'; who was compelled by slender family finances to leave school early in his teens and become assistant at a little shop that was managed by his father; who occupied almost every leisure moment in reading hard or attending evening classes; who presently graduated from the little shop to the post of writer at East India House; who saved out of his salary till he had put aside enough to maintain him while he studied for the Bar; who embarked on that competitive vocation without resources or influential friends; who established so rapid and so rare a reputation that fifteen years later he was wearing a silk gown (and winning election to the House of Commons); who in 1886 became Solicitor-General; who in 1897 declined to become Master of the Rolls; who in 1908 was appointed Privy Councillor; and who in 1914, after half a century of continuous practice, was entertained to dinner by the entire Bench and Bar—a tribute and an honour without precedent in history.

The unaffected book in which Clarke subsequently recorded this remarkable progression would have afforded Smiles additional satisfaction. 'My chief reason for undertaking the task,' he wrote, 'is the wish that such a book may interest lads whose early lives are spent as mine was . . . and who may be encouraged by the story of my happy and successful life to be vigilant to find, and active to use, opportunities of self-improvement by study, by exercise of mind and body, by the habitual companionship of books, by the cultivation of worthy friendships.' And then, with his unfeigned humility, he added: 'As I write I am humbled by thinking how far my life has fallen short of my own ideals. Still I have not been consciously untrue to them; and perhaps the story of my life will help others to a fuller success.'

Despite his extraordinary catalogue of achievement, Clarke's place in the hierarchy of advocates is not altogether easy to assess. As a cross-examiner he certainly was not equal to Russell. As a lawyer he was not the peer of F. E. Smith.

As a tactician a good many have eclipsed him. But then it was as none of these that he excelled. Clarke's endowment was persuasiveness, and his weapon was the speech—not the smooth persuasiveness of wheedling or blandishment, but that powerful persuasiveness that springs from deep sincerity; not the speech of conventional court rhetoric, but the speech informed with the passionate eloquence of genius.

In complex, abstruse, or tricky litigation Edward Clarke might not invariably shine. But when he was concerned as a principal participant with the terrible simplicities that govern life and death, he had it in him to exert an appeal that sometimes bordered on the irresistible.

The Bartlett case presented him with such an opportunity.

3

Edward Clarke, like everybody else, had read newspaper reports of the preliminary proceedings. He was thus already acquainted with the salient features of the story. Although well accustomed to sensational cases (it was the trial of the Stauntons, nine years earlier, that had set the final seal upon his fame) Clarke did not find them pleasing or enjoyable. While some are fascinated by the scandalous, he was sickened and repelled. But there was one element in the Bartlett case which could not fail to attract his sympathy. Like Catherine Ogilvie before her and Florence Maybrick after, Adelaide Bartlett was a friendless woman, hounded by her husband's relatives, deserted by her erstwhile confidants, and by strangers often condemned unheard. Such circumstances operated to excite all Clarke's essential kindliness and compassion.

Having espoused Mrs Bartlett's cause, Clarke acted with characteristic conscientiousness. He was now an extremely fashionable leader; solicitors competed for his services; every term remunerative briefs piled high upon the table in his chambers. He had in fact reached the stage when it is not unknown for counsel to flit each day from court to court; here arguing a point of law, there questioning a witness, arriving elsewhere just in time to make a closing speech.

And though a murder case during its course exacts unremitting attention (especially from those engaged for the defence), busy barristers are often deep in other work right up to the eve of an arduous capital trial.

Not so Edward Clarke, who had his own canons of conduct. The defence of Mrs Bartlett was an immense responsibility; the odds were perilously poised and he could truly say that her life depended on her counsel's skill. All other matters must make way. He postponed some cases, returned the brief in others, and, free from all distraction, settled down to prolonged and anxious study of his client's story.

4

When a wife is charged with murdering her husband the story should begin not later than their marriage. Events, however violent, are seldom totally detached; their roots are to be found, and they themselves interpreted, by the light of personal history and relations. Thus one may sometimes learn *why* murder was committed. Thus one may sometimes learn *whether* murder was committed.

Adelaide Bartlett had married her husband Edwin, a prosperous provision dealer, on the 9th of April, 1875. She was then less than twenty years of age. The circumstances in which they met are not altogether clear, nor are those surrounding Mrs Bartlett's birth and upbringing. It would appear, though, that she was born at Orleans, the illegitimate child of a Frenchwoman and her English lover; that she was taken to England at an early age; that her father, reputed to have been a man of substance, provided liberally for all her needs; that she brought to the marriage partnership an ample dowry that was turned to good account by her husband in his business. In part perhaps through this accession of capital, in part without doubt through his own energy and exertions, Edwin Bartlett's enterprises steadily expanded during the ten years and nine months that composed his married life.

Mrs Bartlett (it may not be wholly irrelevant to state that her full maiden name was Adelaide Blanche de la Tremoille) was too beautiful to be pretty, too pretty to be beautiful. In a language that does not lend itself to the finer distinctions in feminine attractiveness, possibly the half-French 'piquant' comes closest to the mark. She had a slender, graceful figure, though somewhat lacking height; fine, very large and wide dark eyes; unusually heavy but trimly shaped black eyebrows; a pleasantly broad forehead; luxuriant hair that curled in upon the scalp; a strong straight nose with proudly arching nostrils; full lips over a smoothly rounded chin. A charming girl, to become a fascinating woman, baited with allurement for the hungry, youthful male.

At thirty, Edwin Bartlett could not be so described. Nor did the first phase of the union imply any undue extravagance of passion. Mr Bartlett had an almost mystical reverence for formal education, and though his bride was not lacking in the recognised 'accomplishments'—she played and sang and worked skilfully with her needle—he desired her to acquire at least the rudiments of scholarship. In acquiescent deference to his wishes, Mrs Bartlett started married life with the status of a schoolgirl. First at an English boarding-school, then at a convent abroad, she developed her talents and improved her mind, only returning to her husband for the holidays. It was three years before this strange routine was ended and a conventional domestic establishment set up.

These protracted and unorthodox preliminaries had no apparent untoward effect upon the couple's happiness. Mrs Bartlett was devoted to her husband; Mr Bartlett idolised his wife. There is not the slightest evidence that this bond of affection appeared broken, or even loosened, so long as they both lived. The Crown did not suggest it at Mrs Bartlett's trial. 'They seem to have lived,' said the Attorney-General, albeit somewhat grudgingly, 'upon fairly good terms.'

They were not, however, immune from stresses imposed on them by others. Trouble sprang early from a traditional source: the spite and animosity of relatives-in-law. Mr Bartlett's father, a coarse-grained old curmudgeon, with many of the unpleasing characteristics of the sponger, took instant dislike to the wife of his son's choice—mainly, one may assume without unfairness, because of her competing claim upon that son's munificence. This did not prevent him from making his home with them when Edwin unwisely invited him to do so. He stayed for some years in their household at Herne Hill, never shrinking from abuse of this abundant hospitality and weathering at least one serious dissension occasioned by his vicious hatred of his daughter-in-law. In this dissension, to his credit, Edwin did not temporise; he made it plain that his loyalty as a husband must take precedence of his duty as a son. Fearful of losing his free and favoured place, old Bartlett abjectly climbed down. It was not till 1883, when they moved from Herne Hill to East Dulwich, that the married pair at long last shook him off.

They stepped unknowingly towards far deeper shadows. In 1884 they moved again, this time to Merton Abbey, an agreeable spot between Wimbledon and Mitcham. In Merton High Street was a tiny Wesleyan chapel and Mr and Mrs Bartlett often attended service. The minister was a young man by name of George Dyson; he had soft, dog-like eyes, a long drooping moustache, and a wounded expression like that of a spoilt child. He did not look like one who could stand unbowed in adversity, still less sacrifice himself to save or shield another.

The Reverend Dyson in due course called upon the Bartletts in their capacity as members of his congregation. Mr Bartlett took to him at once; Mrs Bartlett was not unfavourably impressed. The triangular acquaintance ripened rapidly into friendship—a friendship that grew ever more intimate and close until death or catastrophe had fallen on them all.

5

Whether Mrs Bartlett ever became the Reverend Dyson's mistress it is impossible to say with anything like assurance. The balance of probability, in my view, points against it. But even if she did—and it could only have happened at a much later stage—it was certainly not she who encouraged him initially. Edwin Bartlett was the one who made the pace; who insisted on the Reverend Dyson's presence; who drew him within the tiny family orbit; who appointed him the constant companion of his wife. 'I want you to be her guardian,' he said. 'I know you'll be a friend to her when I am dead.'

Meanwhile Edwin Bartlett was very much alive, but he still had demands to make upon the Reverend Dyson's friendship. Who better than the latter to tutor Adelaide, to carry further forward still her cherished 'education'? So it came about that presently two, three, four or even five times a week the Reverend Dyson would present himself at the Bartlett home and, while the master was absent at his business, instruct the master's lady in a variety of subjects. There were no children to interrupt their studies; Mrs Bartlett had been once confined, in 1883, but after an agonising labour the baby was still-born. They therefore did their work in the style that pleased them best—in one instance at least, by the testimony of a servant, with Mrs Bartlett sitting on the floor and resting her head on the Reverend Dyson's knee.

Mr Bartlett knew how matters were developing; if not in detail, at any rate in substance. He did not object; on the contrary, he approved. 'Would that I could find words,' he wrote on one occasion, 'to express my thankfulness to you for the loving letter you sent Adelaide today . . . I felt my heart going out to you. Who can help loving you?' And when the Reverend Dyson, tormented by the pangs of a tender Wesleyan conscience, told Edwin that he had conceived an affection for his wife, and asked whether it would not be best to terminate the friendship, Edwin Bartlett countered with an indignant 'Why? I have confidence in you,' he said to the harassed minister. 'I shall be pleased if you will continue as friendly as before.'

The Reverend Dyson continued as friendly as before and Mr Bartlett loaded him with tokens of regard. He confided in him freely and often sought his counsel. He extended the scope of Dyson's future office from that of Mrs Bartlett's 'guardian' to that of second husband. He made a new will, naming Dyson as executor, and—as in his previous will—his wife as his sole heir. (It was said, but never strictly proved, that by this previous will Mrs Bartlett only benefited if she did not remarry. No such condition cramped the later document, which was to be in solemn fact Edwin Bartlett's final testament.)

The Reverend Dyson was flattered by his friend's respect, solaced by his bounty, attracted by his wife. His mild protest had been overruled and now he offered no further resistance. Wherever the Bartletts went, at Edwin's behest the Reverend Dyson followed. Did they contemplate a trip or expedition, then he must plan his cure of souls to make himself available. Did they take a summer holiday by the sea, then he must travel down—at their expense—to stay with them. Did they change their London dwelling, and depart from Merton Abbey, then arrangements must be made and expedients devised whereby the connection could be maintained intact.

And so early in October of 1885 Edwin Bartlett, mindful as usual of his friend's slender resources, bought him a season ticket between Waterloo and Putney in order that he might, without hardship to himself, continue to visit them after they had moved to their new town apartments in a house in Claverton Street.

By an odd irony the owner of this house was a Registrar of Deaths.

6

If today you were to pass through Claverton Street—it runs from Lupus Street to Grosvenor Road—you would find it typical of the seedy neighbourhood that lies between Victoria Station and the river. It is a neighbourhood that novelists like to label 'shabby-genteel,' though in fact it is not nearly so genteel as it is shabby; a neighbourhood that once enjoyed distinction and prestige, but has given up the fight and surrendered to decay. Plaster peels, woodwork rots, broken fanlights are filled up with boards; overshadowing all, and making it seem meaner, is the mammoth modern mass of Dolphin Square.

It is sad because much of the fabric is unchanged; the buildings of Pimlico are still mostly those that saw the district in its pride and heyday years ago. The face is ravaged, but the bones remain.

In Claverton Street itself there is a gaping bomb site now, to commemorate our generation's intellectual progress. Otherwise the houses stand exactly as they stood when the Bartletts occupied their suite at Eighty-five. The house has been converted since into several separate flats but, wear and tear excepted, shows the same front to the world. The windows are the same, and the steps, and the street door; above is the balcony of the Bartletts' drawing room. As you stand and gaze on this ordinary house that became the mise-en-scène of an extraordinary drama, it is possible to feel that the years have slipped away; to grow deaf and blind to the nearby radio and the intrusive motor car; to imagine oneself standing in the self-same place, watching the Victorian tradesmen vanish down the area, watching Mrs Bartlett peer impatiently from the window, watching the Reverend Dyson primly ring the bell, watching the doctors drive up in their sleek carriages.

Especially the doctors. Because a few weeks after they arrived at Claverton Street Edwin Bartlett started to be ill.

This was unusual enough to be disturbing. Mr Bartlett had always been a very healthy man. Some years earlier an insurance doctor had pronounced him a first-class life; otherwise he had had little truck with the medical profession. Lately, however, he had been greatly overworked and had sometimes complained about a feeling of fatigue. On the 10th of December he suddenly got worse; he felt so unwell that he lay prostrate on the sofa and agreed with his wife that a doctor should be called. She selected Dr Leach because his house was close at hand and it was obviously convenient to have a local man. Neither she nor Mr Bartlett had heard of him before.

Dr Leach was in no doubt about his patient's malady. It was mercurial poisoning.

This term need not be construed in its most melodramatic sense. It merely meant that Mr Bartlett had somehow taken more mercury than his constitutional idiosyncrasies would tolerate. But how did he come to take mercury at all? This was the point that puzzled both the doctor and the patient. Mercury is an antidote to a pestilent disease, but that disease had not afflicted Mr Bartlett. The only feasible solution lay in the latter's statement that recently, while feeling indisposed, he swallowed a large pill sent to him as a sample, without ascertaining what it was for or what ingredients it contained. A curious story, but the only one there was, and Dr Leach had no alternative but to accept it. Nor has anything ever come to light to suggest that in so doing he was wrong.

Dr Leach treated and prescribed for his new patient and the symptoms of poisoning rapidly cleared up. But the attack left distressing torments in its wake: weakness, depression, wearisome insomnia. A specially painful sequel related to the teeth; within fifteen days, at four separate sessions, Edwin Bartlett underwent eighteen extractions, and endured into the bargain bouts of toothache both violent and prolonged.

None the less, on an objective view, he gradually made progress and Dr Leach was not dissatisfied. He had no reason to regard the case as intrinsically grave; it was now a matter of rest and care and building up. The idea of getting a second opinion never crossed his mind until it was raised by the Bartletts themselves in words that could not fail to make their mark upon his memory.

It was the doctor's fifth or sixth attendance at the house. He had examined Mr Bartlett, found his state improved, and slightly varied one of the prescriptions. Preparatory to departure, he was exchanging general conversation with his patient when Mrs Bartlett suddenly broke in.

'Doctor, will you excuse what I am about to say?'

The doctor turned courteously.

'Mr Bartlett is very contented with your treatment,' she went on, 'but his friends have on more than one occasion requested him to let them send a doctor of their own choosing.'

'Yes,' Mr Bartlett added quickly, 'but we intend in future, doctor, to manage our own affairs and not to be interfered with by my friends and relations. I am sorry to say they are not kind to my wife.'

'By all means have a consultation,' said the doctor, who may have wished to stem the tide of family revelations. 'As many consultations as you like.'

'No,' Mr Bartlett said firmly. 'I will not see anyone they send, but I will see any gentleman you choose to bring to see me once. I do this for the protection of my wife.'

If Dr Leach was startled by this last remark he must have been dumbfounded by the next one.

'Doctor,' said Mrs Bartlett earnestly, 'if Mr Bartlett does not get out soon, his friends will accuse me of poisoning him.'

The 'friends' referred to existed only in the singular; it was cantankerous old Bartlett who had been round raising trouble, criticising the treatment, crying out for specialists. It was against him that Edwin sought to give his wife protection. It was he that Mrs Bartlett feared would welcome an excuse for taxing her with poisoning her husband.

Her fears were to prove depressingly well founded. But meanwhile the appropriate protection was invoked. Dr Leach invited to the house another physician, who duly confirmed his diagnosis and his remedies.

Any suspicions formed by Mr Bartlett's 'friends' seemed ludicrous when measured against Mrs Bartlett's conduct. Throughout these trying weeks she nursed her husband with unfaltering devotion, herself discharging the most repulsive duties, and foregoing whatever sleep could not be snatched in a chair or on a sofa by his bed. She did not hesitate to hazard her own health until she reached the pitch of near exhaustion. Her concern was deep, her toil unremitting, her affection manifest.

Until, in the last days of the fading year, came a strange and sinister sequence of events.

7

They followed each other, these events, with that metronomic timing seldom found outside a well-constructed play;

indeed they would fit better into the neat world of Sardou than into the untidiness of ordinary life.

On 27th December Mrs Bartlett saw the Reverend Dyson (who was still paying his customary visits) and privately asked him if he could get her chloroform. On his enquiring for what purpose, she told him that her husband had an internal complaint which was shortening his life and which periodically occasioned him great pain; that he was sensitive about the matter, would not discuss it, and would not be treated by anyone but her; that during severe spasms she could only soothe him and enable him to sleep by the use of chloroform; that she usually obtained it from a nurse named Annie Walker, but Annie Walker was at that moment abroad; that she was accustomed to sprinkle the chloroform on a handkerchief, and as it was highly volatile required a large amount—as much as would fill a medicine draught bottle. 'Can't you get it through the doctor?' the Reverend Dyson asked. 'The doctor doesn't know I'm skilled in drugs,' Mrs Bartlett said.

On 29th December the Reverend Dyson handed Mrs Bartlett a bottle of chloroform.

On 31st December Mr Bartlett seemed in better appetite and spirits; he had oysters for lunch, jugged hare for dinner, more oysters and some palatable accessories for supper; then ordered his breakfast with meticulous care. 'I shall get up an hour earlier,' he said to the maid, 'at the thought of having it.'

Nobody, save Mrs Bartlett, saw him again alive. Some time early on 1st January—or possibly late on 31st December—Edwin Bartlett died, in the presence of his wife, from a cause which the doctor could not ascertain. Mrs Bartlett was unable to enlighten him. The bottle of chloroform had disappeared for good.

The mere chronology spoke out for itself.

8

There was to be much more, though, than mere chronology thrown into the scales which were already being set up and in which the fate of Mrs Bartlett would be weighed.

Her own story was simple. She had fallen asleep, she said, in the chair by her husband's bed; she woke up in the middle of the night and found him lying on his face; she was shocked to find him stark cold, and tried to brandy; failing to bring him round, she roused and sent for Dr Leach.

Thus far unchallengeable. But soon suspicions mount. The Registrar landlord, on entering the room, detects a smell resembling ether, as well as that of brandy, in a wineglass on the mantelshelf, and—collecting data with official zeal—deduces that the fire has lately been built up. The landlord's wife, casting her mind back, recalls a conversation on the previous evening when Mrs Bartlett asked her if she had ever taken chloroform, and added that Mr Bartlett took some sleeping drops. 'Ten is a strong dose,' Mrs Bartlett said, 'but I would not hesitate to give him twelve.' Dr Leach, arriving post-haste from a broken sleep, cannot conceal his deep perplexity; not only is there no apparent cause of death, but there had been no reason to suppose the man was going to die. 'Can he have taken poison?' he enquires.

Only two points of light gleam through the cloud of doubts now gathering round the unhappy Mrs Bartlett. The doctor observes a bottle of chlorodyne on the mantelshelf. 'What is this doing here?' he asks. 'Oh, that,' says Mrs Bartlett; 'Edwin rinsed his mouth with it.' 'Rinsed his mouth!' exclaims the doctor. 'Then he must have swallowed some.' 'No, no,' says Mrs Bartlett; 'he only rubbed it on his gums.' She will not accept this plausible solution, she will not grasp the proffered chance to clear herself. There are no poisons that her husband could have had; none he could have got at without her knowledge. And—the second gleam of light—when Dr Leach bends over the corpse he notes the characteristic smell of brandy on the chest; on the chest, down which it would naturally trickle if feverishly pressed against the numb lips of the dead.

But none of this helped to solve the doctor's problem; reluctantly he refuses his certificate. 'Must there be an inquest?' Mrs Bartlett asks. 'I *ought* to report to the coroner,' says the doctor, 'but as I have no suspicion of foul play, we will have a post-mortem, and then, if the pathological cause of death is found, I will give a certificate in due course. . . .'

The post-mortem took place on the following afternoon. It was directed by an eminent pathologist and performed by his assistant, in the presence of Dr Leach and two other physicians. The first thing they noticed on opening the stomach was an overwhelming smell of chloroform—'almost as strong,' said one, 'as a freshly opened bottle.'

For nearly two hours they probed and searched without finding anything to account for death. The vital organs were all healthy. No injury was manifest. They could find, in medical phrase, no pathological lethal cause. There was nothing more that they themselves could do, except carefully preserve the contents of the stomach and patiently wait for a chemical analysis.

'They think it's chloroform,' Dr Leach told Mrs Bartlett. He was blissfully unaware of the dreadful implications. She, whether guilty or guiltless, knowing what she did, may well have been afraid.

9

There followed a period of tense, uneasy waiting—not for the public that were as yet hardly aware of the tremendous drama that was brewing, but for the principal actors in the piece, who were kept in a state of quivering uncertainty about the parts they would be called upon to play. After hearing only formal evidence, the Coroner adjourned his inquest for a month; various relics of the departed Edwin Bartlett were sent to the Home Office in packages and jars; the days went by, but no report was issued; and Adelaide Bartlett and the Reverend Dyson, chafed by the increasing burden of suspense, entered upon a train of conversations that altered their relationship for good and all. It was no longer a question whether he would lead her to the altar; only whether he would send her to the drop.

The Reverend Dyson did not know at first of the suspicions that the doctors had formed at the post-mortem.

Nevertheless he showed considerable apprehension. That very afternoon, as he escorted Mrs Bartlett from the shrouded room in Claverton Street to the home of friends, he asked her pointedly if she had used the chloroform. 'No,' she said. 'I have not had occasion. The bottle is there, just as you gave it to me.' As the Reverend Dyson still exhibited disquiet, she told him to dismiss the matter from his mind.

Any chance of his doing so vanished a few days later after he had had a talk with Dr Leach. The latter, acting of course in perfect innocence, freely disclosed to him the notes of the post-mortem. The reverend gentleman did not waste a minute. He hurried from the surgery straight to Mrs Bartlett. 'I have seen the doctor—I know everything,' he cried. '*Now* will you tell me; what did you do with the chloroform?'

Mrs Bartlett may have felt she had sufficient nervous strain without adding the catechisms of the Reverend Dyson. She certainly did not trouble to dissimulate her rage. She got up from her chair, stamped her foot on the floor, shouted 'Damn the chloroform!' and fumed about the room. But the Reverend Dyson was too frightened to be intimidated. He began to load her with querulous reproaches. She had told him that Edwin had an internal complaint; there was nothing about this in the notes of the post-mortem; she had told him that Edwin's life would be a short one. 'I did not,' snapped Mrs Bartlett. 'Alas!' exclaimed the Reverend Dyson, '*I am a ruined man.*'

In these five words may be found the key to the Reverend Dyson's subsequent conduct. Henceforward he had but a single thought: am I going to get mixed up in this, and, if so, how shall I stand in the opinion of the world? He spared not a moment's solicitude for the woman—the woman to whom he was admittedly attracted, the woman he had accepted as his wife to be, a woman who might well be free from any sin and yet was standing in the deadliest of perils. One might have expected even a less godly individual to be prompted by charity if not by affection. But no words of comfort or encouragement ever rose to the Reverend Dyson's lips. 'I am a ruined man'; that was the scope and measure of his spiritual nobility. It is possible to doubt whether Adelaide Bartlett was a deeply wronged woman; it is not possible to doubt that the Reverend Dyson was an egotistical and sanctimonious man.

The workings of his mind at this juncture are transparent. If *she* is accused of killing him with chloroform, and they find out that she got the chloroform from *me*, and they are able to prove that there is anything between us, then everybody will at once assume the worst. What, then, must I do? Watch my step very carefully in future, try to erase any evidence of the past.

What other interpretation can be placed on his request, made in the midst of such a stormy interview, that Mrs Bartlett should give him back his 'poem'? A stanza from this powerful and inspiring work is quoted by Sir John Hall in his valuable preface to the transcript of the trial:

'Who is it that hath burst the door,
Unclosed the heart that shut before,
And set her queen-like on its throne,
And made its homage all her own?—
My Birdie.'

The Reverend Dyson had presented this poem to Mrs Bartlett with all that its sentimental images implied. Mrs Bartlett now returned it without delay or cavil, apparently unimpressed by his literary gifts. . . .

Having safely recovered the incriminating paper, the Reverend Dyson gave free rein to his nonconformist feelings. Later that day he again saw Mrs Bartlett and told her he intended 'to make a clean breast.' 'I wish,' said Mrs Bartlett, 'you wouldn't mention the chloroform.' 'I shall,' the Reverend Dyson said, 'I am going to tell everything I know.'

He proposed to make this 'clean breast' at the inquest. But he was not called at the first hearing, nor at the second either, and meanwhile a new gravity had invested his intention.

Late in January the Home Office analyst completed his

report. On the 26th Dr Leach had just received it when Mrs Bartlett called. 'I have good news for you,' he said, with genuine satisfaction. 'Had it been one of the secret poisons which may be administered without the patient knowing, you would most certainly have been accused by some people of having poisoned him. But the government analyst says the cause of death was chloroform. That should set your mind at rest.'

10

The Reverend Dyson was as good as his word. When at last his turn came, he made a clean breast at the Coroner's Court. Repeatedly stressing how he had been deceived, he told the story of the chloroform in detail. The effect on the jury, who had already heard the Home Office analyst, was naturally and inevitably immense. When Dyson stepped down, they proclaimed their opinion that Mrs Bartlett (who, on the advice of her lawyer, had declined to give evidence) ought to be placed in custody forthwith.

A week later they met again and concluded their enquiry. A verdict of Wilful Murder against Mrs Bartlett was foreseen. But the Reverend Dyson did not, at this stage, escape with the whitewashing he had hoped and worked for. A verdict was returned against him also; his pastorless sheep in suburban Merton Abbey heard with dismay that he had been arrested and charged as an accessory before the fact.

This sharp series of detonating shocks projected the Bartlett case into that notoriety which was henceforth to be one of its distinguishing concomitants. Public debate became continuous, and in social exchanges to venture no opinion on the innocence or otherwise of the two accused was to confess oneself completely out of touch. About Dyson's complicity there were opposing schools of thought. About Mrs Bartlett there was a greater measure of agreement; on its first impact the clergyman's disclosure was to seem as decisive outside court as it had seemed within. Weighing what they knew as fairly as they could, before trial the majority were certain of her guilt.

Edward Clarke was now to form his own opinion. Having digested every detail of his brief, he pondered long upon their implication. In the austere surroundings of his chambers, or in the library of his house in Russell Square, he would pace to and fro with regular, slow tread; the fine brow furrowed, the firm lips set, the massive mind intent upon arriving at the truth.

Very deliberately he came to a conclusion. He believed that the popular judgment was at fault, and that he sustained upon his shoulders the burden of defending an innocent woman who bore every mark of guilt.

To the very end he never wavered in this view.

11

The defender was indeed faced with a formidable task. He could not challenge the findings of the analyst; he must fight on the footing that chloroform caused death. He could not challenge the substance of the Reverend Dyson's story because Mrs Bartlett did not challenge it herself. And yet their conjunction would assuredly prove fatal unless fresh facts were introduced by way of explanation.

Those were days before a prisoner could give evidence at his trial, so Mrs Bartlett herself could not be heard. She had, however, previously given an account—on 26th January when she visited Dr Leach; and the doctor, a principal witness for the Crown, was obviously bound to repeat it in the box. This, though, did little to improve the prospect. It necessarily dictated the trend of the defence, and Mrs Bartlett's explanation as it stood was much less likely to convince than to astonish.

It had astonished honest Dr Leach, for whom the interview provided a surfeit of amazement. He was almost stupefied at the outset when he found that Mrs Bartlett, instead of showing relief at the analyst's report, at once exhibited symptoms of distress and said: 'Doctor, I wish anything but chloroform had been found.' 'Why?' cried the doctor. 'What on earth do you mean?'

This brief question drew a very long reply. Mrs Bartlett

entered on a closely detailed statement going back to the beginning of her married life. She told Dr Leach of a platonic relationship that was interrupted upon one occasion only; of the happiness she enjoyed with her husband none the less; of his wish that, if he died, she and the Reverend Dyson should be married, and of his 'giving' her to Dyson with that object in view; of his subsequent and unexpected sexual overtures; of her reluctance to submit now she was 'practically affianced'; of her procuring chloroform with the misguided idea of waving it in his face and sending him to sleep on any occasion when he might be importunate ('If you had put that plan in practice,' Dr Leach observed, 'it would have been both dangerous and ineffectual'); of her uneasiness at having the chloroform in her possession ('I had never kept a secret from Edwin in my life') and bringing him the bottle on the night before he died, with a frank declaration of what had been her purpose; of his putting the bottle on the mantelshelf beside him; of them both going off to sleep; of her terrible awakening. Had she noticed whether much was missing from the bottle? 'No,' said Mrs Bartlett, 'I do not know.' Who had got the chloroform for her? She did not answer, and, said Dr Leach, 'I saw it was a question to which no answer would be given.'

This bizarre tale, verging on the unbelievable, formed the dubious base on which Edward Clarke erected one of the greatest defences in the history of our courts.

12

It was clearly a case in which the evidence of experts would play a large, perhaps a dominating, part. Though the cause of death had got to be accepted, much would depend on other scientific points: the effect of chloroform in different modes of application; its scope and limitations as an instrument of murder; the possibilities of administering it in sleep without the victim's knowledge and resistance.

Edward Clarke left nothing to chance. In the reading room of the British Museum he familiarised himself with the relevant literature, and when he had done, there were few in Harley Street whose knowledge of chloroform was greater than his own. Guy and Ferrier's *Forensic Medicine*, Alfred Taylor's *Medical Jurisprudence*, Dolbeau, Wynter Blyth, Wharton and Stillé, Woodman and Tidy, Quimby and Elliott—these and others were enquired into and mastered till even Clarke felt satisfied that his researches had been thorough.

Steeped in the facts, primed with technical knowledge, inspired by the conviction that his client was innocent—no advocate has ever been better equipped for a defence than was Edward Clarke when, on the first day of the trial, he walked into the packed and expectant Old Bailey and took his seat on leading counsels' row. He was a few minutes early, but that was intentional. 'I made a point,' he said afterwards, 'of being in my place every morning before the judge came in, so that when the fragile, pale little woman came up the prison stairs to take her place in the dock she should see in the crowded court at least one friendly face.'

13

Every eye was turned in that direction as the two accused, with their retinue of warders, slowly filed into the legendary dock. With the courtroom crammed and alert with curiosity, their bearing was subjected to a stern and painful test. They responded somewhat differently. Mrs Bartlett, in widow's black, looked drawn but perfectly composed; the Reverend Dyson displayed signs of strain and fidgeted uneasily. It was observed that, though he sometimes stole a covert glance at her, she gazed straight ahead as if unconscious of his presence. . . .

The customary awestruck hush accompanied the appearance of the judge. Though an extremely able lawyer and a recognised authority on circumstantial evidence, Mr. Justice Wills is now chiefly remembered for his brutal sentence upon Oscar Wilde, and the fierce, hysterical terms in which he couched it. He was indeed fanatically puritan, and the mere thought of sodomy deprived him of all balance. The Bartlett case, where the charge was merely murder, did not outrage his instincts to the same degree, and while often expressing horror and disgust, he tried it without prejudice or partiality. . . .

Before the trial opened, the Attorney-General (who was leading for the Crown) announced a decision that changed its shape and course.

Frank Lockwood, Q.C., counsel for the Reverend Dyson, had applied on his client's behalf for separate trials. The lawyers present had been expecting some such move. Statements by one prisoner are not evidence against another (unless made in the other's presence and hearing), but in a joint trial, when such statements are put in, it is hard to maintain that principle in practice. There was a risk that statements made by Mrs Bartlett might injure the Reverend Dyson. There was an even greater risk that statements made by him might injure her, and Clarke accordingly supported Lockwood's application.

It was all unnecessary. The Attorney-General rose, not to object nor to reply, but to apprise the court of an impending metamorphosis. 'After anxious and careful consideration,' he declared, 'we have come to the conclusion that there is no case to be submitted to the jury on which we could properly ask them to convict George Dyson, and after his arraignment we propose to offer no evidence against him.'

By this single sentence the Reverend Dyson was transformed—from prisoner himself on trial for his liberty to potential witness against prisoner on trial for her life. The onlookers were taken completely by surprise. They had got their first big thrill before they had expected.

For a moment the court rocked and murmured like the sea.

The judge was appropriately circumspect. 'I think,' he said, 'that the proper course, for every reason, is that I should reserve any expression of opinion until the case against the other prisoner has been investigated.'

The court moved through the long-established ritual. Both prisoners were arraigned; each pleaded not guilty; the jury were sworn and the prisoners given in their charge; the

Attorney-General briefly repeated his intention of offering no evidence against the male accused; thereupon the judge directed the jury that it was their duty to say at once that Dyson was not guilty; the jury's foreman stood up in his place and pronounced the formal verdict of acquittal.

The Reverend Dyson was free. Eagerly and thankfully he hastened from the dock, without a word or even a glance behind. No bond survived between his former love and him, and yet somehow his departure made her seem still more forlorn as she sat amid the gaolers to face her trial alone.

This was, on the whole, by no means a disadvantage, viewed coldly and heartlessly from the tactical point of view.

14

The Attorney-General, by virtue of his office, is titular leader of the English Bar. Since political considerations influence his appointment, he is not necessarily the country's leading counsel. The Attorney-General of this period, however, stood pre-eminent in every respect; he was not merely the Crown's chief law officer by preferment, he was also the Bar's outstanding figure by acclaim. For the rôle of Mr Attorney in April 1886 was filled by no other than the great Charles Russell, in the fullness of his powers and at the summit of his fame.

That the Bartlett trial involved a clash between Russell and Clarke considerably added to its fascination. Though not as yet upon the same high pinnacle, Clarke was rapidly climbing to a place in which he would be Russell's regular opponent, and with him would constitute the first of those famous pairs that have been such a striking feature of our courts. Like those that followed later—Carson and Isaacs, Simon and Smith, Hastings and Birkett—Russell and Clarke abounded in sharp contrasts. One was born for strife, one for conciliation; one was caustic and impatient, one courteous and suave; one relied on power, one upon persuasion. And yet each somehow avoided the defects of his qualities; Russell's brusque manner seldom alienated juries, and Clarke undoubtedly possessed an inner toughness that enabled him to defy adversity or fatigue.

When both men were at their best and given equal opportunities, Russell was beyond all question the superior. But in the trial of Mrs Bartlett only Clarke was at his best, and only Clarke could deploy the full range of his gifts. Russell's forte was cross-examination, but there was not a single witness for him to cross-examine. Moreover, no counsel can be at the top of his form if there is anything on his mind besides the case in progress, and the Bartlett trial happened to coincide with the first Commons reading of Mr Gladstone's first Home Rule Bill, in which Russell, as Irish nationalist and English politician, was patriotically as well as professionally involved. His long and tiring days in court were followed—and preceded—by equally long and tiring evenings in the House, and it is permissible to assume that even as he spoke of Dr Leach or Mrs Bartlett at the back of his mind hovered Morley or Parnell.

The effect on his performance as an advocate was marked. It became apparent in the early stages of his opening, which was neither so forceful nor so well-knit as his reputation promised. He was handicapped by imperfect acquaintance with the facts, being not infrequently pulled up by Clarke or prompted by his juniors. It is doubtful whether Russell ever made another speech in which the introductory phrase 'I think' occurred so often; he used it manifestly to insure against involuntary mis-statement.

But however much inhibited by uncertainty on detail, Russell was incapable of vague and cloudy speech. Though his opening was in no way memorable or brilliant, it furnished a clear outline of the prosecution's case. He gave a brief history of the Bartletts' marriage and established the Reverend Dyson's relation to the pair. He described how Mrs Bartlett had asked Dyson for the chloroform, and pledged himself to prove that her 'reasons' were all lies: Edwin Bartlett had had no internal ailment; neither that nor any other disease was shortening his life; she had never obtained chloroform from the nurse Annie Walker, nor had Annie

Walker ever been abroad. He pointed out that Mrs Bartlett only put forward the 'extraordinary story' that she told to Dr Leach after she had learnt of the analyst's report.

'And now,' said Russell, emerging with some relief from the complex web of fact, 'I come to what you will probably find is the real question in this case. You will probably have no difficulty in coming to the conclusion that the deceased died from the effects of chloroform, which chloroform somehow found its way to his stomach. *How did it get there?*'

How, indeed? Russell submitted that there were only three alternatives. It might have been suicide, but, he said, 'you will find nothing to support that suggestion. Edwin Bartlett was in returning health, in improved spirits, and before going to bed had made arrangements for his breakfast.' It might have been an accident, 'but it is in the highest degree improbable that, on putting the glass or tumbler to his lips, a man would not at once perceive the mistake that had been made.' And, Russell added, 'Taken with the intention of committing suicide or taken accidentally, the pain it would cause would be so acute that no amount of self-control which anyone can suppose to exist could restrain the paroxysms of pain, followed by contortion and by outcry and by exclamation, which could not have failed to attract attention.'

Russell frankly admitted that this must also be expected if the chloroform was administered by any third person. 'There would be the same outcry, the same acute pain, and so forth—provided that the administration into the stomach was not *preceded by some external application* of chloroform, which might lull into a stupor or a semi-stupor; and in that condition it might be possible—and in that condition alone, as the medical men think, probable—that it could be conveyed to the stomach without it being followed by circumstances and occurrences which must have attracted attention.'

Here, then, was the Crown's third and last alternative—the alternative of murder. The theory was that Mrs Bartlett had first, in the popular acceptation of the word, 'chloroformed' her husband until he was insensible, and afterwards poured liquid chloroform down his throat.

The Crown elected to stand upon this theory as the only one consistent with the facts.

15

The Attorney-General's speech occupied most of the first morning. During much of the afternoon Edward Clarke was cross-examining old Bartlett.

This Dickensian villain, part Quilp, part Silas Wegg, had made up his mind from the start that Edwin Bartlett had been murdered by his wife. Assiduously he worked to procure evidence. 'This cannot pass,' he had cried dramatically as he stood in the room of death with Dr Leach. 'We must have a post-mortem, doctor, a post-mortem.' While bestowing a father's last salute on the forehead of the corpse, he had cunningly sniffed the lips for the smell of prussic acid. He had tried the pockets of Mrs Bartlett's cloak before she departed in it from the house—an occasion on which the cynical old fraud made a point none the less of kissing her goodbye. ('It calls unbidden to one's lips,' his lordship was to comment, 'the name of Judas.')

Old Bartlett had done his best to get her charged. Now, there can be no conceivable doubt, he intended to do his best to get her hanged.

There was little of real substance in the evidence of Old Bartlett; he never touched the main line of the prosecution's case. He had set himself the task of fomenting suspicion, of building up an atmosphere, of conveying to the jury by a host of minor incidents that Mrs Bartlett's behaviour in itself bespoke her guilt. For instance, he was 'refused' (at her command) to see his son while he was ill; for instance, though he had particularly asked, she would not tell him who was his son's doctor; for instance, despite his earnest supplication, she would not call in a physician 'from London' to advise. 'We cannot afford it,' she had said. 'You had better afford it,' Old Bartlett had said amiably.

Such evidence, though without roots and inconclusive, if

allowed to stand unchallenged might influence a jury. Clarke did not intend to take the slightest risk. He had enough ammunition to annihilate Old Bartlett—and though this might not bear on any major issue, it would at least mean the defence had been launched under good auspices. The demolition of a witness, even a mere auxiliary, always benefits the side against whom he is called

Clarke rose to begin his cross-examination immediately the court reassembled after lunch. The air was electric, as it always is in any great trial at the first real clash of swords.

Clarke wasted no time in preliminary sparring; his opening questions struck straight at the heart.

'Mr Bartlett, I believe you were not present at your son's marriage to the defendant?'

'I was not.'

'Did you disapprove of that marriage?'

No attack was ever more direct. Old Bartlett played for time.

'I was not asked,' he said.

'Not asked to the marriage or not asked whether you approved?'

'I was not asked whether I thought she was suitable or not.'

'As a matter of *fact*, did you disapprove?'

Old Bartlett, who was anything but a fool and fully understood the drift of this, tried to make his answer noncommittal.

'Well,' he said, 'I did not much approve of it, but I did not disapprove of it.'

'Were you asked to the marriage?' Clarke enquired.

'No.'

'Why not?'

'Because they knew I was busy,' Old Bartlett answered.

The most gullible jury wouldn't swallow that. Clarke had established his first important point—that Old Bartlett had never been well disposed towards his daughter-in-law.

He proceeded at once to build on this foundation.

'When did you go to live with your son?'

'1877 or 1878.'

'Do you tell the jury that you enjoyed the complete confidence of your son and his wife after that time?'

'We lived on most friendly terms,' Old Bartlett said, but Clarke preferred to keep to his own wording.

'Do you say you enjoyed the complete confidence of your son and his wife?'

Old Bartlett—foolishly—plunged.

'I believe so.'

Clarke's face darkened in reprobation of the lie.

'Very soon after Mrs Bartlett came home to live with your son did you have to write an apology for the things you had said about her?'

'I signed an apology,' Old Bartlett admitted, 'but I knew it to be false.'

'What, sir?'

The ring in counsel's voice might have checked a cooler witness. But Old Bartlett was aflame with his own malice. He went on:

'When I signed the apology it was to make peace with my son. He begged me to sign it because it would make peace between him and his wife, and I did.'

Clarke spoke with the utmost gravity and distinctness. Each word fell separately into the hushed court.

'You say that, because it would make peace with your son, you signed that apology, *knowing it to be false?*'

'Yes,' replied Old Bartlett, hard-pressed but defiant.

'Did your son make use of that apology, and have it printed?'

'At her suggestion.'

'I should think so,' snorted Clarke, permitting himself one of his rare lapses into comment.

The cross-examination was not five minutes old, but already Old Bartlett wore a very different aspect. It was clear—all the more so from his efforts to conceal it—that his hatred for the prisoner was venomous and abiding. It was clear that his hatred did not merely lie dormant, but found a vent in backbiting or calumny. It was clear that he was not above affirming what was unveracious—for either the apology he had signed was false,or else he had lied in saying that it was.

One more question and the picture was complete.

'Have you entered a caveat,' asked Clarke, 'against the will in which your son left everything to his wife?'

'I have,' Old Bartlett reluctantly acknowledged.

So to the hatred and the lying had been added powerful motive—the most powerful that could operate on a man of such cupidity. Only Adelaide stood between him and his son's fortune. . . .

Having discredited the witness with admirable economy, Clarke now turned to his specific allegations, and these, too, soon assumed a different complexion. The old man had to admit that, though he had been 'refused' to see his son on one occasion, on at least one other he had been expressly asked to come—by Mrs Bartlett herself, in one of several letters that she wrote to keep her father-in-law apprised of Edwin's state. He had to recant his earlier assertion that he had 'particularly asked' for the name of Edwin's doctor. ('She seemed reluctant,' he told Clarke, 'to say much about the doctor.' 'Tell me what you asked her?' 'I didn't ask her anything.') He had to expand and clarify his story about the prisoner's unwillingness to take a second opinion; Clarke confronted him with a passage from another of her letters—'I am expecting another doctor, so you must excuse this note.'

'Take that letter,' Clarke said. 'Was it written before or after you had suggested a physician?'

Old Bartlett knew that he was tied down by the dates.

'Well, I suppose after.'

'When you saw Mrs Bartlett soon after that letter did you ask if the doctor had been?'

'They told me that he had.'

'Did you ask his name?'

'No.'

'Did not Mrs Bartlett tell you?'

'I won't undertake to say.'

'Was it not Dr Dudley?' Clarke said with sudden sternness.

'Yes, it was Dr Dudley,' Old Bartlett answered grudgingly.

There was nothing left now; neither credit nor character nor even trumped-up charges. The despicable old man slunk out of the box, conscious that he had wholly failed to promote his wicked purpose. 'Fortunately, as it seems to me,' Mr Justice Wills said later, 'very little depends on the evidence of the senior Bartlett. With the sole observation that, from the hour of his appearance after his son's death, Mrs Bartlett lived under suspicious eyes, I think I may dismiss him from the scene.'

16

That evening, back at home in his quiet library, Clarke could review his first day's work with modest satisfaction. The downfall of Old Bartlett had been crashing and spectacular; an event to rouse the feelings and stir the imagination. But Old Bartlett, after all, had been no more than an outrider. No one knew better than he who was defending that the Crown's main forces were yet to be engaged.

To dispose successfully of these main forces demanded a carefully calculated plan. In advocacy, tactics should be flexible and resilient, strategy almost always definite and fixed. The swift improvisations when new dangers develop, the dramatic counter to an unexpected thrust, the dazzling riposte to the damaging reply, the neat turning movement to protect a punctured flank—such agile and dexterous manœuvres, incomparably exciting in the throbbing heat of court, lack none the less a substance and a purpose unless integrated in a general design.

Having heard Russell's opening speech, sketching the Crown case, Clarke could project his own campaign with something like precision. Russell had said there were but three alternatives, and had then discarded two; Clarke would seek to show that one of the latter—suicide—was not at all unfeasible. Russell had admitted that the administration of liquid chloroform was extremely difficult; Clarke would seek to show that for the medically unskilled it was virtually impossible. Russell had cast scorn upon the explanation Mrs Bartlett gave to Dr Leach on 26th January; Clarke would seek to show, out of the mouths of others, that that 'extraordinary story' was substantially correct. (This was not the least important point, and maybe the most delicate. Juries seldom accept purely scientific evidence if it seems in conflict with everyday horse-sense. 'What did she want the chloroform *for*?' and 'Why did she *lie* to get it?'—these would be the questions preoccupying their minds; questions to which her answers, unless in some degree corroborated, invited rejection as outrageously far-fetched.)

Such were the lines Clarke laid down for himself, and which were to guide and govern his handling of the case through the swelling climax of the next five days.

17

The second day's proceedings were entirely dominated by the Reverend Dyson's appearance in the box.

The Reverend Dyson remains a constant puzzle. It is impossible to reconcile his conduct with his character. We know him to have been a weak, timorous caricature of a man, in love with himself and yet afraid of his own shadow—the last individual to play the smallest part in forwarding a plot to murder in cold blood. Assuming that the Crown case was well founded and that Mrs Bartlett wilfully took her husband's life, I should still be disposed to rule out any suggestion that the Reverend Dyson was privy to the crime.

And yet how furtive, how sly, was his behaviour at the time—ill-according with his subsequent displays of injured innocence. At every step he laid himself open to suspicion. He deliberately distributed the purchase of the chloroform, visiting three different local chemists' shops in turn. From each he bought a small amount, to each he told a lie ('It is for taking out grease stains,' he had casually remarked). At home he poured the aggregate into a larger bottle which he gave to Mrs Bartlett the following afternoon—gave it to her, not in the house at Claverton Street, but when they were out strolling on the Embankment by themselves.

Under the pitiless glare that beats upon the witness box the Reverend Dyson recounted these events. The judge did not conceal the effect it made on him.

'You were asked to purchase a medicine bottle full. Why didn't you ask for it straight out at the first chemist?'

'I do not remember,' said the Reverend Dyson wretchedly. 'I do not remember what was in my mind at the time.'

As at the inquest, so at the trial, the Reverend Dyson spared Mrs Bartlett not at all. While he had at the last moment regained status with the law, he had still to clear his reputation with the public and to re-establish beyond a shade of doubt his eligibility as a minister of God. If in so doing he destroyed Mrs Bartlett, that would be distressing but it just could not be helped. It was she, after all, who had brought this misfortune on him. . . .

'She asked me. . . . She told me. . . . I did what she wanted. . . . I was puzzled. . . . I was perplexed. . . . I was alarmed'—the exculpatory phrases poured forth in abundance. Incessantly the Reverend Dyson sang his brave refrain: It was she, not I; it was she, not I. Compulsively the spectators glanced from witness box to dock. Mrs Bartlett sat bolt upright and gazed into the void. . . .

When the Crown had finished examining the witness, and Edward Clarke rose to his feet, from the purely emotional point of view the case had reached its zenith. Mrs Bartlett's champion now came face to face with the man whose intervention had placed her where she was. His mode of giving evidence could have done nothing to mollify the prisoner's angry feelings, and many expected her counsel to exact a retributive penalty in cross-examination.

It would have been easy enough—easy to crush and blot out the Reverend Dyson if Clarke had been of such a mind. As in the earlier instance of Old Bartlett, ample material lay ready to his hand. An hour or two's questioning on certain hostile lines and the Reverend Dyson might have found few to believe that his association with Mrs Bartlett was platonic or that his purchase of the chloroform was free from bad intent. You are in holy orders, are you not? And expected to maintain a high standard of propriety? Do you consider it proper that you should regularly spend many hours as the sole companion of a young married woman? *I did not ask whether Mr Bartlett thought it proper, sir, but whether you did.* Then why did you do it? Is it usual for clergymen to act in this fashion? To comfort the wives of their absent congregants with kisses and embraces? Or to present them with love poems? Why did you buy the chloroform in three separate lots? Was it not to disguise the fact that the amount was large? Why should you try to disguise it if you thought the transaction was straightforward? What were you afraid might come to light? . . . The questions are easy to devise but difficult to answer, as the Reverend Dyson would have soon discovered. Like many a better man before and since, this selfish weakling would have learnt how frail a shield is innocence when folly, mischance and indiscretion have marked a human being for their own.

It was open to Clarke to send Dyson from the box broken, disgraced and ruined beyond repair. But how would this avail? Clarke's business was not to avenge his client's shabby treatment but to gain her acquittal on a capital charge. Unrestrained attack upon the Reverend Dyson would frustrate rather than promote this end. The more sinful he, the more sinful she; the more evil he knew, the more there was to know. By painting his situation at its blackest, one might win a battle and then lose the war.

The cross-examination therefore called above all else for tact—a quality with which Clarke was liberally endowed. If the destruction of Dyson had been what was required, Russell would have done it with more brilliance and panache. But no one could have judged and carried out with greater nicety the delicate performance that promised most reward.

18

Clarke began his questioning in a quiet, even tone. The spectators—and perhaps the Reverend Dyson too—waited for the storm that never was to break.

'Whatever your relations were with regard to Mrs Bartlett, they were relations that were known to her husband?'

'Oh yes.'

'And did you down to the last day of his life endeavour to reciprocate his friendship and to deserve his confidence?'

'I did.'

'Were you sincerely solicitous for his welfare?'

'I was.'

'And do you believe that every day of that illness you and his wife were both anxious for his welfare and tried to serve him?'

'I do.'

All these answers could be forecast with moral certainty. In the Reverend Dyson's eagerness to clear himself, Clarke had perceived an element of which he could make use. While the witness would not hesitate to incriminate Mrs Bartlett if it appeared to offer an advantage to himself, he would be equally ready to speak up in her favour where his own interests were intertwined with hers. More than once during the cross-examination Clarke properly exploited the points of such identity.

'You became aware at a very early period of your acquaintance that Mr Bartlett had peculiar views on the subject of marriage?'

'Yes.'

'Did he ask you whether you thought the teaching of the Bible was distinctly in favour of having one wife?'

'He did.'

'Did he suggest to you that his idea was that there might be a wife for companionship and a wife for household duties?'

'He did.'

'He suggested to you that a man should have two wives?'

'Yes.'

'That would have struck you as a most outrageous suggestion, would it not?'

'A very remarkable suggestion.'

The scandalised judge could not restrain himself.

'Did it not strike you,' he asked, 'as an unwholesome sort of talk in the family circle?'

'Not coming from him, my lord,' the Reverend Dyson answered. '*He was a man who had some strange ideas.*'

This answer to the Bench was of immense value to Clarke. It furnished the first support for the 'extraordinary story' which Mrs Bartlett had told to Dr Leach. Before anyone could make his mind receptive to that story, he would have to be independently and thoroughly convinced that Edwin Bartlett had had some very strange ideas indeed.

'Did he ever make reference,' Clarke asked the Reverend Dyson, 'to marriage between you and Mrs Bartlett after he should be dead?'

'He made statements which left no doubt in my mind but that he contemplated Mrs Bartlett and myself being ultimately married.'

In strict accordance with his policy of steering clear of any head-on clash, Clarke made a studiously indirect approach to a dangerous part of the Reverend Dyson's evidence—his assertion that he had been told by Mrs Bartlett of an internal ailment which caused her husband spasms and was shortening his life. Clarke neither contested nor admitted this assertion. He simply took steps to demonstrate that such statements might have been made innocently.

'You told my learned friend that you have seen Mr Bartlett put his hand to his side and complain of some convulsive pain?'

'Yes.'

'On more than one occasion?'

'Yes.'

'When his wife has been there?'

'Yes.'

The first point was made. Clarke moved swiftly on.

'Did he ever mention the possible duration of his life?'

'I think he did.'

'When?'

'I cannot say.'

'Was it not when you were on holiday at Dover?'

'I cannot swear that.'

On matters which did not implicate him personally, the Reverend Dyson was scrupulous to a fault.

'At Dover did he mention something about his condition?'

'I think so.'

'What was it?'

'He said he was not the strong man he once was.'

'Did he say what was the cause?'

'He attributed it,' the Reverend Dyson said, 'to overwork.'

Second point made. If the prisoner had indeed talked of an internal disease, there had been overt signs that might excuse such a conclusion; if she had indeed talked of its shortening his life he himself had also been disturbed about his health. Her remarks—if ever made—no longer seemed so damning.

Clarke now struck the preliminary notes of what has been previously catalogued among his major themes. He began to set the stage for his theory of suicide.

'You were with Mr Bartlett, were you not, at the very beginning of his illness?'

'I was.'

'Before this time, had he appeared to you to be getting into an ailing and low condition?'

'He seemed very much worn out at night when he returned.'

'Very weary, very depressed, complaining of sleeplessness?'

'During the actual sickness, yes.'

'As that sickness wore on, did he become more depressed?'

'He varied,' the Reverend Dyson said.

'You've seen him crying, have you not?'

'Once.'

'When was that?'

'The Monday in Christmas week.'

'All that time was he talking about not recovering?'

'He spoke very little.'

Clarke tried another way round.

'Is it not the impression on your mind that at that time he thought he would not recover?'

'Yes, I have that impression.'

'When you went on the following Sunday, was he not even worse?'

The Reverend Dyson demurred.

'No, I thought he was brighter. But '

'But?'

'He . . . contradicted himself.'

'How?'

Then it came out: the perfect answer for Clarke's purpose.

'Well, he asked me whether anyone could be lower than he was without passing away altogether.'

In print, the author can italicise or underline. In court, counsel must use other means for emphasis.

'He asked you whether it was possible for a man to be lower than that without passing away altogether?'

'Yes.'

'According to that expression, he was thinking of himself as one actually on the edge between life and death?'

'Yes.'

Thrice had the Reverend Dyson said it; threefold had been its impact on the jury.

Very grave, very firm, but still without heat or rancour, Clarke now drew the witness to the central point of all. His questions on this subject were deliberately few and heavily insured against an unexpected answer.

'Did you mention to *Mr* Bartlett that you had got the chloroform?'

'Mr Bartlett? No.'

'You understood that Mrs Bartlett did not desire it to be mentioned to him?'

'Not specifically the chloroform,' replied the Reverend Dyson, 'but the affliction for which she wanted it.'

The opening was no larger than a crack, but the able cross-examiner needs no more.

'Then she never asked you not to mention you had got the chloroform?'

'No. But I think,' the minister characteristically added, 'I ought to state, in justice to myself, that there was a visitor there and I could not give it her in his presence.'

The Reverend Dyson's urge to clear himself had intervened again. Now the trick was on the table for the taking.

'At all events, *she* had not asked you to keep it secret?'

'No.'

Although he would have hardly dared to hope so at the time, the Reverend Dyson's ordeal was drawing to a close. One further matter and Edward Clarke had done.

'You said, did you not, that you threw away the bottles you had bought from the chemists' shops on Tooting Common as you were going to church on January the 3rd?'

'I did.'

'Were you then in great anxiety and distress about your position?'

'I was.'

'You were afraid the effect of your having bought the bottles might get you into trouble?'

'Precisely.'

'You had in your mind what might happen to yourself?'

'What might have been the cause of Mr Bartlett's death.'

'What might happen to yourself?' Clarke quietly insisted.

'The thought was in my mind,' the Reverend Dyson said, 'that possibly the chloroform I had bought had been the cause of Mr Bartlett's death.'

'And you thought you would be ruined if the matter came out?'

'I thought I would be ruined if my fears were true.

'That is, if *you* were associated with the matter?'

'Yes,' said the Reverend Dyson, 'I saw that danger.'

Here was another solid gain for the defence. For Mrs Bartlett also had thrown away a bottle—the larger bottle into which the chloroform was poured. She had disposed of this bottle—so she told the Reverend Dyson—through the window of a railway train on January 6th. That was a suspicious and incriminating action which might have been construed as consciousness of guilt. But, Clarke could now say, what of the clergyman himself? This man, against whom the Crown presents no case; this man, against whom I have made no imputation—he too hastily got rid of every article that might tend to connect him with Edwin Bartlett's death. His motive? The fear of false interpretations. Why should Mrs Bartlett's motive not have been the same?

By the only criterion that could be reasonably applied—the effect upon the interests of the woman in the dock—Clarke's handling of Dyson richly justified itself. The spectators, it must be confessed, were somewhat disappointed. There had not been any fireworks; it had all been so subdued.

For exactly the same reason the Reverend Dyson felt intensely gratified. There had not been any fireworks; it had all been so subdued. He had passed through the crucial test comparatively unscathed, and now his protracted agonies were over. Breathing a prayer of thanksgiving he vanished from the box, from the court, from the case, to lose himself for ever in the nameless multitude.

19

Dr Alfred Leach, L.R.C.S., of Charlwood Street, Pimlico, had come to curse the day when Mrs Bartlett invited his attendance on her husband. He was a modest family doctor and had no aspirations to be a Willcox or a Spilsbury. Indeed his scientific attainments were but average and no one was likely to ask him to give evidence as an expert. But because of his short association with the Bartletts, because at all material times he had been the deceased man's medical attendant, because he had been the first qualified physician to appear upon the scene after Edwin Bartlett died, because he had been made the recipient of Adelaide Bartlett's 'extraordinary story'—because of these things he found himself, not merely a witness, but a key performer in one of the most sensational trials of the century.

It was not a rôle for which he was well fitted, either by abilities or temperament, and of this Dr Leach himself was painfully aware. For weeks before the trial he worried himself sick. Obsessed by an anxiety to tell the exact truth, he continually went over every detail in his mind and wrote out long accounts of what he thought had taken place. In the flurry of court he tried to bring to mind these documents, with only intermittent and variable success. Abrupt and disconcerting lapses of memory, irrelevant and unrequested bursts of recollection, a passion for futile and interminable periphrasis, a visible terror lest he might leave something out, a suggestion that he had learnt his evidence by heart—this awe-inspiring combination of defects made honest Dr Leach the very archetype of bad witness. Sorely he tried the patience of barristers and judge. 'This perpetual self-consciousness,' complained the latter at one juncture, 'detracts from the value of what you have to say.'

It was unfortunate that he should cut so miserable a figure when he tried so hard and undeniably meant well. No one recognised his shortcomings more frankly than himself. 'I'm sorry I'm such a bad witness,' he once remarked remorsefully—which would have been disarming in a less austere assembly. Counsel seldom apologise for being bad advocates, nor does his lordship for being a bad judge.

Largely through his own fault, Dr Leach was in the box a good deal longer than any other witness. He was called in the middle of the third day of the trial; his examination-in-chief (conducted by Russell, whom he soon provoked to frenetic irritation) dragged on into the later stages of that afternoon; his cross-examination had only been begun when the judge adjourned proceedings for the day. Clarke's further questions, and a re-examination of unusual length—and tone—occupied the whole of the morning session following. Dr Leach's patients, back in Pimlico, must have been almost as fretful as the lawyers.

Clarke's cross-examination of this unhappy man is the

kind of masterpiece that the lover of dramatic coups so often overlooks. Even its author did not seem to rate it high. In later years he confessed some merit in his tackling of Dyson; of his duels with the experts he felt justifiably proud. But about Leach never a word. And yet in cross-examining this upright, worried doctor Clarke built up one of the main walls of his defence. He made the case for suicide.

He opened with a few broad and general questions, designed to form a frame for what was to come after.

'So far as you could see and judge, during the whole of the time was Mrs Bartlett tending her husband with anxious affection?'

'So far as I could see and judge, decidedly.'

'Could you have wished for a more devoted nurse for him?'

'No. It is only right that I should say that emphatically.'

'You were told that, night after night, she had sat and slept sitting at the foot of the bed?'

'Yes.'

'Was it obvious to you that she needed rest and was suffering in strength?'

'It was.'

Clarke added nothing more by way of preamble. Now—though the fact was not immediately apparent—he embarked upon a great and sustained effort to show that Edwin Bartlett had been ripe for self-destruction. He did not—could not—claim that in those three weeks of December he was on the verge of death. He could—and did—invite the doctor's collaboration in composing a portrait of a man who might well have *wished* to die.

Clarke started by eliciting a sickening description of the conditions which the illness had created in the mouth.

'When you first saw him on the 10th December, doctor, what attracted your attention?'

'He had a blue line round the edge of his gums, and the gums themselves were red and spongy.'

'By the 14th was the blue line beginning to give way?'

'Yes—to a grey sloughing margin.'

'Was that when his sleeplessness got bad?'

'Yes, his teeth were beginning to pain him then.'

'On the 16th and 17th he had some teeth out, and a number of loose roots?'

'Yes.'

'Were they all very decayed and horrible?'

'That fairly describes them.'

'Was there a foul fungoid growth at the roots?'

'In some later extractions, there was.'

'On the 17th were the gums still bad?'

'Yes. In front the grey slough had sloughed off, leaving a jagged margin.'

There was nothing novel about any of these facts, nor had Dr Leach the least desire to hide them. They were, quite literally, there for the mere asking. The artistry lay in their presentation and arrangement; in the way they were linked to make a cumulative impact, which in turn was linked to others as the advocate went on.

'Was it on the 19th you began to talk to him about getting out of doors?'

'Quite as early as that.'

'Did he refuse?'

'He said,' Dr Leach replied, 'that it would kill him.'

The doctor, who had so far been more relevant and concise in answering Clarke than he had been with Russell, now once again got the bit between his teeth. 'He really was so obstinate about going out of doors that he almost at one time made me believe that I had overlooked something serious in him. He was——'

'Doctor——'

'—so reasonable on some points that I——'

'Doctor——'

'—could scarcely have put it down to sheer folly.'

'Just listen to me, doctor. At that time did Mrs Bartlett tell you before her husband that he still talked about dying?'

'It was about that time probably; I'm not sure but that she said it more than once.'

'Did you promise that if he went to Torquay for Christmas you would take him down and place him under the care of a medical man there?'

'Yes; I said I would take him down and I mentioned Dr Dalby because I thought he would like to feel that he would be looked after. He——'

'Doctor——'

'—required no looking after practically.'

'You wanted him to stay in Torquay alone?'

'Oh yes.'

'Why was that?'

'Because he was practically a hysterical patient at the time, and his wife petted him very much.'

'He was getting better physically?'

'Oh yes.'

'Then on the 23rd did something happen that upset the whole thing?'

'Yes. He passed a worm.'

'Was he much depressed and shocked?'

'Yes. He thought it had proved there was something wrong with him.'

'Did he say he now thought there was more mischief about him than you had found out?'

'Yes.'

'Did he tell you a day or two afterwards that he felt worms wriggling up his throat?'

'Yes, the next day, I think, and he kept to it.'

'It was a delusion, I suppose?'

'I don't know.' Dr Leach was nothing if not fair—to the Crown, to the defence, to the dead. 'I don't know. Two or three days ago I saw a worm that did wriggle up a patient's throat and was vomited.'

Delusion or fact, it was all the same to Clarke.

'Then he may have felt that?'

'He may, but in his case I think it was a mistake.'

'The upset imagination of a very nervous man?'

'Yes.'

'And he was in a more depressed and troubled condition after that time, was he not?'

'For a day or two.'

Clarke paused for a moment before putting his next question. His words were measured.

'During that next day or two did a very curious matter take place with regard to mesmerism?'

Dr Leach flew into one of his not infrequent panics.

'I cannot fix the date of it from memory,' he said. 'I think I have notes of it somewhere. I think the Treasury have them. I think I must have parted with my original copy.' He fumbled desperately among his sheaf of notes—most of which, so far, he had not been allowed to read. 'Oh yes, here it is. It was on the 26th; he told me an extraordinary tale.'

'About the possibility of being under somebody's influence from a distance?'

'Yes; he thought he and his wife had been mesmerised by a friend. Shall I relate what he said?' the conscientious doctor asked.

'Do, please.'

'I went to see him that morning and said, "Well, Mr Bartlett, how have you slept?" He said, "I could not sleep. I was nervous and restless when I saw my wife asleep in the easy chair, so I got up and went and stood over her like *this*!" '

The doctor held up his arms in demonstration.

'He was very excited. "I was like this," he said, "for two hours, and I felt the vital force being drawn from her to me. I felt it going into me through my finger tips, and after that I laid down and I slept." '

The ungovernable murmur of astonishment in court testified to the effect created by this narrative.

'Did you imagine,' Clarke enquired gravely, 'that he had stood over her for two hours extracting the vital force from her?'

Dr Leach was moved to unaccustomed raciness.

'I did not imagine,' he said, 'that Mr Bartlett would stay two hours doing anything. . . '

It was growing late and upon this answer ended the third

long day of Mrs Bartlett's trial. The participants went their several ways to private meditation: Clarke to his home, where, buttressed and surrounded by his books on chloroform, he prepared to do battle with the Crown experts on the morrow; Mrs Bartlett to prison, where she passed the torturing night in a turmoil of thoughts that must for ever remain secret; the jury to the quarters which of necessity they shared, where they could ponder at leisure a new-born possibility—that in his last days Edwin Bartlett had been mad.

20

Next morning Clarke resumed his cross-examination and completed his sketch of Edwin Bartlett's mental state. So neurotic, so hysterical did this now seem to have been, so eccentric were his sayings and so unbalanced were his acts, that there was no surprise when Clarke put into words the idea that was floating through everybody's mind.

'Had you suspected him of insanity?' he asked.

'At one time I did,' Dr. Leach admitted.

The doctor had not benefited from his night's repose, if indeed he had been able to get any. It is much more likely that he lay awake for hours, wondering why he had proved such a tiresome witness and planning to give greater satisfaction in the morning. Whatever the cause, he was even more diffuse and long-winded than before; he added to his harvest of judicial reproofs; and it took Clarke two more hours of patient, expert questioning before he had taken him through all essential points.

That which is essential is not necessarily decisive. But one short passage, which appeared that morning of only minor consequence, was destined, in conjunction with the scientific evidence, to play a major part in influencing judgment.

'Did Mrs Bartlett wish,' Clarke said, 'to have the post-mortem made as quickly as was possible?'

'She certainly did,' answered the doctor. 'She chafed at the delay till next day. When I told her that the eminent pathologist we wanted couldn't come that afternoon, she said, "Can't he be persuaded?" '

'Persuaded to come so that he might make the post-mortem on that very day?'

'On that very day.'

'So,' said Clarke, 'if the pathologist had been able to come the post-mortem would have taken place on the afternoon of death?'

'Yes.'

The majority in court may have wondered at the time whether Clarke was not labouring a secondary matter. But it was not secondary, and he had good reason to make sure it was remembered.

Like tigers travelling in the wake of a rabbit, the Crown experts were due to follow Dr Leach. Matters of pure science would have to be thrashed out with them. But Dr Leach after all had academic knowledge and practical experience; here was a chance of reconnoitring the ground.

Clarke picked his steps warily.

'Just a few questions on a different subject, Dr Leach. Have you ever at any time seen a case of death from poisoning by liquid chloroform?'

'No.'

'It is extremely rare, isn't it?'

'It has occurred, of course; it is rare.'

'Have you yourself administered chloroform from time to time?'

'Yes; about two hundred times.'

'Is it an operation that requires to be very carefully and skilfully done?'

'It is an anxious one.'

'Of late years has ether been substituted for chloroform in anæsthesia?'

'Yes.'

'Do you know why?'

'Because it is less dangerous.'

'Not only less dangerous,' suggested Clarke. 'Are not some things incidental to chloroform less often found with ether—vomiting, for instance?'

'Yes, quite so.'

'Is vomiting constantly found with inhalation of chloroform?' the judge interpolated.

'The patient usually vomits afterwards,' Dr Leach explained, 'and even during the administration.'

'In many cases,' Clarke asked, 'does the vomiting begin almost immediately?'

'It depends.'

'On the condition of the stomach?'

'Oh yes; if food has been given previously.'

'I was going to say, if you had made up your mind to administer chloroform to a patient, you would take care with regard to diet six hours or so before?'

'At least four,' said the doctor, feeling a slight revival of confidence now he was being asked to judge instead of being judged. 'At least four, and that must only be beef tea or some liquid easily digested.'

'Suppose you had any indigestible substance in the stomach, such, for instance, as a substantial quantity of mango chutney.' (Evidence had been given that Edwin Bartlett had had mango chutney with the last meal of his life, and the remains of it, *half digested*, were observed at the post-mortem.) 'That would almost certainly produce vomiting, would it not?'

'It might,' said Dr Leach.

'It *would*, would it not?'

The doctor still hesitated.

'I should not like to say it *would*.'

Clarke saw how close he was to yielding. He lowered his demand by a fraction.

'I should not like to ask you to prophesy, but you would *expect* it to?'

It was sufficient. Dr Leach accepted the compromise.

'It is a very likely suggestion,' he said.

Russell, seeing the way that things were moving, irritably tapped his celebrated snuff-box. He had staked his case at the outset on a theory: that the administration of liquid chloroform had been preceded by external application. Only thus, he had admitted, could 'the medical men' explain how the liquid was administered without causing cries and paroxysms of pain. And now here was one of his 'medical men' (though Russell when he had used the term was certainly not thinking of small fry like Dr Leach) giving Clarke one reply after another that tore up the platform on which that theory stood.

Still, the experts will be able to put it in perspective. If only we could get this blundering fool out of the box. . . .

But the defence had advanced further before Edward Clarke sat down.

'Have you ever administered chloroform to an adult in sleeping?' he had asked.

'No,' said Dr Leach.

'Have you ever heard of an authentic case of its being done?'

'No,' said Dr Leach. .

The re-examination (by one of Russell's juniors) was extraordinarily long and extraordinarily contentious. At times it seemed that everyone forgot by which side the witness had originally been called.

At lunch-time Dr Leach was released at last from purgatory to dedicate himself afresh as a healer of mankind. Few men have run inadvertently into such a sea of troubles or contributed so innocently to their exacerbation.

The way was now clear for the prosecution experts to speak in support of the Attorney-General's opening and to back, by the weight of their considerable authority, his reconstruction of the way the crime was done.

21

The cross-examination of scientific experts falls into a peculiar and isolated category. Others are called to testify to *facts*, and opposing counsel is generally concerned to show that they are either untruthful or mistaken. The experts lead the way into the realm of *theory*, of analytical dissertations and deductive reconstruction. Any contest with them may ultimately turn upon niceties of wording or the shape of formulæ.

Some surprise is occasionally expressed because so many acknowledged experts prove unimpressive witnesses; they are moulded like wax by the cunning hands of advocates who do not rival them in specialised erudition. That is because their mastery of the subject under review is not matched by a mastery of the art of giving evidence. They may be profound, but not quick; thorough, but not selective; accurate, but not lucid. They may find it easier to express themselves on paper; they may find the laboratory more congenial than the court. They may be witnesses who are Experts, without being expert Witnesses.

Few have been both in superlative degree; not more than two or three in any generation. But one such, unquestionably, was Dr Thomas Stevenson, and it was he who had performed, at the Home Office's request, the analysis of Edwin Bartlett's remains. Professor of Medical Jurisprudence at Guy's Hospital, one of the leading consulting physicians of the day, a toxicologist of international repute, Dr Stevenson was above all a tough, shrewd witness; honest and fair enough in forming his opinion, but not easily moved to qualify his blunt expression of it. He could not be rattled and he would not be cajoled.

In the Bartlett trial Dr Stevenson appeared amid distinguished colleagues, each of whom contributed a viewpoint of his own. But on all sides he was considered as their leader, and when on the fourth afternoon he stepped into the box everyone present saw in him the instrument of destiny.

Stevenson was not the man to exploit by style or manner the drama inherent in his situation. He gave his evidence with matter-of-fact composure. He told of finding chloroform in the contents of the stomach, and fixed the quantity at 11¼ grams. He described an inflamed patch on the stomach itself—'at the usual spot,' he said, 'after swallowing irritant poison.' He declared unhesitatingly that the chloroform discovered had been the cause of death.

'Could he take a fatal dose,' asked Russell, 'and suppose he was taking some innocent thing?'

'No,' replied the witness, 'I don't believe he could.'

'Is it possible to put liquid down the throat of a person who is insensible, in the sense of being unconscious, but still having the sense of feeling?'

'Yes; you can put liquids down the throat of a person who is fairly moderately under the influence of inhaled chloroform.'

'Would it be difficult?'

'Not if the man was lying on his back with his mouth open.'

Thus was filled in Russell's sketch of the Crown theory. There would be 'no great difficulty' in pouring the *liquid* down if *inhaled* chloroform had taken 'moderate' effect.

But could a person untrained in medical technique produce such a condition, or recognise it when it had been produced? This was the main point Clarke was to take in a cross-examination which he himself regarded as the trial's turning point. . . .

When Russell sat down, Clarke got slowly to his feet.

In front of him was a rampart of massive medical books, the paper markers drooping like a sea of flags becalmed. The moment had arrived—the moment when the close research of many days would bear or stint its fruits.

Signs of the strain inseparable from a long capital trial showed momentarily on the defender's face as he put his first questions.

'Dr Stevenson, you have for many years given your attention to subjects of this class?"

'I have.'

'And you have had a long experience of the administration of chloroform?"

'I have.'

'And you have also given study to the experience of other doctors?'

'Yes.'

'And you have edited *The Principles and Practice of Medical Jurisprudence*, by Dr Alfred Swaine Taylor, who is well known as one of the greatest authorities in that branch of medical science?'

'Yes.'

'And so far as your skill and experience have enabled you, have you taken care that it is complete in the subject with which it deals?'

'Yes; it is fairly complete, I think.'

Deliberately Clarke was reinforcing Stevenson's prestige. Deliberately he was projecting him as the Supreme Authority; the Expert of Experts; the man who, in dealing with chloroform, knew all there was to know. Now he asked the question for which this had dressed the ground.

'Can you refer me to *any* recorded case, *anywhere*, of murder by the administration of liquid chloroform?'

Stevenson answered as Clarke knew he must.

'No,' he said, 'I know of none.'

So if Mrs Bartlett had killed her husband by giving him liquid chloroform, she had performed a feat that was apparently unique.

'There are no recorded cases of murder in this fashion,' Clarke went on, 'but have there not been deaths from the swallowing of chloroform by accident?'

'Yes,' said Stevenson.

'How many?'

'About twenty have been recorded.'

So, by the test of statistics, accident was a more feasible hypothesis than murder.

'You say that liquid chloroform could be administered while a person is under the influence of chloroform inhaled?'

'Certainly.'

'You know that the brain appeared normal on post-mortem?'

'I have heard so.'

'But when chloroform has been inhaled just a short time before death would you not expect a distinct odour in the ventricles of the brain?'

'Not always,' Stevenson said, adding, 'It has been observed.'

'Come,' Clarke persisted. 'Is it not one of the most prominent symptoms recognised?'

'Not according to my observations.' Clarke's hand reached out among the books. The witness anticipated the coming thrust. 'I am speaking from my own observation,' he re-emphasised.

'I do not want to challenge your book by any other,' Clarke remarked politely, 'but you know *Guy and Ferrier*?'

'Yes.'

'Is it a book of substantial authority?'

'Yes.'

Clarke opened the volume at a place already marked. Stevenson waited, outwardly impassive.

'I am at page 550 of *Guy and Ferrier*.' Clarke began to read. ' "The odour of chloroform is perceptible on opening the body. It is especially observable in the cerebral ventricles." '

He paused enquiringly. Dr Stevenson's response was not entirely unevasive, nor did it possess his usual rigid relevance.

'Asphyxia usually arises from giving too much chloroform,' he said. 'There you would expect to find the smell more prominent.'

Clarke seized his advantage.

'I quite agree it may be a question of quantity, but what I am putting to you is—if you are looking for post-mortem indications of chloroform having been inhaled, the odour in the cerebral ventricles would be one of the principal ones?'

'Oh, I should certainly look for it,' Stevenson conceded.

All this, though highly useful, was subordinate. It set the scene; it provided Clarke with a favourable background against which to open the decisive interchange.

'You spoke earlier,' he said, 'of administering chloroform to persons while in sleep?'

'Yes.'

'Did you speak of adults?'

'Yes.'

'As a matter of your own practice?'

'No,' said Stevenson, 'I have not done it myself.'

'You are speaking of recorded cases?'

'I am.'

'In the case of adults, is it the fact that the attempt to administer chloroform by inhalation during sleep almost invariably wakes the man?'

'Not almost invariably,' Stevenson jibbed at the phrase, which was indeed a little strong. 'Not almost invariably. If I may refer to the largest number of experiments that have been carried out by one individual—Dolbeau—he found that three awoke to one that was chloroformed.'

Clarke extracted another volume from the stack.

'Do you know Wynter Blyth's work on poisons?'

'I do.'

'I am reading from page 136. "Dolbeau has made some interesting experiments in order to ascertain whether under any circumstances a sleeping person might be anæsthetised. The main result appears to answer the question in the affirmative, at least with certain persons; but even with these *it can only be done by using the greatest skill and care. This cautious and scientific narcosis is not likely to be used by the criminal classes, or, if used, to be successful.*"'

Clarke stopped. Dr Stevenson nodded slightly, but made no spoken comment. . . .

The afternoon had lengthened into evening, and still this intensive questioning went on. It was conducted entirely on the plane of general principle; no references were made to the case that was being tried. The talk was not of Mrs Bartlett, but of Wynter Blyth and Dolbeau; not of the man who died at the house in Claverton Street, but of patients in Scotland or the United States; not of what the prisoner had or had not done, but of what, in the light of science, it was possible to do. Yet Clarke's purpose was most relevant and consistently maintained. Each question was directed to the self-same urgent end: to show that the operation which, on the Crown theory, Mrs Bartlett had performed would test the powers of a qualified physician and be utterly beyond her capacity and knowledge.

Toe to toe, counsel and doctor fought the matter out. As book after book was produced and scrutinised, as successive authorities were cited and discussed, the Old Bailey seemed transmuted into some scholastic forum where learned professors contended for the truth. But there was one who sat apart, in her sombre widow's garb, to bear constant reminder of the stake upon the outcome.

At last the advocate pushed the books aside. They had served him, and he had used them, well. The witness was not in any way discredited—this would have been the reverse of Clarke's intention—but he was tied, as a result of the long interrogation, to certain important medical premises. On the basis of these Clarke could now venture upon a series of dramatic, and indeed decisive, questions which related all that had transpired to the case before the court, and garnered the harvest he had so astutely sown.

'Let me put it again,' he said to Stevenson, and there was that in his voice that made everyone alert. 'Let me put it again. You say there is a particular point in the process of chloroforming at which the patient would be able to swallow, though he was sufficiently under the influence of chloroform not to suffer from the pain?'

'I do.'

'How would you yourself ascertain that that time had arrived?'

'By the reflex of the eye. I would not like to pour down the throat if the reflex had been abolished.'

'How would you test it?'

'By touching the eye and watching for the closure of the eyelid.'

'Would you mind touching your own eye; just show us how it is done?'

The jury watched the doctor's practised fingers.

'Like this. You separate the eyelids, see? And . . . just touch the conjunctiva.'

Clarke bowed in acknowledgment.

'I am much obliged. That is the test to ascertain if the sensation of pain has gone?'

'Yes.'

It was time for the concluding strokes.

'Suppose you had to deal with a sleeping man and it was your object to get down his throat without his knowing it a liquid which would cause great pain; do you not agree it would be a very difficult and delicate operation?'

The eye; the reflex; the precise stage of anæsthesia. Stevenson had to bear them all in mind. He replied in somewhat guarded terms.

'I think it would be an operation which would often fail, and might often succeed.'

He had gone far enough; Clarke could afford to insist on his own phrase.

'Would you not look on it as a *delicate* operation?'

Stevenson yielded.

'Yes, I should look on it as delicate; I should be afraid of pouring it down the windpipe.'

'If the patient got into such a state of insensibility as not to reject it, it would go down his windpipe and burn that?'

'Some of it might.'

'If it did so, it would leave its traces?'

'I should expect to find traces.'

As the whole world knew, no such traces had been found. The cross-examination appeared to have reached its culminating point. But Clarke was to add a final, unexpected twist.

'If the post-mortem examination had been performed, *as we know from Dr Leach that Mrs Bartlett wished*, on the very day upon which death took place, there would have been a better opportunity of determining cause of death?'

'There would,' said Dr Stevenson.

Clarke sat down amid a buzz of murmurs which leapt into a hubbub as the hearing was adjourned. The cross-examination had been admirably managed, the closing phase spectacular in triumph.

The effect that it produced upon the jury may be gathered from what took place next morning when the court resumed.

22

A word ought to be said about the jury that now held Adelaide Bartlett in their charge.

Notwithstanding official pronouncements to the contrary by those whose high attainments must command respect, a number of juries called to modern murder trials have shown themselves perverse or unintelligent or both. The Bartlett case provided an opposite example. The jury were fair-minded and notably acute, closely following the intricacies of scientific argument and not at all averse to doing some thinking on their own. This was already patent from questions they had put to various witnesses as the trial progressed.

Nine times out of ten an interfering jury is an even greater bane than an interfering judge. But the Bartlett jury earns complete exoneration. Their interventions were, without exception, strictly to the point; they were cast in language that was clear and yet exact; they usually led, and were always meant to lead, towards elucidation of some obscurity. Anyone who, remembering the trial of Mrs Maybrick or of Mrs Thompson or of William Herbert Wallace, feels inclined to regard the jury system with despair, may take fresh heart from the sagacity and diligence of the twelve London citizens who tried Mrs Bartlett.

On the night of Dr Stevenson's cross-examination they must have talked it over at length among themselves. In the course of their discussion they found that there was something more that they would like to know. . . .

First thing next day Dr Stevenson went back into the box for the inevitable anti-climax of his re-examination. It did not last long, and he was about to step down again when the foreman of the jury stood up in his place.

'My lord,' he said, 'there are one or two questions *we* should like to ask,' and he proceeded to ask them in a style of which no barrister need have felt ashamed.

'We desire,' he began, 'to be perfectly clear upon this point.' There was none of that hesitation, that unintelligible stammering that serves to characterise the muddle-headed. Here was a man who knew what he was about. 'If an unskilled person administers chloroform down the throat, must he not do it very gradually for fear of choking?'

Dr Stevenson took a second or so to turn the question over.

'In some cases,' he said, 'I don't think it would be difficult to do it quickly.'

'But the chances are that some portion of the chloroform would remain in the mouth for a little time?'

'A *very* short time.'

'But it must remain there for a little time?' The foreman stuck to his point with the tenacity and coolness of a seasoned silk who has been cross-examining witnesses these five and twenty years. 'It must remain there for a little time, doctor, must it not?'

'Some of it might. If the person were unable to swallow, it would be likely to remain at the back of the throat.'

'And then it will show some signs of having been there, in the same way as if it lay in the intestine?'

The court was following with rapt attentiveness. Such a scene was rare between juryman and witness.

'It would show some sign,' Dr Stevenson repeated, 'if the patient were unable to swallow.'

'You would expect more signs if a person could not swallow than if he were drinking medicine quickly off?'

'Yes.'

'What signs?'

'If a person could not swallow, the chloroform would remain at the upper end of the windpipe, and upon the post-mortem I should expect to find irritation or inflammation.'

'If taken suddenly, you would not expect to find either?'

'I should not.'

The foreman glanced round at his fellows much as the seasoned silk would glance round at his juniors. That what we wanted?

They nodded their assent. . . .

On those rare occasions when a jury speaks, none pays heed more anxiously than counsel; it makes a chink, however slight, in that blank wall of silence that normally conceals the tenor of their thoughts. Clarke weighed and weighed again the purport of the foreman's questioning. He was too wise and circumspect to build hopes on it unduly. But as a straw in the wind he observed it and felt thankful;

it proclaimed that the jury had understood his case and that their minds were at any rate not closed.

From this he could justifiably derive encouragement as he braced himself for the greatest of his tasks.

23

The Crown case had closed. Clarke had intimated that he would call no evidence. Russell, who, as a law officer, could claim a prescriptive right to the last word, showed that he meant to do so by remaining in his seat. On that fifth morning, therefore, in a court not less expectant than it had been on the first, Clarke uttered the first words of what was destined to become a classic of forensic eloquence—the closing speech on behalf of Mrs Bartlett.

He began by referring to Russell's exercise of his 'anomalous privilege' and made legitimate capital out of his own disadvantage. 'Although I call no witnesses,' he declared, 'although I have to content myself with comments on the evidence before you, when I have finished I shall be answered by the leader of the English Bar. He will have an opportunity—I do not say that he will use it—but he will have an opportunity of pointing to topics which I may not have appreciated. If he were to make his statement now I should hear his comments and might be able to answer them, but they will come to you when my lips are closed.'

The beautifully modulated voice—one of the most melodious and expressive that has ever graced the courts—assumed a note of challenge as this protest was developed.

'I hope an Attorney-General may be found some day—unless the law is altered, as it should be—to abandon the exercise of a right which does not seem to me defensible.' As Russell's underlip jutted forward in ill-humour, Clarke was exquisitely disarming. 'I know that my learned friend will endeavour to be as fair in his reply as he was in his opening. But I know so well, by my own experience of forensic combat, how an instinct of antagonism is aroused in which the strongest determination to be impartial could not be trusted by any of us to clear him from prejudice or passion.' Then came a telling stroke. 'My learned friend, *coming from a country distinguished far more for its advocates than for its judges*, may import the combative instinct into the conduct of this case.'

Russell's Irish blood may well have boiled, but he was temporarily rendered impotent. What valid objection could one take? Courteously but firmly, with absolute propriety but infinite finesse, Clarke had spiked the guns he was to fire hereafter.

As a pendant to this preliminary theme, Clarke warned the jury that his speech must be a long one since he had to bear in mind that Russell was to follow him. 'That consideration obliges me to deal with all the topics that are before you, because otherwise I should run the most grievous risk—not for myself,' he added parenthetically, 'for it is a matter of no moment to me what comment might be made on my speech or on my advocacy—but risk to one whose interests are present to me at this moment in far higher degree than any consideration that could attach to myself.'

A look of pathetic gratitude flickered for a moment across the sad young face of the woman in the dock.

The jury would not be in any wise dismayed at the prospect of a long and comprehensive speech from Clarke. They had followed the evidence with unfaltering attention; they earnestly desired to reach a just decision; they would gratefully welcome assistance in their task. And—to adopt a less disinterested approach—recompenses are not lacking for those who find themselves caught up in the grip of a great orator.

The jurors leaned forward receptively as Clarke invited them to hear his grounds for claiming an acquittal.

By way of exordium he summarised the case in a devastating sentence—a sentence that, with one possible exception, was not open to criticism in a single phrase or word, but which held compressed within its narrow compass almost every circumstance in favour of his client. 'You are asked to believe,' he said, 'that a woman who for years had lived with her husband in friendship and affection; who, during the whole time of his illness, had striven to nurse him and to help him; who had tended him by day, and had sacrificed her own rest to watch over him at night, simply sleeping at the bottom of his couch that she might be ready to comfort him by her presence; who had called doctors, that by no possibility should any chance be lost of ascertaining what his trouble was and having the quickest means to cure it; who had watched over him, had tried to cheer him, had talked lightly when they were together before the doctor in order to give him spirits—that woman, you are asked to believe, on New Year's Eve was suddenly transformed into a murderess, committing crime not only without excuse, but absolutely without object, by the execution of an operation which would have been delicate and difficult to the highest trained doctor.'

In theory, Clarke had been outlining the case for the Crown; in practice he had outlined the case for the defence. It was like a simple plan or chart to guide the jury through the multitude of detail, and show how each part was related to the whole.

Perhaps because he knew that it was uppermost in their minds, he elected to deal with the scientific evidence first. He reminded them that there had never been a murder in this fashion—'though there have been murderers equipped with all the medical experience.' Had the unskilled Mrs Bartlett established a grim precedent? Let them realise what such a verdict must involve.

It had been admitted by the Attorney-General that an unwilling person could not be made to inhale chloroform; nor could it be poured down the throat of such a person unless inhalation had first made him insensible. 'And I do not think,' said Clarke, 'that my learned friend will suggest that Mr Bartlett acquiesced.'

'Certainly not,' interpolated Russell from beside him

'Very well,' Clarke rejoined, his gaze still on the jury. 'Now let us see what step this is that you are asked to take.' He recalled the Crown's theory of the double operation: that Mrs Bartlett had first 'chloroformed' her husband, and then poured the liquid down his unresisting throat. 'That is the suggestion,' he said, and shook his head. 'But it is a suggestion which is almost an impossibility.'

He supported this assertion by plain and forceful reasoning. Experiments had shown, as agreed by Dr Stevenson, that if an attempt was made to 'chloroform' a sleeping person he was overwhelmingly likely to wake up and resist. And these experiments, Clarke shrewdly pointed out, were made by skilled chloroformists under the best conditions. 'Is it not,' he asked, 'in the highest degree improbable that an unskilled person would *ever* be able to administer chloroform in sleep without waking the person subjected to the process?'

But it did not finish there. If chloroform was inhaled shortly before death one would expect to find signs of it in the brain; no such signs were remarked at the post-mortem. Again, one would expect to find signs of it in the heart; the examining pathologists declared the heart was normal. And again, as a general rule, chloroform caused vomiting; there was no evidence that Edwin Bartlett had vomited at all.

'I am going by steps, gentlemen,' Clarke said. 'I have shown you the enormous—may I not say the almost insuperable?—difficulty of administering chloroform to a sleeping person without waking him. But now let us assume this . . . *miracle* has been worked.'

He rapped out the word 'miracle' with electrifying effect.

'What happens next? There may be a time, the duration of which no one can measure, the conditions of which it is scarcely possible for the most careful doctor to predict—there may be an instant of time or a few instants in which the second part of the operation might be done. For Dr Stevenson, with all his experience, such an operation would be difficult and delicate.' And what was the allegation of the Crown? 'That one absolutely unstudied in the ways of medicine; who knew little of chloroform, the mode of its administration, the objects it would serve—that she, alone in the room with her sleeping husband succeeded in performing this difficult and delicate operation, and so succeeded that no trace, no spilling of chloroform by the nervous hand, no effects through contact with the soft passages, no signs in the post-mortem condition of the body, remained to reveal the fact that she had done it.'

This constituted the strongest argument at Clarke's disposal. It was founded on the success of his cross-examination, and he had hammered it home with clarity and power. But now there were the general issues to be faced; the string of suspicious incidents, the lies to get the chloroform, the marital relations between Bartlett and his wife in the crucible of which her credibility would be judged.

Clarke had been speaking for the best part of two hours. He had barely reached the fringe of this less favourable ground when the adjournment came.

24

The mounting pressure was taking toll of all, and for the chief actors lunch was a token meal. Each was preoccupied and worn with private cares. Russell felt conscious that he had not been at his best, and that the case against the prisoner could have been more aptly put; as senior Crown counsel he deplored this situation and ransacked his resourceful mind for a means to rectify it. Mrs Bartlett, lodged below the dock for the fifth successive day, reflected that the sixth must surely seal her fate, and wondered for the thousandth time where she would spend the seventh. Clarke, aware that this was now suspended by a thread, summoned up his last reserves of nervous energy and strength. He dreaded, as every sensitive man in his position must, that calamity might result from some shortcoming on his part.

When he re-entered court so large a flock of barristers had crowded in to hear him that it was only with some difficulty he got back to his seat. The public galleries, which had been crammed to bursting-point throughout, now appeared to have accomplished the impossible and packed in even more than had been there hitherto. It is doubtful, though, whether this made much impression upon Clarke. He was not an actor with an audience, but an advocate with a jury, and his absorption in his client's interests was complete.

That afternoon session was entirely his. From beginning to end he remained upon his feet, striving without cease for possession of the jury. Flinching from nothing, ventilating all; commenting, interpreting and placing in perspective; using the facts to illuminate psychology and using psychology to illuminate the facts; allying simplicity of substance with nobility of style, he composed such a picture of this melancholy case as could never be forgotten by those who saw it done. . . .

Very still he stood; pale from his exertions, but straight and sturdy as a pillar, as he opened the last phase of his tremendous fight.

Already he had dealt with what he called 'the smaller matters' of suspicion : the fire that had seemed freshly tended in the middle of the night ('With a patient suffering from sleeplessness it would be the manifest duty of the person watching to build this fire up and make it last for hours'); the conversation about chloroform with the landlord's wife ('That day Mr Bartlett had had a tooth drawn. . . . He had taken gas'). These 'suspicious' circumstances, Clarke had declared, 'do not survive examination,' and Russell himself was later to concede that they were 'insignificant.' But now Clarke met the challenge of a much more serious matter—the excuses for requiring chloroform that Mrs Bartlett was alleged to have concocted.

He reminded the jury that this matter depended on the evidence and recollection of the Reverend Dyson, and adroitly utilised the Crown's endorsement of his innocence. 'I accept the conclusion at which the Crown arrived. There was really no case to be submitted to you against him. But' —and Clarke's voice rang out in indignation—'when you are asked to use against Mrs Bartlett the untruthful statements which she has made, and which come to you on Mr Dyson's evidence, does it not occur to you that if matters of this kind are to have great weight, how fortunate Mr Dyson is that he is not standing in the dock himself?' He took pains, though, to make it crystal clear that he was demanding equity, not denouncing Dyson. 'I beg you to note,' he emphasised again, 'that I do not impeach his innocence in the least. But supposing *his* case were before you, what would you have? Suppose someone who knew him had seen him fling away the bottles on Tooting Common and had had the curiosity to pick a bottle up; suppose it had come out, at the first meeting of the inquest, that he was a habitual visitor at the house, that he had been in the habit of walking out with Mrs Bartlett, that his relations with the Bartletts were of an exceptional character; suppose it had come out by enquiry at the chemist's (whose name is on the label) that when Mr Dyson asked for the chloroform he had told him a falsehood—what would have been Mr Dyson's position?'

Between accused woman and exonerated man the parallel was indeed remarkably exact. 'I use it,' said Clarke, 'to show you that where against him, *an innocent man*, a falsehood told for the express purpose of getting this poison might have been proved in the witness box, it would be hard indeed that a statement from the lips of the very man to whom Mrs Bartlett told a story which was not wholly true to explain her desiring to possess this chloroform—it would be strange indeed if that were allowed to weigh upon your minds as a serious element of suspicion against *her*.'

The form of this plea was singularly persuasive. Dearer to a jury than the most flawless syllogism is the traditional tag concerning sauce for the goose.

Recalling, in studiously temperate terms, that 'there is very good ground for the suspicion that he has been anxious to protect himself without much regard to the actual truth,' Clarke declared it would be unsafe to rely on 'the entire accuracy' of the Reverend Dyson's statements. But—he reinsured himself lest the jury should think otherwise—suppose that Mrs Bartlett *had* departed from the truth. Could she have told Dyson what she later told Dr Leach? Could any woman of delicacy have done so? 'She gave him some reason for wanting the chloroform,' said Clarke. 'Mr Dyson's idea, he says, was that she would sprinkle drops upon a handkerchief and use it for the purpose of soothing Mr Bartlett. Well, it is not far from the explanation she gave to Dr Leach; and is it not perfectly intelligible that she should desire to veil by that sort of account the real truth which she could not be expected to communicate to Mr Dyson?'

Perfectly intelligible—always provided that the real truth *was* contained in the story Mrs Bartlett had told to Dr Leach. The difficulty of making that story even credible—a difficulty that did not exclude its authenticity—had haunted Clarke since before the trial began, and he cannot have been wholly free from qualms as he came to grips with this least tractable of problems.

He spoke, though, as ever, with a burning sincerity that was the mirror of his faith in Mrs Bartlett's innocence. Her story, he said, had received corroboration at every point where it was possible to test it. It was in evidence that Edwin Bartlett had held strange views on marriage, and had harboured the idea that a man might have two wives. It was in evidence that he had fostered, as far as he was able, the growing affection between Dyson and his wife. It was in evidence that he had written to the former expressing his 'thankfulness' for 'the loving letter you sent Adelaide today,' and subscribing himself 'yours affectionately, Edwin.' Clarke attached great importance to this letter, which he roundly described as the key of the whole case. 'Of all the strange things that this court has heard,' he exclaimed, 'there has been nothing stranger than that letter, where "yours affectionately, Edwin," is with apologetic humility thanking the man who had written a loving letter to his wife.'

Moreover, Clarke insisted, Mrs Bartlett's story was entitled to the greater credence as she had never intended nor expected it to be made public. 'I claim for that statement this: it was not a statement offered to an accusing world as an explanation of circumstances that had cast suspicion on her; it was a private communication of the most private matter to the physician in whose skill she was trusting for her treatment. It was a statement which comes to you in such circumstances as to bear with it the almost irresistible presumption that it is true.'

It is instantly apparent when a jury has lost sympathy with counsel, when they find an argument entirely unacceptable even at the very moment of its exposition. Their concentration breaks. They begin to fidget. They glance at one another and occasionally exchange conversation in a whisper. They are again twelve separate, unrelated individuals instead of twelve members of an integrated team.

Subconsciously, but none the less intently, Clarke watched for any of these signs while he steered through this most perilous passage on his course. There were none. The jury, whatever they might later come to think under stress of other pleas and after time for meditation, were at present following him without hint of resistance. They sat quiet and almost motionless, absorbed in every word, their eyes never departing for an instant from his face.

Heartened, he moved on to the theme of suicide. (It had never, of course, been incumbent upon him to offer the jury an alternative solution, but he knew very well that the absence of one would inevitably operate to his client's prejudice.) He recited the now familiar catalogue of Edwin Bartlett's disabilities and woes: the overwork, the illness, the depression, the insomnia, the visits to the dentist, the appearance of the worm. But to these Clarke linked, as a potential climax of the husband's anguish, Mrs Bartlett's confession about the chloroform. 'She told him to what extremities she had been driven, and gave the bottle into his hands. . . . On this night, when he has suffered during the day, when he has undergone this operation, and must undoubtedly have suffered from his condition, he is told by her, substantially, that the consent which he has given with regard to Dyson is regarded by her as an irrevocable decision, that she has taken him at his word.'

This led him into a vivid reconstruction of what took place upon that New Year's night. A pictorial gift is invaluable in advocacy; pictures stay in the mind after abstractions disappear; and Clarke's superbly evocative account, rooted in fact but crowned with imagination, must have fought a mighty battle for his client in the jury room. 'Suppose,' he said, 'that Mrs Bartlett had left the bedroom as usual to wash, and he had placed the bottle of chloroform on the mantelshelf. There was a wineglass there, the glass that was found afterwards, and while she was away it was perfectly easy for him, without leaving his bed, to pour some chloroform into this wineglass and to drink it off. If he swallowed it quickly, there would not be—as there were not—appearances of long exposure of the softer substances of mouth and throat.' Thus Clarke took up the point the jury themselves had made.

'Having drunk it, he reassumes his recumbent position; the chloroform passes down his throat and reaches the stomach.' (No word, though, of the predicated agony and uproar.) 'Within two or three minutes after that he might be passing into a state of coma. . . . Then she herself goes to sleep, and her husband's coma deepens into insensibility, and insensibility passes into death. . . . The hours go by. She has heard them, happier than she, in the other parts of the house speaking to each other of the brighter hopes of the New Year that is beginning, but the first thing she awakens to in that New Year is the sad consciousness that the husband who might not fully have deserved the love that he received, but who, at all events, had treated her with affection, with confidence, with the desire to protect her—she awakens to find that husband apparently cold and dead.'

His delivery quickened with the narrative. 'She springs to his side. There is close to the end of the mantelshelf—for we know it—the wineglass from which he has taken that fatal draught; the woman's instinct is at once to administer brandy in hopes to restore him. She pours into the glass some brandy and tries to pour it down his throat. I am not sure she does much; with shaking hand she spills some brandy on his chest which the doctor smells afterwards. It is no use; she puts back on the mantelshelf, where it was found when they came into the room, this wineglass with the brandy in it. The landlord, on smelling the glass, may well have detected the odour of chloroform, though it was only brandy it contained.'

The momentum of the speech was now almost irresistible. It tore along torrent-wise, engulfing and sweeping forward everything in its path. 'There was no scientific miracle worked by the grocer's wife. There was unhappily the putting within reach of a man who was broken by illness, and upon whom there had come this disappointment, there was the putting within his reach of the poison which he might have used, and probably did use; but there was nothing more, and from that moment there was not a word of hers, there was not an action, not a look, which was not the look or the word or the action of the loving wife who had nursed him through his illness to this point, and who now found him suddenly gone for ever.'

The end of Clarke's stupendous effort was in sight. For weeks he had worked and lived for Mrs. Bartlett, hardly allowing himself one extraneous thought, but soon he would be powerless to lend her further aid. This was his last chance, and the strong flame of his advocacy burned white as he spoke his final words for the client whom he believed.

'This woman has not had the happiest of lives. She has been described to you as a woman who had no friends. But she had one friend—her husband. In his strange way he stood by her and protected her. He was affectionate, and when her reputation was assailed he defended it as only her husband could. And to her at this moment it may seem most strange that he to whom she had given persistent affection should be the one of whose foul murder she now stands accused. And if he himself could know what passed among us here, how strange, how sorrowful, it might seem to him—how strange that such an accusation should have been formulated and tried in court in spite of the efforts which he made to prevent it—efforts which he perhaps defeated by his own despairing act.'

It was a bold and moving image, giving rise to the memorable appeal which was to be his close.

'Gentlemen, that husband has gone, but she is not left without a friend; she will find that friend here today in the spirit which guides your judgment and clears your eyes upon this case. It is a great responsibility for men to be called suddenly from their business and their pleasures to decide upon matters of life and death. I believe that, as a case like this goes on from day to day, there comes into your hearts a deep desire which is in itself a prayer that the spirit of justice may be among us and may guide and strengthen each to play his part. That invocation is never in vain. The spirit of justice is in this court today to comfort and protect her in the hour of her utmost need. That spirit will speak in firm and unfaltering voice when your verdict tells to the whole world that in your judgment Adelaide Bartlett is not guilty.'

He had finished, after speaking for close upon five hours. As he sat down the strength ebbed out of him; he felt almost dazed by an onrush of fatigue. He closed his eyes and rested his head for a moment on his hands, barely conscious of a sound seldom heard inside the courts—the billowing thunder of tumultuous applause.

25

For all practical purposes the trial was at an end. The defence, which from the start had made uninterrupted progress, exceptional in hard-fought trials outside the realm of fiction, had now attained the peak. Clarke had started with a case that it was generally expected he would lose. With his cross-examination of Old Bartlett the adverse current, which had been flowing fast, was stemmed. With his cross-examination of the Reverend Dyson, he reversed the tendeney and was no longer losing. With Dr Leach he began to win, though he was not yet winning. With Dr Stevenson he was winning, though he had not yet won.

The speech clinched all. There was still another night for the jury's second thoughts, there was still another day for argument and review, but the spell of that eloquence persisted unimpaired. Whether they knew it or not, whether they minded or not, the twelve were no longer free to make their own decision.

A thirteenth member had been added to the jury.

26

This only becomes clear, however, in the light of history. Until the verdict all remained in doubt, and the tension prevailing in the last hours of the trial was even greater than had gone before.

Clarke himself was a prey to deep misgivings. 'I do not think,' he said afterwards, 'that anyone who has not been through it himself can realise the mental strain of the last day of a trial for murder upon counsel for the defence. As he listens to the reply for the Crown, and to the judge's summing-up, he finds little comfort in the thought that he has done his best.'

Outwardly calm but with every nerve on edge, the defender perforce sat silent hour by hour in the court that yesterday had been quickened with his voice. He heard Russell's reply, vigorous and pithy, only marred by a last-minute attempt to substitute a brand-new theory of the murder for that which had been so badly blown upon. He heard a careful summing-up of exemplary fairness, though the judge did not disguise his personal opinion that the proper verdict would be to convict. And ever and anon he heard the shouting and the clamour from the huge throng waiting in the streets outside. . . .

The jury retired a few minutes before three. An hour passed, an hour of restless agony. Just before four they came back into their box—but merely to ask the judge to verify some minor points of detail, which being done they once again withdrew.

They were out a further hour. It was precisely five o'clock when the rustling and whispering of an overwrought assembly died upon the instant as the jury reappeared. They bore themselves as men do who have reached a great decision, but what decision few then would have ventured to predict. . . .

The prisoner was brought back into the dock and the figures were disposed for the most nerve-racking of ceremonies. Mrs Bartlett showed an iron self-control, but it was hard to determine whether she or her counsel looked more white and strained.

The Clerk of the Court rose with due formality.

'Gentlemen, have you agreed upon your verdict?'

'We have,' said the foreman.

'Do you find the prisoner guilty or not guilty?'

Nobody breathed. Time stood still. Then the foreman began to read from a sheet of paper.

'We have considered the evidence,' he said, 'and although we think grave suspicion is attached to the prisoner——'

The qualifying clause told all. A spontaneous cheer went up and could hardly be suppressed.

'—we do not think there is sufficient evidence,' the foreman continued, 'to show how or by whom the chloroform was administered.'

The dock door opened, Mrs Bartlett stepped forth to freedom, and for the first and last time in his fifty years of practice Edward Clarke broke down in court and wept.

27

And now the cheers burst forth again, and would not be denied. In vain did the ushers scurry to and fro; in vain did the judge speak of insult and of outrage. His remonstrances were drowned in the ever-growing din, which spread like wildfire through the corridors and courtyard, and was presently being echoed back from the overflowing streets.

This demonstration was not for Mrs Bartlett. It was Edward Clarke who was the idol of the hour. It was he for whom the jury waited by the steps to shake his hand before he left the court for home; it was he who, as his carriage passed out of the gates, found it surrounded by a demonstrating crowd which ran alongside all the way down Holborn where passers-by called tribute from pavement and from bus; it was he who, on attending a theatre that same evening, was immediately picked out and accorded an ovation.

So in a more leisurely and spacious age than ours was homage paid to the triumph of a great counsel.

28

For Russell a less exhilarating sequel lay in wait.

Three years later he was to figure in a not dissimilar case that acquired equal notoriety—the trial at Liverpool of Mrs Florence Maybrick. She too was charged with murdering her husband; she too was alleged to have used poison; she too drew the scientific fire of Dr Stevenson; she too had to endure a minute scrutiny of her private life. But there was this striking contrast between the plight of the two women: Mrs Bartlett had Russell ranged against her, Mrs Maybrick had Russell enlisted on her side. That the evidence against Mrs Bartlett was stronger than that against Mrs Maybrick is, in my opinion, not open to doubt. Yet Russell, the most formidable counsel of his day, failed to obtain a conviction against the former and failed to secure an acquittal for the latter.

The one woman was as luckless as the other fortunate. Mrs Maybrick had cause to curse the fate that gave her a perverse jury and a mentally sick judge. Mrs Bartlett had cause to bless the gods that laid at her disposal the selfless endeavours and persuasive voice of Edward Clarke.

Hay Wrightson

EDWARD MARSHALL HALL

EDWARDIAN TROMBONES

Marshall Hall defends Robert Wood

1

Since the beginning of this century many London districts have completely changed their character. Such is not the case with Camden Town. There are superficial differences, of course, but in essentials it remains what it was in 1907, the year of the murder distinguished by its name. It is a place where underfed and overcrowded thousands wage perpetual battle on the poverty line; where dubious lodging-houses jostle modest homes and working folk commingle with shady fly-by-nights; where squalor animates as it deforms, and lends to ugliness a crude enchantment; where social commerce flourishes in the steamy pubs from which couples, casually met and matched, depart each night at closing time to furtive privacy. It is a place of pungent contrasts—of dull monotony and indiscreet adventure, of dingy greyness and flashy colour, of gay excitement and unrelieved despair. It is a place that provides its own escape from its own horror. It is the poor man's West End.

Even in this restless spot, however, there are backwaters and byways where at least on the surface life is lived at slower tempo. One of these may be found behind Royal College Street by anyone turning eastward at The Eagle. He will pass under some railway arches, dank and cavernous; over a crossing where traffic lights strike a solitary modern note; and thence into a long ascending road along which a few trees import a faintly rustic air. Known as St Paul's Road in its days of notoriety, this thoroughfare has since been unaccountably re-christened.

The houses in St Paul's Road now are mostly bruised and battered. A cheerless tale of penury or indifference can be read in the missing gates and broken gateposts, in the numbers rudely chalked on splintered doors, in the rubbish dump that fills the space intended for a garden. Few make St Paul's

Road their permanent abode; it is a temporary stop on the way up—or the way down.

In appearance, Twenty-nine does not differ from the rest. It has the same depressing, unattractive air. Children may clamber up and down the steep stone steps; a couple of milk bottles may stand upon the sill; but these indications of harmless domesticity, while tempering the gloom, accentuate the commonplace. Not a house, you would think, to draw anyone's attention, to be worthy of the slightest notice from the passer-by. And yet there are still those who would make a special journey just to gaze on Twenty-nine—and particularly at the window of the first floor front.

That window grips and chills and terrifies. Fancy likes to make of it an eye that constantly looks inwards, scanning the room it has learnt to know so well. The scene there, one imagines, never changes to the Eye; it is frozen into a macabre tableau, and has been so now these many, many years. Whole generations have passed through it unheeded—have lived, loved, quarrelled, worked and died; to the Eye they were but phantoms, it is the tableau that is real.

You and I, if privileged to penetrate this room, might see a large family at the ritual of tea; the Eye sees only empty liquor bottles and the broken meats of a supper laid for two. You and I might see a lively bunch of youngsters, playing on the floor with their cheap and simple toys; the Eye sees only the steady drip of blood, soaking through the bed into the boards below. You and I might see a genteel widow, toasting at the fire, while outside beats the hubbub of a golden afternoon; the Eye sees only a torn and naked girl, motionless in the silence and the slate-cold light of dawn.

For the Eye sees the room in which The Murder was committed; the Camden Town Murder that destroyed Phyllis Dimmock and came within an ace of destroying Robert Wood. It is a room that has held its secret more than forty years; a secret shared with none—except the murderer and the Eye.

2

The women of the streets draw a sharp distinction between prostitutes (prompted solely by the profit motive) and whores (who, while not indifferent to monetary reward, practise promiscuity because they relish it).

Phyllis Dimmock was a prostitute who had turned into a whore. Born into respectable poverty at Walworth, and christened more prosaically Emily Elizabeth, she grew up into a pretty, pleasant-mannered girl. The combination of good looks and bad prospects set her upon a well-worn and platitudinous course. First as a factory worker flirting with her 'boys,' then as a domestic servant flattered by her 'followers,' she quickly learnt how to exploit the fascination it was in her power to exercise over the other sex. Economic pressure, combined with youth's predilection for the raffish, ensured that this power was in due course capitalised, and Phyllis abandoned irksome thriftiness for the relative prodigalities of the prostitute's half-world.

Few who tread this demoralising path ever get a chance to retrace any of their steps. Phyllis Dimmock furnished an exception to the rule. At the age of twenty-one, already a veteran of the brothels and the streets, she made the acquaintance of a man named Bertram Shaw, who was employed on the railway as a dining-car attendant. Despite the corrupting effects of her profession, Phyllis still retained considerable charm and Shaw was stirred to more than passing interest. The girl being not unwilling, a liaison was established. Perhaps because of his knowledge of her past, Shaw would not enter into a contractual alliance, but in every respect save that of legal ceremony he conferred on Phyllis Dimmock the status of a wife.

They lived together in modest but agreeable apartments, dividing responsibilities as married couples do. Phyllis got the meals and did the household chores. Shaw earned the money and paid the household bills. It was an orderly existence and, as Shaw was a steady man and genuinely fond of her, Phyllis could look forward to a protracted partnership.

Even if the menage was not, technically, respectable, at least it offered her escape from the degrading accompaniments of haphazard harlotry.

But Phyllis, being Phyllis, did not see it in that light. Harlotry was not only a trade, it was a pleasure. The joint home with Bert was quite convenient in its way—as a base, a jumping-off ground, the tranquil centre of a wild and vicious vortex. Though she did not despise the comforts of the new life, she lusted after the excitements of the old.

The nature of Shaw's work presented her with a solution. Most afternoons he went out at four o'clock, travelled north during the evening with his train, slept at Sheffield overnight, and travelled back next morning, arriving about noon. This gave Phyllis freedom and immunity during the hours that for her purpose counted most. In one regard she was better off than she had been before; provided that she acted with reasonable caution she had now what her sisterhood refers to as 'a place,' without the necessity of settling the rent.

So night after night, as the unsuspicious Shaw expertly manœuvred down the rocking restaurant car, Phyllis set forth from the sombre street she lived in, seeking places better served with noise and light—and men.

Her favourite hunting ground was the pavements and the public houses of the Euston Road.

3

Any one of several reasons may prompt a man to cultivate the company of those whose morals and behaviour are less seemly than his own. It may be curiosity; a consuming thirst for first-hand knowledge of phenomena absent or suppressed in his habitual milieu. It may be titillation; the undeniable stimulus of entering a world where normal values are inverted or annulled. It may be a pernicious taste for coarse debauchery that appears to be endemic among the most fastidious; this weakness is exemplified by Oscar Wilde and Dowson, and has been dramatised by Emlyn Williams and Pinero.

There is reason to surmise that all three motives combined

in Robert Wood. He was a well-educated, intelligent young man, with an inquisitive and restless disposition. He had a high degree of talent as an artist and designer, betokening a temperament responsive to impressions. And though he held a well-paid post with a reputable firm, and though he lived with the most virtuous of parents in a middle-class environment of unpretentious worth, from very early manhood Wood had shown a propensity to seek out the companionship of public courtesans.

For some time this propensity was largely satisfied by his association with a girl named Ruby Young—a name that he was presently to make for a brief space almost as familiar and notorious as his own. Ruby described herself as an artist's model, but like numerous other ladies in that estimable profession she spent most of her evenings on the prowl in Leicester Square. Wood was well aware of this; it may indeed have kindled rather than subdued his ardour; certainly he and Ruby maintained a close relationship hardly distinguishable from that of any courting couple—save perhaps in the omission to contemplate a marriage, and in the readiness with which favours were demanded and bestowed.

It was Wood, though, not Ruby who first tired of the arrangement. It seems likely that the kindly, amiable artist had a fancy to inspect more thorough-paced depravity. When at last Ruby moved from Liverpool Street, King's Cross (which was only a few yards from his home off Gray's Inn Road) and withdrew to the less accessible region of Earl's Court, Wood seized the chance to start a gradual cooling off. He saw Ruby less and less, and frequented more and more a stratum of the half-world in comparison with which the girls of Leicester Square constituted an élite.

His favourite hunting ground was the pavements and the public houses of the Euston Road.

4

The precise date and hour at which the artist Robert Wood and the harlot Phyllis Dimmock first crossed paths on their common hunting ground was the subject of vigorous contention at the time and can now never be finally determined. It may be that, as some of the girl's associates asserted, it occurred as early as April 1906, and that thenceforward for a space of eighteen months the pair met frequently on the friendliest of terms. It may be that, as Wood consistently maintained, it did not occur until September 1907, and that their brief acquaintance mainly hinged on fortuitous encounters. Whichever version is accepted, of this there is no doubt: whether by chance or whether by design, Robert Wood was in Phyllis Dimmock's company on four of the last six evenings of her life.

Phyllis was murdered early on Thursday, 12th September. On the previous Friday, Wood was with her at The Rising Sun. On the Saturday he was with her at The Eagle. On the Monday he was with her at The Rising Sun again. On the Wednesday once again he was with her at The Eagle.

On this last occasion they stayed at least an hour. They were not, however, narrowly observed. The bar was full, and others were busy with their own affairs. No one gathered any clue to their precise relationship; no one noticed whether they left singly or together. Even the watchful staff could only say that, before the closing hour, both of them had gone.

That Wednesday night when Phyllis Dimmock stepped out of The Eagle to all intents and purposes she stepped out of this world. A gap begins—a gap in which nothing can be learnt of her actions or companions save by reconstruction both laborious and fallible.

The gap extends for twelve hours; then terminates abruptly.

5

At half-past eleven on the morning of the Thursday, Bertram Shaw, refreshed by his short walk from St Pancras, came striding briskly up the slope of St Paul's Road. He was in excellent spirits. His train had been on time. The day had turned out sunny. His afternoon was free.

He whistled as he trotted up the steps of Twenty-nine, latchkey in hand, ready to open the front door.

Usually Phyllis ran downstairs to greet him. Instead the landlady met him in the hall.

'Oh, Mr Shaw,' she said, 'your mother's just arrived.'

His mother lived some sixty miles off at Northampton, and her advent in London was entirely unexpected. She had in fact made the journey on a sudden impulse, being eager to inspect the lately acquired 'wife' whom her son had mentioned in his letters.

The Fates never acted with more cynical brutality than in prompting the poor lady to choose that very day. . . .

'I'll go right up,' Shaw said.

'She's below,' said the landlady. 'I took her to my room.'

'Why?' Shaw asked.

'Because,' said the landlady, 'we can't get into yours.'

Shaw looked puzzled, as he was; puzzled and inquiring; but before he could give his perplexities a shape his mother had appeared and hurried to embrace him. The reunion banished the matter from his mind.

'Come up and meet Phyllis,' he said, without a qualm.

Chattering lightheartedly they climbed the stairs together.

The apartment Shaw and Phyllis shared consisted of two rooms, linked and divided by a pair of folding doors. They had a key to these and to the door on to the landing, but it was not their habit to lock either.

Shaw tried the landing door and found it would not open. He rattled the handle. He banged upon the panels. He called Phyllis's name, loudly and repeatedly. He pressed his ear to the narrow slit and listened. Inside there was not a stirring, not a breath.

All Shaw's unformed misgivings now returned in sharper outline. Leaving his mother bewildered, he tore downstairs again. In a moment he was back with the landlady's spare key.

What Shaw expected to see when the door opened depended on his idiosyncratic mental make-up. Each of us in such circumstances fashions his own nightmare.

What Shaw actually saw was but the prelude to a nightmare. The sitting-room had been incontinently ravished;

furniture shifted, drawers upset, the contents overturned. But there was no human occupant—none, alive or dead. Beyond, the folding doors stood shut, blankly non-committal.

They also were locked. But Shaw had grown too apprehensive to be patient. He used his sturdy shoulders and cracked the doors by force.

It was then that he saw what he must now have feared to see; the nightmare itself, stark and unforgettable.

6

The police moved fast. In a matter of hours they believed themselves on the verge of an arrest.

All their data pointed in the same direction. The medical evidence—based on the advance of rigor mortis—fixed the girl's death between four o'clock and six. Nothing suggested that there had been a struggle; her face was peaceful; her body lay at ease. And since Shaw could produce an alibi from his colleagues and employers; and since inquiries soon established beyond a shadow of a doubt that Phyllis had been bringing men home almost every night, smuggling them in after the landlady's retirement and smuggling them out again early in the morning, the police were irresistibly impelled to this conclusion—that it was one of these stray visitors who had murdered Phyllis Dimmock; taking her unawares—maybe as she slept—and, with one tremendous slash from a sharp and powerful weapon, cutting her throat from ear to ear right back to the spine.

So investigation turned to the taverns she had haunted and among whose patrons she had angled for admirers. Foremost among these was The Rising Sun, and here straightaway the police came upon a man acutely conscious of his own predicament.

He was a ship's cook, lately paid off from a voyage. In accordance with the mariner's immemorial tradition, he had set out to spend his accumulated wealth upon a round of amorous conviviality. In pursuit of this aim, he fell in with Phyllis Dimmock, meeting her first in Euston Road on

Sunday, 8th September. The couple having made themselves sufficiently acquainted, they drank together in The Rising Sun; thereafter the ship's cook escorted Phyllis to her rooms, where he remained with her till seven the next morning. This programme proved so profitable to one and so enjoyable to both that it was repeated on the two succeeding nights. . . .

Sunday, Monday, Tuesday.

'And Wednesday?' the police asked.

'Oh no,' said the ship's cook, instantly defensive. 'I never saw her Wednesday; not after I left her at her place in the morning.'

'Where were you Wednesday night?'

'In The Rising Sun,' the ship's cook answered promptly. 'But Phyllis wasn't there; she didn't come in all night. I stayed till after twelve; anyone'll tell you that.'

'And where did you go from there?'

'To the place where I'd been stopping; it's a temperance hotel. I walked back with a friend—a chap; he was staying there too. The old girl let us in and she locked the front door after us.'

'What's the name of the hotel?'

He told them, and they hurried off to verify his statement. It was confirmed and vouched for by unchallengeable witnesses. Had it been otherwise the ship's cook might have paid high for his pleasures—in the shape of a trial and maybe a conviction. It would not have been the first time that an innocent man was hanged.

As it was, the police acknowledged the inevitable and crossed off the only name upon their list of suspects. They may be pardoned if they did so with professional reluctance. For lately the ship's cook had almost monopolised the girl and thus reduced the number of potential candidates. In those last few days, what other men had been around with Phyllis?

Some frequenters of The Rising Sun did speak of a man: a man with a long, thin face and sunken eyes; a well-spoken man; a man of education. He had been in with her more than once, they said, in the days before the murder; but they had never seen him since and did not know who he was.

7

Wood worked hard to make certain that they never should. As the Camden Town mystery filled the columns of the press and excited speculation both in public and in private, the artist with the long thin face and sunken eyes took steps to cover up the tracks that linked him with the victim.

Provided he kept well away from Camden Town there was only one person he had valid cause to fear. That was Joseph Lambert, a bookseller's assistant, whom he knew on pleasant terms but only seldom met. By an irony of the Fates (different in kind but comparable in degree to that which timed the visit paid by Mrs Shaw to London), one of these rare meetings between Wood and Lambert had occurred in the bar of The Eagle public house on the evening of Wednesday, the 11th of September. Lambert had dropped in by chance. Wood was with Phyllis. He introduced her by her first name to his friend, and before Lambert left they all had a drink together.

Nine days later, when photographs of Phyllis were appearing in the papers, Wood called at the shop where Lambert worked. He took the latter aside and asked him if he had heard about the Camden Town affair. 'Yes,' said Lambert, 'I have, but what about it?' He had not, after all, recognised the photographs, and was somewhat mystified that Wood should seek him out for an idle conversation about a shocking crime.

Wood might have refrained from committing himself further. But the hue and cry was dangerously insistent; at any moment more and better pictures might be published; Lambert's enlightenment might only be postponed. Better that his friend should hear who Phyllis was from him—and hear at the same time his reasoned plea for silence.

He went straight to the point.

'I want you to do me a favour. That night I saw you in the pub—last week—remember?' Lambert stared, nonplussed by Wood's urgency of manner. 'Well, if anyone says anything to you about it, say we met and had a drink. But leave out the girl.'

'Leave out the girl,' Lambert repeated.

'Yes,' said Wood.

Lambert cast his mind back. He recalled that curious meeting at The Eagle, and the little group the three of them had formed; himself, Wood and the girl—the girl, on whom he had never since bestowed a single thought. He had forgotten her; she whom he was being entreated to forget. His response was human; he tried to recollect her. Tall, slender, a rather pretty face. . . . *Have you heard about the Camden Town affair?*

The two men looked steadily at one another. No word passed; but at that moment Lambert knew—and Wood perceived he knew.

'She was Phyllis,' the latter said at last. 'That girl was Phyllis Dimmock.'

'Yes,' Lambert said. There didn't seem anything else to say.

'Of course, I don't want to get mixed up in this affair,' Wood continued. 'Think of the publicity. Think of my people.'

Lambert did so. He thought of Wood's father, lately in poor health; thought of how he would take a public revelation that his well-respected son had been a prostitute's familiar. With the gentle and likeable Robert Wood before him no theme more sinister entered Lambert's head.

'I can rely on you?' Wood asked.

'That'll be all right,' Lambert said.

Wood pressed his hand and left

But this was only the negative side of Robert Wood's precautions. On the positive side he enlisted his old sweetheart, Ruby Young.

8

Ruby Young was in love with Robert Wood. She had been so from the start; she remained so to the end; it complicated equally her actions and reactions, and drew her, unwilling, to the centre of the stage. She is indeed the third tragic figure in this drama, and her sufferings, though less conspicuous and fearsome, are not one whit less pitiful than the sufferings of the pair that underwent a crucifixion more spectacular.

By the September of Phyllis Dimmock's murder, Wood's alliance with Ruby Young was virtually quiescent. A quarrel in July about another woman—Ruby was inclined to be jealous and possessive—precipitated a breach that had already been foreshadowed. Since then they had only seen each other once, and that through an accidental meeting in the street. But Ruby still hankered after her former flame and when, out of the blue, on the 20th of September she received a telegram asking her to meet him at their old rendezvous, she decked herself out in all her finery and went to the appointed place in pleasurable elation.

Wood's greeting was flatteringly warm, but his subsequent behaviour proved a little disconcerting. He showed gallantry, affection, remorse for his neglect—but seemed to be obsessed by an undisclosed anxiety. He could hardly wait till they had sat down in the teashop before he appealed to her to help him in his 'trouble.'

'But what sort of trouble is it?' Ruby asked.

'Remember this,' he said, side-stepping the query: 'if any questions should be put to you, say you always saw me on Mondays and on Wednesdays.' He patted her arm tenderly. 'On Mondays and Wednesdays. Will you?'

'But what for?' she demanded.

'Will you do it?' he said.

Ruby felt resentful. If he didn't trust her, if he didn't want to tell her what he had been up to—very well, he needn't; that was as he liked; but then why should she put herself out to help? 'And it's sure to be something to do with a girl,' she bitterly reflected.

'Will you do it?' Wood repeated gently.

It was on the very tip of Ruby's tongue to say she wouldn't—and thereby to save them both unutterable torment. But as she looked at him, her mood suddenly changed.

Here was the way to conciliate the loved one; once she had this hold upon him he would have to see her—see her often to make sure of her goodwill. 'And if I can only see him,' Ruby thought with the female's timeless faith, 'if I can only see him, I know I'll win him back.'

'Well,' said Wood, 'will you do this for me?'

Ruby heaved a sigh.

'Oh, all right,' she said. . . .

Having muzzled truth and sown the seeds of falsehood, Wood could face the future with less disquietude. Day by day he went about his business, patiently waiting for the tumult to die down.

9

So it might well have done had not the ship's cook, dead end of one trail, opened up another.

He told the police a story that could not be disregarded. Before he left Phyllis on the Wednesday morning—after the third and last of his nightly visits—he had picked up a letter that had come with the post and been thrust under her door. She took it, read it, then showed part of it to him. That part he remembered. 'Dear Phyllis,' it had run. 'Will you meet me at the bar of The Eagle at Camden Town 8.30 tonight, Wednesday—Bert.' He was sure about that; sure of the very words—just as he was sure that Phyllis had struck a match, set fire to the letter, and thrown it in the grate.

What impressed the police most about this revelation was the fact that it could be at least partially confirmed. Some charred paper had been salvaged from the grate, and such writing as could be deciphered seemed corroborative. One could say no more than that; it was too vestigial to be read consecutively—or to furnish a fair sample of the correspondent's hand.

There remained, however, a further chance of coming by the latter, and here once again the ship's cook was instrumental. Phyllis had had a hobby; she collected picture postcards, most of which she kept in a big, old-fashioned album. She had shown him one such card, the ship's cook said, immediately after she had let him see the letter. At her prompting he had read the message written on it—another, not dissimilar, request for an appointment, somewhat unexpectedly signed with the name 'Alice,' and charmingly embellished, by whoever sent it, with an expert little pencil drawing of a rising sun. The ship's cook was certain that the writing on postcard and letter were the same.

The police could now indulge in an attractive chain of reasoning. If you knew who wrote the postcard, you would know who wrote the letter. If you knew who wrote the letter, you would know who was with Phyllis on Wednesday at The Eagle. If you knew who was with Phyllis on Wednesday at The Eagle, you would know who took her home. And if you knew who took her home . . .

This chain might not seem flawless to a trained logician, but in a case almost devoid of other clues it made a hopeful basis for renewed investigation, or would have done if the police had not been frustrated from the outset.

The postcard itself was nowhere to be found.

Methodically they sifted the contents of the album—pathetic little trophies of a brief and sordid life; mostly contributed by sometime paramours dispersed among the ports and docks and barracks of the world. There were cheap comic cards, cheap sentimental cards, cards with ardent postscripts, cards with waggish innuendoes—but none that was signed 'Alice' and none that had been decorated with a rising sun.

The police thought they knew why. Indeed, the very absence of the postcard might explain a feature of the crime that had been so far inexplicable. When Shaw burst through the folding doors that morning he found the shutters of the bedroom window incompletely closed; the gap admitted a narrow shaft of light trained exactly on the dead girl's sewing machine. On the top of that machine was the album, lying open; some of the cards lay scattered on the floor below. It now seemed nearly certain that, before he left, the murderer had recalled to mind the card that might betray him, that might serve as proof of his connection with the girl; that he had had the nerve to search for it, the good fortune to find it, and the prudence to destroy it or take it out of reach

Another trail was closed. The days passed. The tumult lessened, and at last began to die.

10

Bertram Shaw was packing up. He had not slept here since the night it happened; always up North, or at an hotel, or with friends. Now, thank God, he had got another place.

He packed rapidly, keen to get it over. Shirts, his week-end suit, some personal belongings—he crammed them into the bag just as they came to hand. Phyllis's few possessions had already been removed. Soon no visible trace remained of either to show that they had ever occupied the room—except a sorrel stain which no scrubbing would erase.

Shaw took a quick look round to make sure nothing had been left. Mindful how small articles like studs and links secrete themselves, he felt under the paper lining of the drawers. He found no studs nor links; only a picture post-card, signed with the name 'Alice,' and charmingly embellished, by whoever sent it, with an expert little pencil drawing of a rising sun.

11

The flagging hounds revived; once more the hunt was up. Next Sunday, at the wish of Scotland Yard, a replica of the postcard was displayed in national newspapers, backed by an appeal to the civic spirit of anyone who might chance to recognise the writing. Reinforcing this inducement, one enterprising paper made an offer of one hundred pounds reward

One may wonder whether there has ever been another postcard delivered to the breakfast table of so many millions. They studied it with the care befitting its credentials ('believed to have direct bearing on the case of Phyllis Dimmock'); examining the postmark ('9 Sept. 4 a.m.'); reading and re-reading the now notorious address (Mrs B. Shaw, 29 St Paul's Road, Camden Town'); brooding over the seemingly innocuous invitation ('Phyllis darling, if it pleases you, meet me 8.15 p.m. at the——' and there the words gave way to the celebrated drawing: a perky, rather bibulous sun coming over the horizon, one eye closed in a Rabelaisian wink); musing solemnly on the facetious close ('Yours to a cinder, Alice').

Fired with the zeal of amateur detectives, eager to assist in tracking down a malefactor, the millions were baffled; they did not know the writing.

But Ruby Young knew it—knew it the moment her eye fell upon the paper.

12

'It *is* your writing, isn't it?' she said, even before the front door had been closed.

'Of course it is,' Wood answered.

He spoke almost lightly, but Ruby shrank back as if she had been struck.

'Why have you come? What has happened?' she whispered. 'Oh, Bob, what have you done?'

Wood smiled reassuringly.

'Have patience,' he said. 'Let's go up to your room, and I will tell you all.'

Ruby had passed through a day of mental torture, beset by thoughts she hardly dared to form. The newspaper, unread, was folded back to show the postcard, and every few minutes she stared at it again. So this was the 'trouble' in which Wood had sought her help; this was why she had to say she always saw him Wednesdays; this, too, was the reason for his renewed attentiveness—the kisses, the gifts, the visit to the play. He had been keeping the right side of her, fostering her devotion, using every trick to make his shield secure.

Not even fear and horror and foreboding insulate a woman from the pangs of wounded pride.

She sat down and waited. He paced about a little, then suddenly began.

'Ruby, it's just sheer bad luck,' he said. 'I'd only met the girl a week before, and all we ever did was pass the time of day. I was nothing to her and she was nothing to me.'

'Then why,' Ruby asked, 'did you send her a postcard asking her to meet you?'

'I didn't,' Wood exclaimed. 'That's the terrible part about it. It was meant as a joke.' He shook his head slowly. 'It all happened on the Friday before . . . before the murder: meeting her, and the postcard, and everything.'

He stopped, as if to see whether he was being heard with sympathy.

'Go on,' Ruby said.

'I was with a friend of mine and, entirely by chance, we went in The Rising Sun. There was a girl there; she asked me for a coin to start the electric organ. I gave her one, and—well, naturally, next time I was ordering I stood her a friendly drink.'

'And that was Phyllis Dimmock?' Ruby asked.

'I just knew her name was Phyllis; you know what it is in a pub.'

'And you'd never seen her before?'

'Never in my life.'

'What about the postcard?'

'I was just coming to that. After my friend left—he had to catch his train—a boy selling postcards came into the bar. They were rubbishy stuff, and I happened to have some really good ones in my pocket—some I'd brought back from my holiday at Bruges. So when I saw Phyllis was going to buy one from the boy I suggested she chose one of mine instead. She had a look at them, she picked one out, and she said, "That's pretty; send it me and write something nice on it." '

'How did you know where to send it?'

'She dictated her address.'

'And why did you write . . . what you did?'

Wood ran a hand through his hair.

'Well, Ruby, what *was* I to write? Something nice, she said. I used the first thing that came into my head. Before my friend left I'd arranged to meet him again at The Rising Sun, so I wrote down the words of that appointment, and drew a picture to make it more amusing. It didn't seem to matter. I was going to sign my name, only she said, "Don't; the governor might cut up rough; put 'Alice'—that's the name of a woman that I know." I put "Alice," ' Wood said, throwing wide his arms, 'and now you know the story of this miserable postcard that looks as though it's going to bring me to my ruin.'

Ruby's heart was growing lighter. He didn't do it, then; of course he didn't do it; her deepest instincts had told her all along. He was the prey of circumstances, and as such to be pitied—but he was still not absolved for his duplicity with her.

'What happened next?' she said, coldly inquisitorial.

'I hadn't a stamp,' Wood said, and smiled forlornly, 'so I said I'd post it later. I finished my drink, I said good night, and I walked out of the pub.'

'Did you see her again?'

'I saw her on Saturday—next day. I was up in Camden Town, on business, and I met her in the street. She said, "You haven't sent my postcard," and she was right, I hadn't; truth to tell, I'd forgotten the whole thing. I promised I would, and we talked for a bit, and then I left her. I posted the card next night.'

'Did you see her again?'

Wood hesitated.

'Once more—on the Monday. She was in The Rising Sun. She came over to speak to me; I stood her a drink; then she said goodbye and joined some other men. That was the last time—the last time I ever saw her.'

'She was murdered on the night of the Wednesday,' Ruby said. Her voice was strained.

'I know.' Wood looked graver now than he had done throughout. 'I know, Ruby. That's why you must stand by me. I was out walking by myself that Wednesday night, and I can't bring anyone to prove just where I was. *You must say I was with you.*'

There was a pause. They were both very still and quiet.

'It might get me into dreadful trouble,' Ruby said, 'if other people proved that I was . . . somewhere else.'

'No, no,' Wood insisted. 'Your word and mine together, we can defy the world.'

'If you went to Scotland Yard——' Ruby began.

'—they wouldn't believe me. Not without a witness.' He sat down beside her. 'I know I can trust you, Ruby.'

'I'm not the only one who knows your writing,' Ruby said.

'They won't spot it at home,' Wood said, 'and you're the only other one who knows it well enough.' He put his arm about her. 'You'll be my own girl, won't you? Promise me, dear? Promise?'

Ruby gazed straight ahead.

'I promise,' she said at last, and her lip began to quiver as the burden of the day's events grew more than she could bear.

13

During the months that were to come Ruby Young was widely regarded as a female Judas. This judgment—based in part upon the incorrect assumption that she had betrayed Wood for the newspaper reward—was wickedly unjust to one taxed beyond her strength. Initially she did more for Wood than could have been expected. Having given her promise, she was resolved to keep it; having entered into conspiracy, she meant it to succeed; and it was actually Ruby, not Robert Wood himself, who constructed in detail the mendacious alibi. That she later was the cause of Wood's exposure is a fact; that she became so deliberately is unwarrantable inference. Hers was not a case of broken faith, but of breaking nerve.

There were two phases in the process of attrition. At first she was in a continuous state of dread lest someone else should have recognised the writing. But in this respect Wood's optimistic surmise proved well founded; no one else apparently formed even a suspicion—except one business colleague, a Mr Tinkham, who was satisfied when Wood gave him the selfsame explanation, and about whom Ruby Young did not even hear. But as her justifiable and substantial fears receded Ruby conceived others, not less grim because less tangible; fears of some unforeseeable contingency in which they themselves would effect their own undoing. Her distress was not diminished by Wood's understandable but harassing insistence on their compact. 'Be true,' he would adjure her each time that they met. 'Yes, yes,' she would say, 'but don't bother me; it's getting on my nerves.'

Ruby's ultimate concession to this pressure followed precedents established by her sex. She sought the solace of a confidant. Her choice was unwise—indeed, calamitous. Thinly disguising it as someone else's story which was being presented for its academic interest, the foolish girl recounted the whole episode to a man whom she described as 'one of my gentleman friends.' This friend in turn had a friend who was a pressman; next day the latter was brought into this oblique discussion; he grasped its real significance—and also its potential value to himself. Almost before Ruby realised what she had done she found herself being questioned by an officer from the Yard.

There was then no alternative; she had already gone too far; Ruby had to admit that she knew Robert Wood to be the author of the postcard. But as full comprehension of her grievous blunder dawned, and she foresaw the consequences it might have for Wood, the anguish of remorse completely overcame her. She could not go on; she could tell them nothing more.

For the police, however, that was temporarily enough. Dropping dark hints about what can happen to accessories—especially accessories who don't repent in time—that afternoon they took Ruby with them to wait for Wood as he came out from his work.

It was a painful scene. The girl, half stunned by now with misery and terror, stood near the office door in accordance with her orders. The police kept watch from a short distance away. When Wood appeared, Ruby, leaden-footed, moved into his path.

He smiled at the sight of her.

'Sweetheart,' he said, and put his arm through hers, 'this is nice. I'm glad to see you. You're pale, though; what's the matter? You've not been crying, have you?'

Ruby almost choked.

'Of course not,' she said. 'I . . . I'm all right.'

'Well, you look a bit downhearted,' Wood said chaffingly. 'Come on, we'll go and have some tea and cheer you up.'

Still arm in arm, they walked along together. A burly man came from an alley opposite and moved towards them purposefully. Wood tightened his grip on Ruby's arm.

'See that fellow there?' he muttered. 'I believe he's a detective.'

'Take no notice,' Ruby said. She was going through it compulsively, as one does through a bad nightmare.

The burly man approached.

'Mr Wood?' he asked.

'Yes,' said Wood.

'I am a police inspector and I wish to speak to you.'

'Certainly,' said Wood.

The two men withdrew a little.

'I've been making enquiries into the murder of Phyllis Dimmock,' the inspector said, 'and I have reason to believe that a postcard sent to her was written by you.'

'Quite right,' said Wood.

'Then I shall have to detain you pending enquiries into your movements on the night of 11th September.'

Wood was perfectly calm. Had he not an unassailable alibi?

'Very well,' he said. 'You will allow me to say goodbye to my young lady?'

The inspector nodded. Wood went to Ruby and took her in his arms.

'I have to go with him,' he said. 'Don't worry, dear.'

Ruby was like stone.

'Goodbye,' he said again, and kissed her on the lips.

It broke her strange, somnabulistic trance. She began to sob, loudly, hysterically, clinging to him as though she would never let him go.

'Don't cry,' he whispered, greatly touched. 'Don't cry. But be true, dearest. Be true.'

14

Wood's belief that Ruby would be 'true' led him still deeper into the morass. Invited to recount how he had spent the evening on 11th September, he strictly adhered to their concocted alibi. He told the police that he had been out with 'Miss Ruby Young, my sweetheart'; that they had had tea together in a Holborn café; that they had afterwards strolled about in the West End; that it was late before he parted from her outside Brompton Oratory—all upon the confident assumption that Ruby, when questioned, would tell this story too.

But meantime the police were hard at work on Ruby, who was pitifully demoralised and almost unresisting. Between passionate storms of weeping she confessed what had been done, and Wood's carefully plotted alibi became a boomerang.

The whole flock of lies and subornations and suppressions now came home to roost. The police discovered Lambert. They discovered Tinkham. And from the former—as Wood's friend, an unimpeachable source—they learnt that their man had been with Phyllis on Wednesday at The Eagle. . . .

On the 6th October—two days after his original detention—Robert Wood was formally charged with murder. His employers instantly and generously donated a handsome sum earmarked to meet the expense of briefing counsel. His solicitor was thus without restriction in his choice; he could select the man best fitted to the task; and so was brought into the case its most potent element—the giant personality of Edward Marshall Hall.

15

The legend of Marshall Hall is the strongest ever woven round a figure at the Bar. With his impressive height, handsome face and superbly stalwart bearing, his burning eloquence, selfless courage and manifest sincerity, he fulfilled, better than any before or since, the popular conception of the ideal advocate. As Spilsbury in his time was undeniably The Pathologist, so Marshall Hall was undeniably The Barrister —and for many so remains, and so will remain for ever. When history is forgotten, legend is remembered.

No purist, shocked by Marshall Hall's unorthodox performances, can blot out or invalidate the long tale of his triumphs. To specify the gifts he lacked is to stress those he possessed. One should not, therefore, hesitate to say that there were serious flaws in his technical equipment. One might disregard an imperfect acquaintance with the law, which he never attempted to disguise, and which was not a major handicap in his usual sphere of work. But even as an all-round jury advocate he never reached the very highest rank—that sparsely tenanted and exclusive rank where Russell, Carson and Rufus Isaacs stand. Marshall Hall fell short of these because he suffered the defects of his great qualities. The eloquence could degenerate into indiscreet loquacity; the courage could induce a mood of fierce recklessness; the absolute belief in the cause for which he fought could lead to quarrels with an unsympathetic bench and to bitter feuds with influential parties—quarrels and feuds that did not always serve his client while frequently inflicting injury on himself.

This made Marshall Hall a variable and uncertain asset in ordinary cases—even when playing his destined rôle of criminal defender. But there was one situation that hardly ever failed to evoke his highest powers, and in which he surpassed most of those who were otherwise his superiors. Place him in a trial where the outcome must depend upon probing and interpreting the springs of human conduct, put into his care the interests of a prisoner struggling in the net of State or circumstance, make the prospects dark and the stake his client's life—and then Marshall Hall could be a champion beyond praise. In such an atmosphere and such a setting his faults appeared trivial, his virtues magnified; errors of tact or judgment were offset and wiped out by his magnetic intensity and dynamic force. Marshall Hall was at his best where some are at their worst—fighting back to the wall in a dramatic murder case.

That he should take up Robert Wood's defence was altogether fitting, but that he would be offered the opportunity was no foregone conclusion. For several years, as a result of friction with the appellate courts and a long-standing conflict with a newspaper proprietor, Marshall Hall had been in comparative eclipse, and though by 1907 his fortunes were reviving he had not yet regained his former eminence.

It so happened, however, that Wood's solicitor was one of his staunch adherents. He took the course suggested by both loyalty and sense, and presently Marshall Hall, zealously assisted by the young men in his chambers, was delving deep into the details of the case—the case which (says Edward Marjoribanks, his biographer) was to restore him to his old position at the Bar.

16

It is obvious why the trial of Robert Wood caused a tremendous popular sensation. It is not, however, easy to see why—unlike most sensational murder trials—it became a fashionable society event. No member of the clergy was involved, as in the earlier case of Mrs Bartlett. No member of the wealthy classes was accused, as in the later case of Mrs Barney. There have been settings as shocking, crimes as grisly, mysteries as inscrutable—and the modish world has been content to read of them in the papers. But a desire to attend this trial, to be present in person at the Old Bailey, gripped the best derived and the most distinguished.

The court, in consequence, presented an unusual spectacle. When on the first morning Marshall Hall took his seat in counsels' row and cast a quick glance round him, he found that his eyes could hardly turn to any spot without lighting on some celebrated face. Leading actors, like George Alexander; leading novelists, like Hall Caine; leading playwrights, like Pinero; leading journalists, like George R. Sims; dozens of nameless and yet well-established figures from the landscape of St James's Street and the pages of Debrett—they squeezed against each other in uncomfortable congestion, and their presence somehow added to the tensions that had drawn them.

No one felt these tensions so much as Marshall Hall. At all times a man of highly strung temperament, with nerves of almost morbid sensitivity, he reacted to the strain of a capital defence more perhaps than any other advocate. This was one reason—maybe not the least—why he generally excelled in conducting such defences; his own emotions grew so heavily charged that they doubled and trebled his impact on the jury. It is also a reason why he was prone on such occasions to indulge in outbursts of anger and excitement; the smallest episode, immaterial and irrelevant—a whisper overheard, the grimace of a spectator—might have entirely incalculable effects upon a man keyed up to such abnormal heights.

In the trial of Wood, partly because of its intrinsic characteristics, partly because of the atmosphere created by the audience, Marshall Hall was keyed up to these heights before the start. He maintained himself upon them throughout six arduous days, and the results—in every way—were what might have been expected.

17

As leading counsel instructed for the Crown, Sir Charles Mathews was for those six days the defender's chief opponent.

In appearance and physical endowments Mathews might have served as Marshall Hall's antithesis. He was short, in contrast with the other's towering stature; spare and slight as his adversary was massive; unenvied possessor of a high-pitched voice that grated unpleasantly on the cultivated ear. Even so, his quality as an advocate was high. He had a lucid mind, a firm grasp of essentials, an immense capacity for assimilating facts. In an age when cross-examination still ranked as an art, Mathews was one of its most notable exponents. Moreover, he and Marshall Hall, otherwise such opposites, shared one gift of immeasurable importance. Each had a strong yet subtle sense of drama. Marshall Hall backed his with his natural advantages; Mathews backed his with his natural defects. The crouch which gave him a semblance of the dwarfish; the draping of the black gown upon the spindly form; the skilful use of that diabolical voice so that it rose on words like 'kill' and 'death' to a bloodcurdling shriek—these were not to be despised among the attributes that had made Charles Mathews leader of the Old Bailey Bar. Marshall Hall was the last man to underestimate him.

One who was by nature so prone to histrionics might easily have made an over-zealous prosecutor. But though colourful in style, Mathews knew how to be fair, and his opening address was moderately couched. None the less, it was a formidable indictment. The Rising Sun postcard, the fragments of the letter, the lies, the false alibi, the tampering with witnesses—these, as ingredients of a single composition, acquired a force far greater than their sum as separate parts. They produced an effect upon that overcrowded court hardly diminished by Mathews's acknowledgment that there was ample testimony to Wood's good character—especially as the prosecutor did not deny himself a slightly acid comment. 'Whether those who thought so highly of him,' he said, 'knew the way in which he spent his leisure time is doubtful.'

These already familiar inculpations did not exhaust the Crown's case against the prisoner. It was proposed to put the issue wholly beyond doubt; in due course the jury would hear the evidence of a man who, shortly before five o'clock on the morning of the murder, *had seen Robert Wood leaving Phyllis Dimmock's house.* 'His name is Robert MacCowan,' Mathews said. 'He is a carman, who was unemployed and had gone out early that day in the hope of finding work. As he went up St Paul's Road he saw a man coming out of Twenty-nine. MacCowan doesn't pretend that he could see his face, but he noticed an odd peculiarity in his gait—a curious jerk of the shoulders as he walked—and this peculiarity held MacCowan's attention. . . . Now the accused has just such a peculiarity in his walk. The police will tell you that. Ruby Young will tell you that. And several weeks later, at an identification parade, as soon as the men assembled were required to walk, MacCowan without hesitation picked out Robert Wood. "There," he said, "that is the walk of the man I saw that morning." .

To Marshall Hall, as he sat listening to that unmelodious and yet compelling voice, the shape of his own tasks became clearer momently. First, he must convince the jury that all Wood's desperate and dishonest efforts to conceal his association with the girl might feasibly be ascribed to a natural anxiety that no one should know the kind of company he kept. Secondly, he must convince them that the burnt pieces of paper from the grate (although it could not be denied that they bore his client's handwriting) were not necessarily part of a letter of assignation—nor indeed part of any letter at all. Finally, he must knock MacCowan right out of the case.

By his very first intervention in the trial Marshall Hall began to move towards fulfilment of this latter aim.

18

Mathews hurtled to a strident climax and sat down. His junior rose and called the name of Arthur Grosse. A plain-clothes detective, carrying some papers, progressed importantly to the witness-box.

It is customary for a prosecution to introduce its formal evidence first. Photographers and surveyors prove their photographs and plans; officers specially detailed for the purpose tender the fruits of their expert observations. There is thus often created, between prologue and first act, an unintentional but marked breathing space in which spectators can relax, counsel scan their notes and reporters thankfully rest their aching wrists.

But in the trial of Wood such intermission was short-lived. While Mr Grosse apprised his lordship and the jury that it was precisely one mile three hundred and eighteen yards from Twenty-nine, St Paul's Road, to The Rising Sun, and that opposite Twenty-nine, parallel with the street, was a railway siding lighted up by arc lamps, Marshall Hall was seen to be studying intently a copy of a plan that the witness had put in. The more he gazed on it the darker grew his brow. Now and again, with a gesture of displeasure, he would point out some particular feature to his juniors.

When Mr Grosse ran out of information and junior counsel for the Crown had no more to ask, Marshall Hall withheld the usual gesture of dismissal. Instead he stood up and confronted Mr Grosse with an expression on his face that was far from cordial. The reporters instinctively again picked up their pencils.

'When was this plan prepared?' asked Marshall Hall. The ring of challenge in his voice was plain.

'Last week,' said Mr Grosse.

'Was the object of it to show how the light from the railway lamps affected St Paul's Road?'

'It was.'

'Do you think this is a fair plan?'

'I do.'

'What?' Marshall Hall shook Mr Grosse's work contemptuously. 'I put it to you, have you ever seen a more misleading plan in your life?'

The detective withdrew into complacent silence. 'Shout away,' his look implied; 'you won't get anywhere with me.'

'Wouldn't anybody, looking at this plan, conclude that the light from the railway siding was reflected on the front of Twenty-nine?'

'Not on the front,' said Mr Grosse, 'but in the neighbourhood.'

'Look at it!' Marshall Hall commanded. 'Look at it, sir! Is there anything to show that on the opposite side of the road, between the siding and Twenty-nine, there stands a continuous row of dwelling houses?'

'It is not continuous.'

'Not continuous? Do you say that there are not houses all the way along?'

'They are in pairs,' said Mr Grosse. 'There are spaces in between.'

'But from the optical point of view,' put in the judge, 'would the line not be continuous?'

'Yes,' Mr Grosse reluctantly admitted.

'Of course!' Marshall Hall cried heatedly. 'And therefore the only light would have to be projected above the building and down into the street. Wouldn't it? . . Wouldn't it?'

It took Mr Grosse some time again to answer yes.

'There is a tree right in front of Twenty-nine?'

'Yes.'

'You know that, on the morning of the 12th September, the street lamps were extinguished before twenty to five?'

'Yes.'

'So if MacCowan was there just before five the street lamps would be out?'

'Yes.'

'Yes.' The defender's voice was very hard. 'And, that being so, you were specially asked, weren't you, to prepare a map that would show sufficient light to be coming from the railway—the railway which is forty feet below the level of the road?'

Mr Grosse was once more silent, but his complacency had gone. The body blows now landed thick and fast.

'Have you heard it was a dark and muggy morning?'

'Yes.'

'That would reduce the reflecting power of the arc lamps to a minimum?'

'Yes.'

'Is there by the railway a wall that's nine feet high?'

'Yes.'

'Is that shown on the plan?'

'No.'

Marshall Hall, who all this time had been holding the plan stretched out between his hands, now crumpled it up and threw it pointedly aside. . . .

By this cross-examination he achieved a dual effect. He

had not only prepared the way for discrediting MacCowan. He had also in some measure discredited the Crown. Their very first piece of evidence had made a bad impression; if not actually manufactured and contrived, it appeared deliberately prejudicial and tendentious. Henceforward the jury could never repose full faith in the prosecution's impartiality. Their suspicions were aroused; they were on their guard, taking nothing upon trust; they were far more receptive than they might otherwise have been to Marshall Hall's subsequent charges of distortion and mis-statement.

One doubts whether there has ever been a trial of similar prominence in which cross-examination of an apparently formal witness gave the defence such a brilliant flying start. It is an example to advocates—and a warning to detectives.

19

The advantage had been dexterously seized. It was Marshall Hall's problem to retain it and exploit it.

After that first fierce fusillade he husbanded his fire while several unprovocative witnesses came and went. From the landlady—stock figure of respectable dismay; 'in *my* house, indeed'—he asked nothing at all. From the doctor he sought only some slight clarifications. From Bertram Shaw, who was candid and forthcoming, he obtained what he required without appreciable trouble.

'What is the name by which you are known to friends?' he asked.

'Bert,' answered Shaw.

'And that was the name that Phyllis always called you?'

'Yes, it was.'

This short passage, seemingly so trivial at the time, was to prove a powerful weapon at Marshall Hall's disposal when, in the waning hours of that December afternoon, he attacked again with unrestricted force. His prey was the ship's cook.

The defender's interrogation of this witness—a classic instance of a man who was bent upon secretiveness being driven from his covert and pitilessly exposed—owed its form and method of approach to one whose name does not appear in the official record. But naturally the brief in any important case is read by all the juniors in leading counsel's chambers. The Wood papers, indeed, had been particularly earmarked for the attention of Marshall Hall's youthful 'devil,' Wellesley Orr, who was later himself to win distinction at the Bar and become stipendiary magistrate at Manchester. It was Orr who, by a blend of industry and intuition, hit upon a point that had eluded Marshall Hall, and without which the latter's attack on the ship's cook could not have been one half as devastating.

The danger in the ship's cook's evidence was patent. If, at St Paul's Road on the Wednesday morning, he had really seen a letter such as he described, then Wood's meeting with Phyllis in the evening was not accidental but had been pre-arranged. Honest mistake in such a matter was unlikely; might the story, though, be deliberately untrue? The ship's cook himself had been under suspicion: had he tried to transfer that suspicion somewhere else? It would be easy enough, of course, to suggest that he had done so, and that this had led to his perversion—or invention—of the letter; but the suggestion would doubtless be indignantly denied and, as things stood, could not be carried further. What the defence sought was some definite sign that the ship's cook in his fright had taken active steps to ensure that the murder would not be pinned on him.

Wellesley Orr found such a sign—in an unexpected quarter. Among those interviewed during police enquiries was one May Campbell, who had known the murdered girl. She had made a long statement, highly damaging to Wood. She claimed to recognise in him a person called 'Scotch Bob'—Wood was Scottish born and retained a slight Scots accent—who had been going with Phyllis and had frequently ill-used her. May Campbell said that Phyllis, on the day before her death, talked of a letter she had had from Scotch Bob, asking her to meet him; that Phyllis expressed anxiety because Scotch Bob had a great grievance against her; that Phyllis also volunteered the information that she had shown a part of Scotch Bob's letter to a sailor who had slept with her upon the previous night.

This statement of May Campbell's had been passed as an act of courtesy to the defence; but the woman herself was not being called by the Crown because much of what she said was demonstrably false—not least her account of the talk she had had with Phyllis, which she fixed at a time when the latter was with Shaw. It thus became possible, and even probable, that she didn't see Phyllis on the Wednesday at all.

As May Campbell was not to be a witness, as nothing that she said would be brought before the jury, many barristers would have thought it wasting time to bother about her and her statement any further. But Orr was thorough, patient and intellectually inquisitive. Constantly he turned the matter over in his mind. Why had May Campbell—whom it did not seem to benefit—gone out of her way to be vindictive towards Wood? How did she know, if Phyllis didn't tell her, that the girl had had a letter and that a sailor saw it? The answer to the second question had imposed itself: she must have got it direct from the ship's cook—although there was no evidence that they were acquainted. But Orr's imaginative stroke was in perceiving that the answer to the second question really solved the first—that the ship's cook must have confided in May Campbell and enlisted her help in shifting the suspicion. They pooled their knowledge and acted in concert. Hence her vindictive lies. Hence his story of the letter.

So Wellesley Orr construed the situation and he struggled to convince Marshall Hall that he was right. The great defender first resisted and demurred; it was too remote, it was too suppositional, there wasn't enough to go on. But Orr, strong in his belief, continued to argue stubbornly and at last converted Marshall Hall to his own view.

Had Orr proved wrong, the attack upon the ship's cook would probably have failed, with consequences that one cannot calculate. But Orr proved right; and his flash of inspiration, turned to full account by a matchless fighting advocate, developed into one of the great forensic coups of history

The ship's cook was a tough and hefty fellow—not at all the type to be easily overawed. He answered Sir Charles Mathews with dogmatic assurance. Yes, Phyllis had shown him the postcard and a letter; yes, he had read all of one and a portion of the other; yes, he could remember that portion very well. He recited it to the jury as he had done to the police: 'Dear Phyllis, Will you meet me at the bar of The Eagle at Camden Town 8.30 tonight, Wednesday—Bert.' The Crown lawyers, following him in the depositions, observed he was word perfect.

'Just look at those.' Mathews handed up a slide; secured in the glass were some wafery shreds of paper—all it had been possible to rescue from the grate. 'Do you know what they are?'

'Yes,' said the ship's cook. 'They're pieces out of the letter that I saw.'

When Marshall Hall got up to cross-examine he stood for several moments before putting any question. Under his penetrating gaze, that might well strike fear into the heart of one who had not been wholly frank, the ship's cook straightaway seemed ill at ease. He shuffled his feet and tried to turn his eyes elsewhere.

The crowd in court was absolutely quiet, as if instinctively aware of an impending crisis.

'Tell me,' said Marshall Hall at last, 'do you know a woman called May?'

The effect on the ship's cook was extraordinary. His jaw dropped; his fingers twitched; a perceptible tremor shook his bulky frame.

'No, no,' he stammered. 'No.'

It needed no psychologist to tell that he was lying. That was apparent to everybody present, though why and what it portended most could still only conjecture. But Wellesley Orr's heart beat a little faster as he noted the frightened appearance of the witness and knew he was going to be vindicated right up to the hilt.

'Think again,' said Marshall Hall. 'And think hard. Do you know May Campbell?'

The ship's cook looked almost stupefied.

'May Campbell?' he repeated.

'May Campbell.' Marshall Hall never relaxed that hard, relentless gaze. 'Do you know her?'

The ship's cook hesitated long.

'By sight,' he faltered.

The first—and the most difficult—obstruction had been cracked. Now, one by one, the barriers tumbled down.

'Have you ever spoken to her?'

'Yes.'

'Where?'

'In The Rising Sun.'

'When did you first speak to her?'

'I think it was the day of Phyllis Dimmock's funeral.'

'Did you talk about the case?'

'It was common talk.'

'Did *you* talk about it?'

'Yes.'

'Did May Campbell give you a description of a man who, she said, was known as a friend of Phyllis Dimmock's?'

'Yes.'

'Did that description correspond very much with the description of the accused?'

'Yes.'

'And after that you picked him out as a man you had seen with Dimmock?'

'Yes.'

The success of this reconstruction transcended expectations, and it stands for all time as a superlative example of the relationship that may temporarily exist between star advocate and inconspicuous 'devil'—if the one is resourceful and the other receptive. It is the relationship between every playwright and his virtuoso actor. Wellesley Orr could not have done it quite like that himself; without him Marshall Hall would no have done it at all.

The defender continued, on the swell of a fast-running and favourable tide.

'When you heard of the murder,' he asked, 'were you not in a great fright?'

'No,' said the ship's cook, though he was certainly in one now.

'You knew that the habitués of The Rising Sun were well aware that you had been with this woman on the Sunday, the Monday, and the Tuesday nights?'

'Yes.'

'It was a very unpleasant situation,' observed Marshall Hall. 'Wasn't it? *Wasn't it?*'

How did you contradict this dominating man, who knew every detail of your personal affairs?

'Yes,' the ship's cook admitted. 'It was unpleasant, yes.'

The witness had undergone a metamorphosis and was now cutting a very different figure with the jury—the figure of one who was, or had been, afraid for his own skin and whose evidence must be weighed and valued in that light.

'On the Wednesday morning,' Marshall Hall went on, 'you say the girl showed you a letter she had just received?'

'Yes.'

'And gave you The Rising Sun postcard to compare with it?'

'She did.'

'Why on earth should she want you to compare them?'

'I don't know.'

'You don't know.' Marshall Hall echoed him satirically. 'Look at the slide again; look at that piece of paper. You say that is part of the letter that you saw?'

'Yes.'

'Do you see the faint blue lines upon it? . . . Look.'

The ship's cook looked as best he could; his hand was not too steady.

'Yes, I see them,' he said.

'Isn't that paper torn from a notebook, from a scribbling book?'

The ship's cook perceived what was coming. He was desperately uncomfortable.

'Well, I saw the letter,' he mumbled, with head bowed.

'Look up, man!' thundered Marshall Hall. 'Look up and speak up! We are in a court of justice. I put it to you that the story of this letter is an invention, and that the fragment you have there might have come from anywhere and certainly never come by post.'

'It did,' maintained the ship's cook, but the sweat poured from him.

'You say the letter was signed "Bert"?'

'Yes.'

'Where did you get that name?'

'It was in the letter, I tell you.'

'Did you know that the man whom Phyllis lived with was called Bert?'

'Only after the murder.'

Marshall Hall spoke very slowly.

'If it had been the object at that time to put suspicion upon *him*, to say the signature was "Bert" would have been useful, wouldn't it?'

The defender waited, but no answer ever was forthcoming. With a faultless sense of timing, the curtain forthwith fell, both on the ship's cook and on the first day of the trial.

20

The second day's proceedings revolved round the evidence given by MacCowan. He was the one Crown witness who could hang Wood by himself. If the jury thought him honest; if they trusted in his powers of observation; if these twin conclusions led them to believe that he had indeed seen a man leaving Phyllis Dimmock's house shortly before five on the morning that she died, and that he was able to identify him afterwards as Wood—why, there would be the virtual finish of the matter. For it was certain as anything can be in this world that if MacCowan had seen anyone leaving Twenty-nine, it was Phyllis Dimmock's murderer he saw.

MacCowan was a wiry little man, bred in the country,

seasoned in the town; his face reflected his mental composition—a curious admixture of naïveté and cunning; he had heard all about these lawyers, especially Marshall Hall, and he was ready for 'em, any time they liked. They'd best not try any of their gammon upon him.

He replied to Sir Charles Mathews with the cheerful air of one who believes that his evidence is incontrovertible. 'I was going through St Paul's Road at twelve minutes to five,' he said. 'As I passed Twenty-nine I saw a man leaving the gate. His left hand was in his pocket, and he jerked his right shoulder forward as he walked. I turned round several times; I had him in sight for thirty yards.'

Left hand in pocket, right shoulder jerking forward; they were the very words that had been used by Ruby Young in describing to the police the walk of Robert Wood—words that the Crown would invite her to repeat when her turn came to go into the box.

It is not always possible, even in retrospect, to pick out the real turning point of a lengthy trial. In this case, however, there can be little doubt. It came when Marshall Hall joined battle with MacCowan. . . .

Unlike the ship's cook, MacCowan did not quail as the defender rose to face him. He, after all, had no underhand transaction to conceal. Nor had he been in court during the former's overthrow, which—notwithstanding his own less vulnerable position—might have exercised a chastening effect.

As it was, he began the engagement almost perkily.

'Did you know at the time,' Marshall Hall had asked him, 'that the gate from which the man came out was the gate of Twenty-nine?'

'No,' said MacCowan, as if it didn't matter in the least. 'I read it in the papers and identified it afterwards.'

'Did you say before the coroner that you were passing Twenty-nine at *five* minutes to five?"

'Yes.'

'And the same before the magistrate?'

'Yes.'

'And yet you now say it was not five minutes, but *twelve* minutes to five?'

'That's right,' said MacCowan. 'I knew I'd left home at twenty to, and I've stepped it out since then and found that I was wrong.'

'Oh, you were wrong, were you?' Marshall Hall's voice suddenly deepened. 'Didn't you alter the time because you were cross-examined before the magistrate as to when the street lights were put out?'

'No,' said MacCowan, a trifle more defensively.

'*Were* the street lights out when you were passing Twenty-nine?'

'No, they were in.'

'Do you know we have had evidence in this court that they were put out that morning before *twenty* to five?'

'They were in,' MacCowan persisted.

'When you made your original statement to the police did you say you saw a man coming not out of the gate but *down the steps* of Twenty-nine?'

'No.'

'Did you not? Wasn't your statement read over to you after you had made it?'

'Yes.'

'It was?' Marshall Hall read aloud from his own copy. '"I looked round and saw a man coming down the steps of Twenty-nine." . . . Did the police invent that?'

For the first time MacCowan showed signs of harassment.

'When we go to make a statement,' he protested, 'we aren't so fly as when we come to be cross-examined.'

'"Fly"? "Fly"?' repeated Marshall Hall in anger. 'What do you mean by "fly"?'

'I wasn't so particular,' MacCowan said defiantly. 'I didn't listen particularly to what was being read over.'

Never was advocate offered such a gift. Never did advocate accept one more wholeheartedly.

'You were "not so fly,"' said Marshall Hall with stinging scorn. 'Do you mean to say that, knowing a man's life might depend on your description, you did not take particular notice of what was read over to you? Have you no regard for human life?'

MacCowan had had time to realise his blunder. He tried to extricate himself by misplaced flippancy.

'One life is as good as another,' he retorted.

He could hardly have made a more inopportune observation. Those in court looked almost fearfully at the defender, anticipating another outburst of explosive wrath. But with sound tactical and keen dramatic sense Marshall Hall restrained what must have been his natural feelings. He was to make full use, though, of the episode later on—in his final speech, when he would stigmatise MacCowan as 'not only a careless, but a callous, witness.'

Meanwhile he still held in his hand the latter's statement. He displayed it ostentatiously as he resumed his questions.

'According to your story you only identified the man by some peculiar twitching of the shoulder?'

'The peculiarity of his walk,' replied MacCowan warily.

'The peculiarity being this twitching of the shoulder?'

'Yes.'

'Did you mention that peculiarity when you first talked to the police?'

The sheets of typescrift fluttered a clear warning.

'No,' said MacCowan, 'but I did tell 'em that the man had a swaggering walk.'

'Oh,' said Marshall Hall. 'Do you wish the jury to understand that when you said "swaggering walk" you meant "a peculiar twitch of the shoulder"?'

'Yes,' said MacCowan. His rather impudent and cocksure manner had passed into one of uncertainty and mistrust.

'Did you describe the man you saw as one of stiff build with broad shoulders?'

'Yes.'

'Wood, stand up. . . .'

The stage folk present must have watched the resulting scene with envy. No production effect, no theatrical contrivance, no arrangement of curtains or of mirrors or of lights could have occasioned so sudden and intense a concentration as that which now was focused on the figure of the prisoner. No one had eyes or thought for anyone but he as he got slowly to his feet from his chair inside the dock.

He looked very serene, very self-possessed—and very narrow shouldered.

Nobody spoke. Nobody moved. Marshall Hall waited till the silence was oppressive.

'Now,' he said. 'Do you describe *that* man as broad-shouldered?'

MacCowan was on the run, but would not capitulate—not because of any animus he felt against the accused, but rather because of his own uncompromising pride. He was an egotistical man who conceived the whole trial in terms of a joust between himself and the defence. And, though he was getting the worst of it, he wasn't giving up; he meant to get one back on this lawyer fellow yet.

'He'd look broader if he wore his overcoat,' he said.

'Then he *shall* wear it,' Marshall Hall declared.

The overcoat was brought; the prisoner put it on. It made very little difference. His slim, almost puny build could not be concealed.

'Would you describe *that* man as broad-shouldered?' asked Marshall Hall again.

MacCowan made one last throw.

'He has broader shoulders than I have,' he contended.

'Would you call a bluebottle an elephant,' said Marshall Hall instantly, 'because it is bigger than a fly?'

Not even the Old Bailey's sombre setting could deaden the effect of this annihilating thrust. A gale of laughter swept across the court—a gale in which MacCowan and all his high pretensions were tossed derisively before being blown away.

21

That second day, marked by such a signal triumph, had also a less satisfactory side for Marshall Hall. It brought the first overt and unmistakable sign of a strained relationship between the defender and the judge.

Marshall Hall's weakness for wrangling with the Bench has already been noted, together with its source—that state of hypertension and emotional absorption that possessed his whole being throughout the longest trial and made him the outstanding advocate he was. One may accept this explanation without being blind to the fact that in these wrangles Marshall Hall was very often wrong, and was sometimes gratuitously offensive in addition. But when he fell foul of authority during the trial of Wood, Marshall Hall was almost invariably right; and if he did put his points with greater vehemence than respect, one must say in fairness that authority had asked for it.

Mr Justice Grantham was a keen sportsman and therefore popular with the public, a learned lawyer and therefore admired by learned lawyers. There are, however, attributes of which a High Court judge stands more in need than readiness with a gun or even proficiency with precedents. One is an open mind; another a regulated tongue. Grantham possessed neither. He was prone to form strong and stubborn preconceptions, which he would freely ventilate in the hearing of the jury. He was equally prone to garrulous interruption which more often confused than elucidated issues.

It is not surprising that there was no love lost between him and Marshall Hall, and those best acquainted with their past encounters had probably expected trouble to begin before. In the early stages, though, both men were on their best behaviour: Grantham silent and seemingly impartial, Marshall Hall directing all his salvoes at the witness-box.

It was the judge who brought this period of concord to an end. . . .

Marshall Hall was cross-examining that friend of the ship's cook who had returned with him on Wednesday night to the temperance hotel. The defender did not essay to break this alibi, but to stress and expand his previous suggestion that the ship's cook had been seeking cover for himself.

'How long had you known him?' he enquired of the witness.

'Since the eighth of September.'

'What, only the Sunday before the murder?'

'Yes.'

'After the murder did he tell you he was very anxious to prove where he had been on the Wednesday night?'

'No.'

'Did you *think* he was anxious to prove it?'

'No.'

The man clearly supposed that the ship's cook himself still stood in danger of the gallows and intended to do all he could to help his new-found friend.

With a master's intuitive sense of what was coming, Marshall Hall cast his next question in peculiar form.

'Did you hear,' he asked, 'that he had slept with Phyllis Dimmock on the Monday, Tuesday and Sunday nights?'

'Yes,' said the witness. He knew that the ship's cook had admitted so much all along.

'Did he tell you in the course of conversation?'

'Yes.'

'A curious conversation,' Marshall Hall went on, 'to hold with a man who had only known you for three days—curious, wasn't it, for him to tell you he had passed the three previous nights in such a way?'

One may logically deduce the next step contemplated: a suggestion that these intimate matters came to be discussed only because the ship's cook was expressing apprehensions, and that the preceding denials of this witness had been false. But, as events befell, that step was never taken, for at this point the witness suddenly caught fright. Whether he, too, could anticipate developments and foresaw some difficulty in explaining things away; or whether, puzzled by Marshall Hall's transposing of the days and his subsequent reference to 'the three previous nights,' he wrongly believed he had been trapped into admitting that the ship's cook had said he slept with Phyllis on the *Wednesday*; or whether, for some other reason more obscure than these, he decided to repudiate what he had already sworn.

As he hovered on the brink of this effrontery, Marshall Hall pressed for an immediate reply.

'Curious, wasn't it?' he repeated, 'for him to tell you he had spent the three previous nights in such a way?'

'He didn't say that,' said the witness shiftily. 'He just mentioned he'd been with her.'

'But for three nights?'

'No.'

Marshall Hall flared up at the barefaced lie.

'Why, I put the three nights to you specifically. I placed them in the wrong order so as to mark the question.'

'I never heard it,' said the witness.

For some moments the judge had been irritably fidgeting. Now he sprang to the witness's support.

'No, nor did I,' he said.

If Mr Justice Grantham was speaking the literal truth—and any other view would be less charitable still—he had simply not been paying the requisite attention. One may sympathise with Marshall Hall if his self-control was taxed.

'I'm absolutely positive,' he shouted. 'I'm as sure I put that question as that I'm standing here. We shall see soon enough from the shorthand note. I call for the shorthand note.'

Even the judge, who had suffered before from Marshall Hall's quick temper, looked taken aback by the storm that he had roused. He sat in sour silence as the shorthand writer turned over the pages of his book. The jury, and indeed most other people in the court who had been listening more closely than Mr Justice Grantham, felt fairly certain that Marshall Hall was right, but awaited final demonstration by the record.

The shorthand writer found the passage. He read aloud haltingly, made nervous by his unexpected leap to prominence.

' "Question: Did you hear that he had slept with Phyllis Dimmock on the Monday, Tuesday and Sunday nights? Answer: Yes. Question: Did he tell you in the course of conversation? Answer: Yes." '

Marshall Hall swung round in triumph towards the jury. They had their heads together and were talking in low tones. The judge observed the spectacle with obvious displeasure.

'Very well,' he said, 'if the witness misunderstood it, I misunderstood it too.'

This singularly graceless piece of sophistry at once brought Marshall Hall back into the fray.

'But your lordship has heard the note read,' he said sharply, 'and I mentioned the three nights.'

'There's no need to get excited,' said the judge in cold reproof.

The injustice of this stubbornly unreasonable attitude might easily have driven the impetuous advocate into some excess of speech that could not have been repaired. It probably would have done so had there seemed no other recourse open in the interests of his client than an outright accusation of judicial unfairness. But however impassioned Marshall Hall became, one part of his mind automatically registered the slightest signs of feeling exhibited by the jury. He knew that so far in this dispute he had their sympathy. He knew that one intemperate act might throw it all away.

There was a short and tense pause while judge and advocate regarded one another with unconcealed hostility. Then the latter turned towards the witness, who was patently dreading a resumption of his questions.

Marshall Hall addressed him quietly and gravely.

'Will you base the truth of your evidence,' he said, 'on the statement that I did not ask you about those three nights?'

'Yes,' said the witness, who now had only one idea—to get out of the box.

'Very well,' said Marshall Hall, 'I will ask you nothing more.'

As he sat down he remarked with satisfaction that the jury had once again put their heads together.

22

None the less, that evening Marshall Hall brooded over the incident, and though he could find little or nothing with which to reproach himself, he could not altogether suppress a flicker of disquiet.

No matter what the rights and wrongs may be, there are always dangers lying in wait for any advocate who gets involved in repeated conflict with the judge. His lordship holds cards not available to barristers. A jury, looking on at a continuous rebellion, may gradually turn against the rebel whom they once admired. Above all, the added pressure may adversely affect counsel's discharge of his prime responsibilities.

So it seemed to Marshall Hall, meditating in the calm repose of his own room, that any further clashes must at all costs be eschewed. He still bitterly resented Grantham's mischievous intervention, and would certainly not sit passive if there should be more. But the prisoner's cause could best be served without them altogether, and Marshall Hall made up his mind to promote this end. Although the injured party, he shelved his personal pride and planned a generous gesture to make peace with the judge. . . .

Next morning when the court resumed he shaped his course accordingly.

'My lord,' he said, 'may I mention a purely personal matter?' Everyone leaned forward. 'There appears to have been an impression,' Marshall Hall went on, 'that there was some friction yesterday between your lordship and myself. I would like to make it clear that I had not the smallest intention of questioning anything that was said from the Bench.'

The olive branch had been held out without a reservation. Grantham, who in private was not an ill-natured individual, seemed willing to accept it.

'It is not for me to assume there is any friction,' he said affably.

'Friction with the witness,' said Marshall Hall, 'I don't repudiate, but I am most anxious to repudiate friction with your lordship.'

'I don't think you should take the trouble,' said the judge.

Upon this friendly and agreeable exchange was ushered in

the third day of the trial—a day on which discord between the two men reached its peak and produced at least two scenes of uninhibited antagonism.

23

In the first of these the fault again entirely lay with Grantham.

The Crown had called Wood's departmental chief. This gentleman agreed with Marshall Hall that the prisoner had been on his staff throughout the past five years; that he had not the least peculiarity in his walk; that on the 12th September he came to work as usual and showed no trace of perturbation or excitement; that he was an exceptionally amiable, upright and industrious young man.

'Do you know anything,' asked Marshall Hall, 'that would lead you to believe he was capable of committing a dreadful crime like this?'

'Most certainly not,' the witness said emphatically.

Such evidence should never count for more than it is worth; dreadful crimes are committed not infrequently by those who would have been deemed incapable of them by their friends. A so-called 'double life,' of body or of mind, is not by any means an exceptional phenomenon. To some degree Wood himself was a confessed example; by day he earned golden opinions of his rectitude, by night he amused himself with the lowest sort of trollop. The judge was fully entitled to demonstrate this point.

'At the works you thought him a high-minded man,' he said. 'Had you any idea of the immoral life you have now heard he was leading?'

'No,' the witness said.

Whether 'immoral' was an entirely justifiable word, whether 'disreputable' would not have been better, might now be considered at least open to debate. At the time, however, to demur would have been fruitless. Mr Justice Grantham's chosen epithet was backed by the ethical criteria that obtained in 1907. Whatever he may have thought, Marshall Hall kept silent.

'It is admitted,' the judge continued, 'that, though nominally under Shaw's protection, this woman was receiving men. *Had you any idea that Wood was living with such a woman?*'

This time there was no question; Mr Justice Grantham had gone very much too far. In his eagerness to drive home what was a legitimate point against the prisoner—to whose case he was now displaying himself consistently inimical—he had lapsed into flagrant error and injustice. No witness had been called, no witness would be called, to say that Wood had ever lived with Phyllis Dimmock. It was the purest surmise presented as proved fact.

In an instant Marshall Hall was on his feet.

'I do not understand your lordship's question,' he declared.

'Are you addressing me or the jury?' Grantham replied irately. 'If you are speaking to me, I wish you would not look at them.'

Many counsel—and Marshall Hall was undoubtedly among them—incline to watch the jury, when, by strictest etiquette, their eyes should be elsewhere. This habit on occasion may merit a rebuke—but not, perhaps, most fittingly at a moment when the judge himself has just done something infinitely worse.

'I am addressing your lordship,' said Marshall Hall, unflinching. 'I said that I did not understand your lordship's question.'

'I am taking the accused's own statement,' Grantham barked, and as Marshall Hall, still standing in protest, endeavoured to fathom this astonishing assertion, the judge repeated his injurious blunder.

'Had you any idea he was living with such a woman?'

The situation was intolerable. Marshall Hall broke in without ceremony.

'There is not a tittle of evidence——'

'I am addressing a witness,' said the incensed judge. 'Counsel must not interrupt when I am putting questions on the evidence in the interests of justice.'

'In the interests of justice——'

'I must ask you not to argue with me.'

'My lord——'

'I shall permit no argument,' decreed Grantham with fierce finality, 'as to the way I am putting my questions to him.'

The conflict of wills had reached a pitch which did not admit of compromise. One or the other must now accept defeat.

It was not to be Marshall Hall.

'With great deference,' he said—and Grantham, despite himself, felt constrained to listen—'I only wish, *in the interests of justice*, to point out that there is not a particle of evidence that the accused ever stayed with the girl or had improper relations with her.'

When he had finished, and only when he had finished, the courageous and resolute advocate sat down. The judge glared at him but said nothing more.

As the witness was suffered to retire, Marshall Hall boldly turned his face towards the jury.

24

The personal ascendancy that Marshall Hall had won stood him in good stead a little later on.

Wood's friend Lambert had been into the box to tell of his meeting with the prisoner and Phyllis at The Eagle. He was followed by one of The Eagle's barmaids who, though able to identify the girl she saw as Phyllis, could only say that she had come in with 'a man' and that presently 'another man' had joined them.

'Did you hear her speak to this second man?' asked junior Crown counsel.

'She said, "Excuse me being untidy; I had to come and meet——"'

'I object,' interposed Marshall Hall, and the court, barely recovered from the last pitched battle, was plunged again into a fever of excitement. 'I submit that since the witness has identified neither of the two men who were with Phyllis

Dimmock, her statement as to what Dimmock said cannot be evidence.'

Marshall Hall was invoking the rule that, in the process of a prosecution, one person cannot report another's words unless those words were uttered in the hearing of the accused. You have not proved Wood was there, the defender argued; therefore the conversation is not admissible.

But we *have* proved he was there, the Crown retorted; we proved it earlier through the mouth of Lambert. 'And,' counsel added, 'Lambert's statement as to what Dimmock said was to the same effect.'

'No, it was not,' said Marshall Hall, jumping up once more.

The judge's displeasure was immediately revived.

'Do you want me to decide against you without further argument?' he said.

'No, my lord.'

'Then you had better sit down.' The pedagogic reprimand soothed Grantham's pride, still smarting painfully from his previous rebuff. 'We can soon see what the witness Lambert said.' He searched his notes, turned up the place, and frowned. Marshall Hall, so it appeared, was right again.

'Lambert said that Dimmock's remark was: "I hope you will excuse my dress, *as I have just run out.*" That *is* different,' the judge conceded.

'Very different,' said Marshall Hall, 'and I submit you cannot accept the evidence of this witness.'

It raised a delicate point on adequacy of proof. The judge thought it over.

'I do not agree,' he said. 'I think the evidence is admissible.'

Marshall Hall was not content.

'Will your lordship make a note of my objection?'

'Yes.'

The defender appeared to think the judge's tone perfunctory.

'I implore your lordship to note that this witness has *not* identified these men——'

'You have said that before.' Grantham tried to close the matter. 'I have not forgotten it.'

'I thought,' said Marshall Hall deliberately, 'your lordship did not *appreciate* it.'

And once again he was left with the last word.

25

The *atmosphere* of a trial is as important as its substance. It determines the mental and the moral standpoint from which—and by which—the accused is judged. It determines the interpretation of his mind and character. It determines whether, given two alternatives, a good or bad construction will be placed upon his acts.

Due in large measure to the work of Marshall Hall the atmosphere in Wood's case had gradually changed. Where earlier had mostly been antipathy or indifference, now there was a sympathetic feeling for the prisoner. The scales against him had seemed unfairly weighted; too many, for motives perceptible or otherwise, had disclosed concern to encompass his destruction. The effect was not diminished by those bringing up the rear—Ruby Young (often in tears, but fulfilling her bitter rôle), and an unsavoury set of prostitutes and brothel keepers whose bias against Wood was as plain as their depravity. The privileged spectators crushed inside the court, the crowds that loitered every day in the surrounding streets, the masses that followed the proceedings from afar—all, or nearly all, were modifying their views. Without necessarily holding that Wood *ought* to be acquitted, they found themselves irrationally *hoping* that he would be.

Maybe a mood of optimism engendered by this atmosphere induced Marshall Hall, when the prosecution closed, to submit to the judge that no case had been made out.

26

There is always some danger in a submission of no case. That is because the jury—who must perforce sit listening—seldom comprehend exactly what is going on. Upon these occasions the defender is contending that there is no evidence on which one could *possibly* convict; that the Crown has made out no case even calling for an answer; that, in fact, the prosecution has utterly collapsed. But juries, unfamiliar with the niceties of procedure, are apt to suppose that the judge is being asked whether *he* believes the prisoner innocent or guilty. Consequently, if his lordship turns down the submission, though he is saying no more than that the jury must decide, the latter body often too readily assumes that he is giving them a broad hint to find the prisoner guilty. 'Ah! the judge thinks he did it,' they whisper to each other.

It follows that such submissions ought not to be made unless they enjoy a solid prospect of success.

Only one of Marshall Hall's sanguine disposition could have discerned such a prospect in the trial of Robert Wood. He argued with all his usual urgency and warmth. There was 'an absolute and utter want of any evidence' that the accused was ever seen at Phyllis Dimmock's house; the evidence of identity was 'weak beyond thought, of a kind to which no attention should or can be paid'; no motive had been attributed to Wood, 'not one iota even of a suggested motive. I ask your lordship to say,' he concluded, 'that the accused ought not to be put in any further peril.'

No fault could be found with the judge's decision nor with the way in which it was pronounced.

'Taking all into account,' he said, measuring his words, 'I cannot say there is no case to go to the jury. I cannot say that there is no case.'

'As your lordship pleases.' Slowly Marshall Hall turned towards the jury-box. He looked like a man who had been labouring in chains but was now suddenly freed. 'Gentlemen.' His voice rang out almost triumphant. 'Gentlemen, for four days you have heard the prosecution. Now, at long last, I can open the defence.'

27

In any trial this was Marshall Hall's great moment.

Some counsel regard the jury as lay figures, impersonal and inanimate accessories of the court, only springing into temporary life when ultimately called on for their Aye or Nay. Such counsel neither feel nor seek a close relation, even when going through the motions of addressing them. Like actors wholly absorbed in the performance, they hardly heed their audience until the end.

Marshall Hall lay at the opposite extreme. From first to last, from the moment that the jurors took the oath in turn until they finally withdrew upon their solemn business, he was acutely conscious of their presence; conscious of them, not only as a corporate entity, but also as defined and separate individuals; conscious that any single one of them might come to hold the key to his client's fate; conscious that at any time the smallest incident might sway their judgments and tip the balance either way; conscious above all of his own responsibility for charging both their emotions and their thoughts. That, rather than any reprehensible intention, was the cause of his constant preoccupation with the jury, to which Mr. Justice Grantham had objected. That, too, was why he felt his powers run highest when he could legitimately meet them face to face; when he could talk to them directly, not obliquely; when, without diversion by opponents or by witnesses, the jury passed into his absolute possession.

'His tall, commanding figure,' one reporter wrote of him while the Wood trial was in progress, 'his outstretched arm, his white set face, communicated his spirit of intensity to the court.' Never was this more manifest than in his opening speech. All the pent-up forces of that energetic nature were released and fused in one tremendous effort to sweep his client clear of the hazard that beset him.

He began by adroitly turning to account his various embroilments with witnesses and judge. 'You may have thought,' he said, 'that, now and then, I was pressing unduly, that I took an unfair advantage, that I asked a question that might appear unworthy. If I seemed to exceed the proper limits I implore you to forgive me; my whole anxiety was for my client. Gentlemen, his life is at stake. I cannot rob the Crown witnesses of theirs. *They* have far less to lose at *my* hands than *he* has at *yours*.' There followed a passage of sustained and brilliant rhetoric in which he dramatised with harrowing vividness the duty which they were sworn to discharge. 'I am proud to boast myself a member of the Old Bailey Bar, to whom are entrusted the lives of their fellow citizens of London. . . . This burden has been lying very heavily on my shoulders. Gentlemen, it will pass to yours all too soon.'

He turned now to the facts, and told them at once what all were keen to learn. 'Wood is going into the box.* He will speak for himself and it will be for you to judge his story.' Boldly the advocate faced and grappled with his chief remaining task. 'Gentlemen, I do not close my eyes to this. We will put him in the box, but he will go into it tainted—tainted because he has spoken untruths in the past. It was wrong; it was unfortunate; the man has suffered greatly for it, heaven knows—but is there not a simple and a natural explanation?

'Assume his innocence; then everything becomes clear.' Superbly Marshall Hall rose to the height of his own challenge. 'Think of it, gentlemen; think of it. He knew that within a few hours of his leaving that young woman she had been foully done to death. He foresaw that his name would be dragged through the public press as one who had been in company with a prostitute. He foresaw the ruin of his reputation. He foresaw the injury to his father's health. So he did what many other foolish folk have done before. He thought a lie would be better than the truth. He asked his sweetheart to save him—not to prove that he did not commit the murder, but to prevent him being publicly inculpated with a harlot.

'That isn't mere surmise. You can test it for yourselves. *The Ruby Young alibi does not cover the crime*. Phyllis Dimmock was killed between four and six a.m.; *we* know this from the doctor—*but the murderer, whoever he is, has*

* Although prisoners had been permitted to give evidence on their own behalf since 1898, the practice had not yet become almost obligatory.

known it all along. Now Wood asked Ruby Young to say that he was with her until eleven o'clock—a useless alibi for the murder, but a perfect alibi for the meeting at The Eagle.'

This very effective point—obvious enough once attention has been called to it,but how many of us would perceive it for ourselves?—produced a visible impression on the jury. More, perhaps, than any other feature of the case, it lent colour and convincingness to the proposition that the charitable view of Wood's behaviour was correct.

Having thus dealt with his greatest difficulty—for, as the judge was to remark in summing up, 'the main evidence against the accused is his own conduct in endeavouring to get people to tell lies'—Marshall Hall swept on to amplify his earlier gains. The burnt paper in the grate? Wood himself would tell them how the girl could have acquired these fragments of his writing; they might be the remains of some scribbling and sketches he did in the public house to amuse himself and her. Certainly they were not the remnants of a letter; there had never been a letter; there was no one but the ship's cook to assert otherwise, and the ship's cook—thanks to Wellesley Orr this could be said with confidence—was palpably a man who did not always tell the truth. MacCowan? His was the flimsiest evidence ever presented in any court of justice in the world. Put aside his chopping and his changing, his barefaced prevarications, his disregard for accuracy when life might hinge upon it; even without these no one could believe that a murderer, with the body of his victim lying in the house, would choose to come out—and to come out, according to MacCowan himself, under the full glare of the electric lamps—at a moment when somebody's feet were clattering past.

Under this slashing and spirited attack the Crown case assumed a new and sicklier complexion. Marshall Hall was well aware of it; in all these matters he felt infinitely strong, buttressed as he was by his cross-examination. But there still remained for him one source of some anxiety, although it lay beyond the strictest boundaries of relevance. Throughout he had been considerably perturbed at the possible effect of his client's admitted laxity. Wood had not scorned the society of prostitutes; one (Ruby Young) had undeniably been his mistress. To what extent would this be held against him by the jury? There were some melancholy precedents—notably Mrs Maybrick, only recently released from gaol after serving fifteen years—of persons convicted upon a murder charge where the evidence was plainly insufficient but their sexual morals had been open to reproach. True, this vindictive and inequitable sanction was more often imposed on women than on men. But even male prisoners could not hope to be immune from the vengeance of a puritan society—for any group of twelve, however tolerant individually, forthwith becomes society in miniature.

Marshall Hall firmly grasped this nettle in the concluding passage of his speech. 'He may have been immoral,' he said very earnestly. 'His relations with women may not always have been pure. In that respect, gentlemen, do not let us be unworldly; in that respect he is only one of many thousands. But what has it to do with the case that brings you here? Nothing; precisely nothing. Were he twenty times as immoral as he is, that would not even begin to prove he was the author of one of the most atrocious and skilful murders of our time.'

28

The speech had done more than project the prisoner's case. It had equally projected the prisoner himself. Over and over again, in a variety of ways, Marshall Hall brought Wood and the jury into contact. 'The murderer was mad. Does *he* look mad?' he once demanded, pointing dramatically at the figure in the dock. (It was like an echo of Governor Robinson's famous stroke—'Gentlemen, does she look it?'—in the Lizzie Borden trial.) The jury found themselves, at Marshall Hall's behest, glancing from client to advocate and from advocate to client—that unruffled client who, under their survey, did not interrupt his sketching of celebrities in court.

This increased awareness of Wood as a human being, not

merely as a bloodless cypher in a mystery tale, had one immediate and one remote result. The latter was to make them more reluctant to convict. The former was to make them still more eager for the moment when Wood would tell his own story from the witness-box.

Their eagerness survived the intermission of a night. It survived the succeeding morning, during which Wood's father, brother and a neighbour swore that he came home at midnight on September 12th; they were patently honest but confused in recollection, and Mathews expertly cast doubt upon the date. It survived the advent of a St Paul's Road resident who had gone on early shift at five on the morning of the crime; he attributed to himself 'a peculiar swinging walk' and Marshall Hall announced him as the man MacCowan really saw. It survived attestation by two Rising Sun habitués that they had seen Phyllis Dimmock with a man not the accused at half-past twelve upon the night she died. It survived all this and indeed delay fomented expectation, not more among the jury than among those looking on.

The feelings of the latter finally found expression through an incident unique in British criminal trials. When at last, towards mid-afternoon on the fifth day, Marshall Hall called the name of Robert Wood, a breathless hush descended on the court. Then, as with one accord, the whole assembly rose, and the prisoner picked his way from dock to box like some high priest amid his reverent congregation.

29

How a prisoner is received when he goes into the box is primarily the business of his advocate. How he fares while he is there is primarily his own.

From a lawyer's standpoint a 'good' witness is one who answers briefly the questions that are asked, does not volunteer unsolicited information, and above all refrains from argument or comment. Any sort of histrionics are regarded with peculiar apprehension and abhorrence.

It was soon apparent that, by these criteria, Wood's merits as a witness were very, very few. Refinement he possessed, and a certain delicate charm that made the notion of him as a brutal murderer incongruous. But with this charm went affectations and conceits that could easily be construed as a technique of evasion.

Right from the start he gave trouble to his counsel.

'Did you kill Phyllis Dimmock?' Marshall Hall had asked him.

This classical propounding of the theme invites one, and only one, response—a simple and unhesitating 'No.' But Wood chose to decline the obvious lead. Instead he thrust his hands out in mute expostulation, flung his head back, and rolled his eyes to heaven.

This foolish exhibition caused acute embarrassment. The jury shifted awkwardly, and Wood's friends looked at one another in dismay.

'Did you kill Phyllis Dimmock?' Marshall Hall repeated with expressive emphasis.

Wood arched his brows theatrically.

'Ridiculous,' he said.

Obtuseness of this kind on the part of his own client is the recurrent nightmare of every barrister. It raises difficulties almost insurmountable. You are forbidden to put the appropriate answer in his mouth; you cannot subject him to cross-examination; you can hardly seek to treat him as a hostile witness.

Marshall Hall went as far as settled practice would permit.

'You must answer straight,' he told Wood solemnly. 'I will only ask you perfectly straight questions. Once again—did you kill Phyllis Dimmock?'

'No,' Wood said belatedly, 'I most certainly did not.'

There was an audible sigh. Even those indifferent to the outcome somehow felt relieved. .

This, though, was but the first of many occasions. Wood refused to tread the path his counsel indicated. He paltered; he digressed; he struck melodramatic attitudes ('If I am lying, I hope God will destroy me at this moment.'); he threw off chatty and intimate asides to the twelve men who were engaged in trying him ('I dare say some of *you* will know what goes on in public houses'). 'I wish you would answer me and not talk to the jury,' said Marshall Hall in fruitless remonstrance; as imperturbable as he was mannerised, the accused would not alter nor modify his course. Perhaps he could not; perhaps his personality forbade; perhaps this was the price that he paid for being 'artistic'—which, many people noted, was his favourite adjective.

Only by patient and arduous endeavour did Marshall Hall succeed in drawing from his wayward client something that resembled a coherent narrative. Before he had finished it was almost evening. The single-handed duel between accused and prosecutor—one in which the parties seemed pathetically unequal—was postponed until the sixth and last day of the trial.

30

If Mathews had seemed subordinate so far to Marshall Hall and had not competed with him as the focus of attraction, that was largely due to the restrictions of his rôle. Now most of those restrictions were temporarily cast off; next morning as he stood up in his place, hands upon his hips, eyes piercing as needles, shrewd mouth very tight-lipped and determined, he made a powerful bid for mastery of the court.

He at once passed up to Wood the celebrated postcard, without which there would have been neither prisoner nor trial.

'Look at that postcard, if you please. Look at what is written on it. On its face it is a note of assignation, is it not?'

The harsh voice rasped the nerves like tearing metal. Of all who heard it Wood seemed least affected, although today he looked fatigued, as well he might. A week may be more restfully spent than on trial for your life, with a Mathews lying in wait for you almost at the close.

'It looks like a note of assignation, does it not?'

'Yes,' agreed Wood, wearily resigned. We've been through this, his manner hinted, so many times before.

'A note that was written by you unquestionably?'

'Yes.'

'And addressed to the woman by the name in which she lived?'

'Yes.'

'At the house where she was killed?'

'Yes.'

'You posted it on the night of the Sunday?'

'Yes.'

'You would expect it to reach her on the morning of the Monday?'

'Yes.'

Mathews drew his gown about him ominously.

'Did you keep the assignation made upon that postcard?'

Wood hesitated. The court was still and soundless.

'I did go to The Rising Sun on Monday night,' he said, 'but later—later than 8.15, it was.'

'Do you suggest that the appointment which you kept was not made by that postcard which you wrote?'

The facts had not changed, yet somehow they now wore a different aspect. Wood felt uncertain of his ground. He stumbled badly.

'There was no *seriousness* attached to it,' he said. 'It was immaterial to me.'

Mathews pounced.

'My question is not directed to materiality. It is directed to fact. Did you keep the appointment made on the postcard?'

There could be no turning back.

'Well, it was hardly a promise,' Wood protested.

'An understanding?'

'So mild,' said Wood, 'that it was only by the way.'

But an admission that the message on the postcard had implied even the mildest 'understanding' was in open contradiction to what Wood had said before—that the words were utterly meaningless and empty; only set down, as the first that came into his head, when Phyllis had asked him to 'write something nice on it.'

It had, of course, no direct bearing on the crime; it disclosed another lie, but he had confessed to many lies; none the less, this enforced reversal of a statement that he had made only yesterday on oath could not be considered a hopeful augury.

Wood did indeed quickly go from bad to worse. Mathews turned next to the fragments from the grate, which the Crown still maintained were the remnants of a letter. He gave Wood the slide, asked him to examine it, and pointed out a half-decipherable sequence: '. . . ill you . . . ar of the . . . e . Town . . . Wednes . . .'

'Take that in your hand,' the prosecutor said. 'Let us try to reconstruct this passage.' Memories went back to what the ship's cook said he saw: Will you meet me at the bar of The Eagle at Camden Town 8.30 tonight, Wednesday.—Bert. 'It seems to begin "Will you," does it not?'

'I'll give you the "w," ' Wood said, 'if you wish.'

'Then there is something illegible followed by "ar." Tell me, as it originally stood, didn't this run: "Will you meet me at the bar?" '

'Are you imagining that?' Wood ironically enquired.

'No, no.' Mathews rapped out a sharp repudiation. 'No, no. I am imagining nothing. I am asking you, who admit you were the writer, what the wording originally was. Can you help me?'

'No, I can't.'

'Well, I don't propose to dismiss it quite so readily.' Once more the deadly little man pulled and flapped his gown. 'Please look at it again. I put it to you that it originally ran: "Will you meet me at the bar of The Eagle." '

'You are imagining it,' Wood reiterated. 'I didn't even know then what the place was called.'

'The public house where you went with Dimmock on the Saturday?'

'Yes.'

'You say you didn't know its name?'

'I have been to many houses in my life,' said Wood, 'but I didn't know and I don't know the names of all of them.'

That was not implausible. Mathews astutely reverted to the slide.

'You see that next is a blurred space, and then follows the word "Town." Didn't "Camden" come before the word "Town" in the letter?'

'Sir Charles, it was *not* a letter.'

'And next is "Wednes . . ."—obviously "Wednesday"?'

'Yes.'

Mathews deliberately paused.

'Wasn't the Wednesday referred to the 11th of September?'

'Not to my knowledge.'

'Consider. You had only known this girl, you say, for five days altogether, beginning on the Friday before she met her death?'

'Yes.'

'She died early in the morning of Thursday, 12th September?'

'So I understand.'

'Mustn't the Wednesday referred to here be September the 11th?'

A flat denial was now virtually impossible.

'It might have been,' Wood said.

Mathews folded his arms.

'So these words which remain, when critically read, are consistent with the making of an assignation?'

'That's what *you* suggest, Sir Charles.'

'Let us see what *you* suggest.' The words shot out with the speed and militancy of machine-gun bullets. 'Did you say that it was something you had written in her p ?'

'I said it might be. I honestly can't make head or tail of it. I can only imagine it was something of the sort.'

'Something of what sort?'

'Oh, just sketches and amusing phrases.'

'Can you find any sketches on it?'

'No.'

'Or any trace of a sketch?'

'No.'

'Or any amusing phrase?'

'No.'

'Or anything which might conceivably be part of one?'

Wood turned the slide between his fingers helplessly. 'No.'

'When do you say you gave that document to Dimmock?'

'I don't know that I gave her anything.'

'Then where do you suggest she got it?'

'I don't know . . . except that she looked through the letters from my pocket when I pulled out my sketch book in the bar.'

'Do you suggest she *took* it?' Mathews asked icily.

'Yes,' Wood said, then added pitifully, 'She was very forward. Those girls are. . '

All that morning Mathews kept Wood upon the rack. Fashions change, even in the practice of the law, and such remorselessness by counsel for the Crown might not pass uncriticised today. No one, however, could reasonably complain that, as such, the cross-examination was improper. Mathews never stooped to a questionable device; he was inexorable but scrupulous, hard-hitting but correct. His triumph over Wood—for triumph, by any measurement of scoring points, it was—seemed the proper due of a brilliant cross-examiner whose gifts had dazzled everyone in court.

But while the limelight thus beat on his opponent, the defender did not retreat far into the shade. It is a peculiar attribute of the greatest advocates that they can exert authority by their very presence. During the three hours in which Mathews questioned Wood, Marshall Hall uttered hardly a dozen words. But he was there; a vibrant, active force, refusing to cede the dominion he had won. Not for a moment were the jury permitted to forget him—nor what he had said, nor the cause for which he stood.

31

The general public now was with Wood to a man. It furnished ample proof of the defender's grip upon them that

Mathews, despite his virtuosity, had not been able to reverse this favourable trend. Within and without the crowds seemed of one mind; they were no longer sympathetic, they were frankly partisan; they were not merely hoping for but *willing* an acquittal. As the minutes of the afternoon ticked by, and the trial steadily drew towards its close, this emotion sometimes passed out of control; hysterical demonstrations took place in Newgate Street, and when the judge, who had begun his summing-up in a manner markedly adverse to the accused, unexpectedly said something in his favour, the notabilities in court forgot themselves and cheered.

No jury could have been insensitive to the pressure of this mass anxiety. But that did not necessarily mean the jury shared it, nor that they would feel any compulsion to give way. Between those who are free from responsibility and those upon whom responsibility is thrust the approach to a verdict may be radically different. It is of no avail to carry thirty million with you if you fail to carry the adjudicating twelve.

Marshall Hall need have entertained no fears. His conquest was to be complete. By a memorable feat of all-round advocacy, in which his splendid talents were extended to the full, he had transformed the losing battle of a week ago into the winning battle of today. He had saved Wood from the gallows and the processes of justice from the shame of grievous error. . . .

It was exactly eight o'clock when the jury returned after fifteen minutes' absence. A few seconds later pandemonium broke loose.

32

That night, though, the Old Bailey was the quietest place of all.

The town was running wild. Men shouted and waved hats; women wept and fluttered handkerchiefs; groups formed impromptu processions of rejoicing; traffic was held up in scores of streets. It seemed, said Marshall Hall with surprising understatement, less like the end of a trial than the result of an election.

But the court, after its frenzied climax, stood silent and empty. Those who had daily gathered there were gone their separate ways—the actors to their theatres, the journalists to their papers, the authors to their studies, Robert Wood to a new life under a new name, Marshall Hall to the next of that long line of cases which was to keep him in the limelight for a further twenty years. The Camden Town drama was at last played out and abandoned for good by its cast of characters.

Only one was bound to it for ever; one who had not been present at the trial at all. She lay now, as she lay then, six feet underground, and her throat had been cut from ear to ear right back to the spine.

P. A. Reute

PATRICK HASTINGS

MODERN SUITE FOR STRINGS

Patrick Hastings defends Elvira Barney

1

Every outstandingly successful advocate is to some degree the creation of his age. By natural instinct or by conscious acquisition he reflects the temper and the ethos that prevails among the society in which his work is done. Failing this, no technical equipment will attain the topmost heights.

Patrick Hastings—who unquestionably takes rank among the greatest jury advocates who have ever adorned the Bar—is the supreme example of a forensic master precisely attuned to the requirements of the time. In any generation his exceptional talents would have won acknowledgment: his extraordinary acuteness as a cross-examiner; his agility and resourcefulness in argument; the vigour of his quick and lucid mind, keenly intelligent rather than deeply intellectual, which made him more at home—as befits a jury advocate—with people and affairs than with theories and ideas. But to these was added a decisive factor that served to set the lasting seal on his success and fame: a worldly knowledge that was rooted in the moment. This worldliness, this fund of contemporary sense, directed his approach to every case he undertook; to those for whom he fought, to those he fought against, to those upon whom rested the outcome of the fight. That approach can be defined in a single word, used in its best and most recent connotation. More than any other counsel of comparable eminence, Hastings was a *sophisticated* advocate—in fashionable practice when fashionable people were setting new standards in advanced sophistication.

Sophisticated people do not care for strident emphasis; they stand on guard against assaults on the emotions; they like effects to be subtle and power to be concealed. In the language of the theatre, they prefer to have their dramas underplayed.

Hastings introduced, or at any rate perfected, the art of

underplaying in the English jury courts. He utterly discarded the barnstorming technique; nobody has ever been more unlike Marshall Hall—nor, one suspects, more pleased to be unlike him. Hastings never stormed nor shouted; never waved his arms about; never gave any sign that he felt at all excited nor that he wished to cause excitement among others. And yet, in the sphere of high life litigation, there has never been a more exciting advocate, nor one who could exert a more mesmerising spell. The personality, cool, self-contained, rather offhand, slightly cynical; the voice, no organ throb moving listeners to tears, but smooth and even purring with an undertone of sarcasm; the manner, informed with that assurance and that ease which, in a public performer, masks the highest art—they enthralled and fascinated London Special Juries, particularly in the years between the two world wars. Here was an advocate whose individual style accorded with current cultivated taste. Hastings was a portent and an influence at the Bar analogous with and parallel to du Maurier on the stage.

Like du Maurier, and for not dissimiliar reasons, Hastings' professional home was the West End—which includes, for these purposes, the east point of the Strand but does not extend as far as the Old Bailey. During his great years in the very highest flight, when he was seldom missing from a civil *cause célèbre*, Hastings engaged in little criminal work and hardly ever accepted a capital defence. 'I have always hated trials for murder'—so he wrote after retirement; and one might well imagine that such trials would repel a genius of his type and temperament.

This did not mean, though, that were he once involved he would not defend a murder case with dazzling ability. Especially a murder case falling, however remotely, into his chosen province; a murder case with a sophisticated setting and, at least upon the surface, a sophisticated twist.

2

Murder is rarely a sophisticated act; and suspicion of murder is generally aroused by the presence of unsophisticated passions. Greed, hate, jealousy and lust—these are universal impulses to action; but in a highly civilised and sceptical community one expects them to remain under reasonable control. It is therefore not surprising that, in contrast to the Borgias of fourteenth-century Italy and to the Medicis of sixteenth-century France, the well-to-do classes of twentieth-century Britain did not go in for killing, except with motor cars. Their murder rate was low, their murder charges few, even in proportion to their restricted numbers. During the last two decades of their existence—for since 1940 they have been virtually wiped out in the redistribution of property and wealth—they found ample employment for their favoured advocates by libel, slander, probate squabbles, and divorce.

This had become such a convention of the epoch that its one great murder trial which did involve the rich came to many as a bolt out of the blue. It gave an entirely unexpected handle to those who disliked and denounced sophistication, but had formerly had no grounds for connecting it with violence. Even now, unless qualified, the implication was unwarranted. For the tiny band of debauchees and profligates that formed the human background to the case of Mrs Barney was no more than a foul offshoot, a leprous excrescence, of true sophistication. They enjoyed—either at first or second hand—the wealth so helpful to sophisticated living; they used what passed for sophisticated language; the simple were deceived by their sophisticated front. But theirs was sophistication that had run riot and turned rotten; sophistication that had gone into reverse. Idle, drunken, emotionally unstable, crude in conduct as they were coarse in spirit, they made a natural forcing bed for frenzy and convulsion.

Out of the rank soil of this Mayfair saturnalia sprang the most vivid murder trial of 1932. It gave the upper strata of society a shaking, seized the undivided attention of the lower, and involved all England in a passionate debate about the character and morals of the woman they accused.

3

Life had showered many favours on Elvira Barney. She was well-bred; her titled parents, with their house in Belgrave Square and their country seat in Sussex, occupied a position of dignity and respect. She was affluent; money raised no shadow of a problem and her pleasures never had to be curtailed through lack of means. She was attractive in the style her contemporaries preferred—a face that was pleasing rather than beautiful; large grey eyes; a tip-tilted nose; blonde and fluffy hair; a boyish figure (though by the time of her trial, when she was only twenty-six, both figure and face were paying for indulgence). She had animal energy and natural intelligence. All these assets she threw heedlessly away.

From her very early womanhood the writing on the wall grew steadily more visible. The existence she led, the diversions she sought, the friends she cultivated—every one was trivial, rackety and exhausting. For a period she did toy with the idea of being an actress, and once even appeared on the stage of the Gaiety in some tiny part in a musical play; but hard work enticed her less than superficial glamour, and she did not press ahead with a theatrical career. She married, with characteristic levity and caprice, a cabaret singer who had performed at a function in her father's house and whom she decided she had fallen in love with at first sight; this marriage turned out badly—Mrs Barney later spoke of it as 'hell'—and the couple separated, never to re-unite. Mr Barney returned to the United States whence he had come, and contributes nothing to this story but his name.

The break-up of her marriage expedited Mrs Barney's downward course. London's Bright Young People claimed her for their own. You still sometimes meet survivors of this long extinguished set; they are mostly male and now almost invariably perverts. Gin-soaked, fish-eyed, tearful with self-pity, these middle-aged derelicts haunt the bars of Kensington and Chelsea, calling down curses on their present lot and feebly lamenting the gay days that are no more. It is hard to believe, looking at them now, that anyone could have ever found them tolerable. But youth, while it lasts, is a potent alchemist, and for Mrs Barney certainly they were not without appeal. Her home in William Mews, near Knightsbridge—a converted cottage—became one of their recognised resorts and her black and red two-seater an addition to their transport. There were many parties; there was much dashing to and fro; there was a brisk traffic in sexual partnerships, from which Mrs Barney did not hold herself aloof.

Her lover, who had no genuine occupation (he vaguely described himself as a dress designer), rented an apartment room on Brompton Road. Everyone called him Michael, although that was not his name. Like Mrs Barney herself, he was respectably derived; but his father, a prominent magistrate and banker, in disgust at his son's conduct, had cut off his allowance; Michael had lately kept himself supplied with cash by 'borrowing' alternately from his mother and his brother. He was now apparently quite content to be kept by his new mistress.

There were several other things besides good family and a taste for dissipation that Mrs Barney had in common with this handsome wastrel. They were exactly the same age. They both drank far too much. And each was prone to sudden fits of jealousy, his petulant and sulky, hers unbridled and consuming.

As in all the circumstances could have been foreseen, their relationship was marked by wildly fluctuating phases. There were times of mutual rapture, all the more intense for being so perilously poised; times when they made love with fierce abandonment or wrote each other tender letters in the idiom affected by adults when addressing infants. There were also times of mutual agony, when they tore themselves and their shallow love to tatters; times when they had painful and degrading scenes in public and quarrelled bitterly far into the night. Neighbours in the mews, mostly chauffeurs and their wives, suffered whichever condition was prevailing; the din of recrimination and dispute was matched by the din of exultant celebration. Resentment aroused by these continual disturbances was not without its bearing upon subsequent events.

If that resentment fixed upon the woman, not the man, the causes were manifest and comprehensible. She, not he, was the tenant of the cottage. She, not he, was in constant residence, the human storm spot of a peaceful neighbourhood. And she, not he, was the dominating partner; even the least discerning could perceive that at a glance. Hers was the more possessive and explosive nature; the more self-willed; the more accustomed to impose itself on others. Of Elvira Barney it might be said with literal truth that she would rather die than be deprived of her own way.

4

One has forgotten the smart jargon of 1932, so it is impossible to say whether the party Mrs Barney gave on the 30th of May was divine or marvellous or super or terrific. There were, however, abundant indications that it gave great pleasure to the persons who attended, and it presented the neighbours with a further opportunity of studying their social betters at close range. From shortly after six the racing cars rattled and roared into the mews; their occupants, loudly shouting to each other, vanished one by one through Mrs Barney's door; the hubbub floating through the windows steadily increased as the female voices grew more shrill, the male more stentorian; sometimes a solitary guest, appearing overtaxed, came out into the mews for a few minutes' fresh air; and once or twice, keen-eyed observers noted, a couple would emerge, drive off in one of the cars, and, half an hour later, return and go inside again. Mrs Barney did nothing by half measures; she entertained her friends in the style to which they were accustomed.

By half-past nine, though, all of them had gone. Michael—who had been handing drinks assiduously—and Mrs Barney—who had been assiduously taking them—now sat alone amid the residual débris. They drank some more—he faster, in order to catch up. When they had put themselves entirely in the mood they set off together on their usual nightly round.

Soon after ten o'clock they were seen having dinner in the Café de Paris. Soon after eleven they were seen at a well-known night resort in Dean Street—the management of which indignantly complained when the papers so described it in the days and weeks that followed. ('We are a high-class social rendezvous and members' club.') Soon after twelve they left this club and so far as is known went straight back to William Mews.

They were certainly there at three, when yet another of their quarrels broke the silence of the summer night. Sleepers in the mews reluctantly awakened; swore at the nuisance; prayed it would die down. But instead the uproar gathered force and swelled in volume. Woman's voice; man's voice; woman's voice; man's voice; separate and distinct at first, then jumbled together. The mews pulled its sheets round its infuriated head; but could not shut out this obliterating row. Groans, abuse, tears, entreaties—and was that the sound of a struggle, of a fight?

Somewhere about four there was a piercing crack. People sat up, startled. No, it couldn't be. Crazy as that woman was, it couldn't be. .

Most of them had dropped off again to sleep before the doctor's telephone began to ring.

5

'I have been cautioned that I am not obliged to make this statement. I have known Michael for about a year. We were great friends, and he used to come and see me from time to time.

'He always used to see me home. He did so last night as usual. Immediately we got in we had a quarrel about a woman he was fond of.

'He knew I kept a revolver in the house. I have had it for years. It was kept in various places. Last night it was under the cushion of a chair in the bedroom, near the bed. I was afraid of it and used to hide it from time to time. He knew where it was last night.

'He took it, saying, "I am going to take it away for fear you kill yourself." He went into the room on the left. I ran after him and tried to get it back.

'There was no struggle in the bedroom. It was outside in the spare room, in the doorway. As we were struggling together—he wanted to take it away, and I wanted to get it back—it went off. Our hands were together—his hands and mine. .

'I did not think anything had happened. He seemed quite all right. He went into the bathroom and half shut the door, and said, "Fetch a doctor."

'I asked, "Do you really mean it?" I did not have the revolver then. I think it had fallen to the ground.

'I saw he looked ill, so I rang up a doctor, but no one answered. I went upstairs again and saw him sitting on the floor.

'I was upset and began to cry. I again rang up the doctor and he said he would come. I went upstairs again. Michael asked, "Why doesn't the doctor come? I want to tell him what happened. It was not your fault."

'He repeated that over and over again. I tried to cut his tie off, put a towel on his chest and got towels. I again rang up the doctor, and they said that he was leaving.

'I again went upstairs and saw he was dead and just waited. I don't remember what I did afterwards. I was so frantic. I am sure—as far as I know—there was only one shot fired.

'Michael and I have quarrelled on previous occasions, but not often.'

Mrs Barney leaned back. Her face was ashen and her breath came heavily. While the Inspector read over her statement in official monotone, for the first time she allowed her eyes to wander over the bleak and bare police station room.

The foolscap sheets were put in front of her. Mechanically she signed.

It was morning, almost ten o'clock in the morning, after a night packed full with horror and distress. When the doctor arrived in response to Mrs Barney's summons ('There has been a terrible accident; for God's sake come at once!') he beheld a scene that might have been pleasing in a mystery novel, but was apt to harrow the steadiest nerves when encountered in real life. Michael sprawled at the top of the stairs, a bullet through his lung; it was obvious to the doctor that he was already dead. Close beside him lay a pistol; it contained five cartridges, two of which were spent. Mrs Barney herself was uncontrollably hysterical and only intermittently coherent. 'He cannot be dead, he cannot be dead,' she cried time and again. 'I will die too; I want to die. I loved him so. I loved him so.' As the doctor, stooping low over the corpse, confirmed his initial melancholy conclusion, she ran aimlessly to and fro, calling the dead man's name and trying to explain what had occurred in disconnected fragments.

The arrival of the police (whom the doctor as in duty bound immediately informed) seemed to drive the unhappy woman clean out of her mind. She said afterwards that she had no recollection of this episode, and quite conceivably she was in some sort of delirium; if not—whether innocent or guilty—her conduct would have surely been less hurtful to her cause. She cursed and fulminated against the officers, calling them 'vile swine' and ordering them to leave; when they used the telephone, she snatched it from their hands; when told that she must go to the police station for further questioning, she gave her interrogator a blow across the face. She shrieked, stamped, laughed and wept alternately. She was, said the doctor, absolutely frenzied.

No spark of frenzy lingered in Mrs Barney now. It had died when they took her away from the cottage that had been her home and where now her lover's body lay. Thenceforward she was calm but patently exhausted; what woman could be otherwise who in so few hours had passed through so many prostrating events? While she made her statement, under the horrified eyes of her distracted parents who had been apprised and had hurried to her side, Mrs Barney must have been close to collapse from sheer fatigue.

The clarity of her account thus becomes the more remarkable. Moreover, it entirely corresponded in essentials with all she had so far said and all she was yet to say. There were one or two omissions, probably deliberate. It would have been painful to reveal in the presence of her parents that she and Michael had been lovers many months; that the quarrel had developed after they had gone to bed; that Michael had threatened to leave her, got up again and dressed; that it was then she had talked of committing suicide. She hoped—no doubt expected—that the matter would soon drop without necessitating these intimate disclosures. But substantially the story that was outlined in her statement was the story that the doctor had already pieced together from her paroxysmal and confused ejaculations; nor was it changed in that excruciating hour when, with two prison wardresses beside her, she told it to a packed and palpitating court. . . .

The police conferred together. Her own statement exculpated Mrs Barney, and they had no evidence yet to suggest it was untrue.

'Very well,' said the Inspector, 'we will not trouble you, madam, any more just now. You are free to go.'

'She will come home with us, of course, Inspector,' said her mother. . . .

The respite was a short one. Only three days afterwards, as the troubled family prepared for dinner, the police came visiting the house in Belgrave Square. They had now been able to make a full investigation and, as a result, were no longer satisfied. Data in their possession could not be made to tally with the statement that the lady gave them earlier in the week.

That evening Mrs Barney, who had said she wished to die, stood in grave danger that this wish would be fulfilled.

6

From the moment of her arrest the popular press was in full cry; their headlines sometimes read like a satirical burlesque. 'West End Flat Mystery,' 'Society Tragedy Sensation,' 'Mayfair Beauty in Shooting Drama,' 'Banker's Son Dead after Cocktail Party,' 'Knight's Daughter on Murder Charge'; variations revolved round these titillating words—save in one instance, where a banner frankly promised 'Mrs Barney: The Biggest Thrills.' The prisoner herself, on her first appearance at the preliminary proceedings in the police court, unintentionally added to the atmosphere of melodrama by falling to the floor of the dock in a dead faint.

Mrs Barney had good reason to feel deeply apprehensive. The police had not at all overstated their position; the new evidence—if accepted—made her story of an accident untenable. One female neighbour was fully prepared to swear she had heard Mrs Barney shout 'I'll shoot you' just before the shot. Another female neighbour was equally prepared to swear that she had heard more than one shot being fired (an assertion that appeared to gain considerable force from the presence of a bullet mark on the cottage bedroom wall). Both women also spoke of an incident some days earlier when, as they declared, Mrs Barney from the window fired at Michael in the mews. And to all these presumed facts was added the opinion of two exceptionally influential experts, Churchill the gunsmith and Spilsbury the pathologist; each independently had come to the conclusion that Mrs Barney's version of the shooting was improbable. The former attached special significance to the type of pistol. 'It requires both a long and heavy pull,' he said.

The Crown thus had a formidable case and the prisoner sore need of a formidable defender. For once in a murder trial money was no object. The brief for Mrs Barney was offered to Patrick Hastings.

One may surmise that that distinguished advocate, then a little over fifty and at the very peak of his dazzling career, thought hard before he undertook this burden. It was in the middle of the summer term, and a dozen heavily marked briefs were on his desk. He was representing one of the great trusts in a claim for £60,000 from one of the great banks. He was retained by a leading theatre management in a suit for damages brought by a leading lady. He was concerned for the co-respondent in an aristocratic divorce with Eaton Square addresses and an adultery charge at Cannes. He was also concerned in a big probate action (disposed of four days before the Barney trial began), in a newspaper libel on a popular peeress (settled three days after the Barney trial concluded), and, as leader of a string of eminent counsel, in an appeal by the directors of a company against a verdict of £250,000 imposed upon them for conspiracy and fraud. (This last case actually started on the final morning of Mrs Barney's trial, and continued uninterruptedly thereafter for a fortnight.) There were certainly ample demands on Patrick Hastings—and there was, of course, his confessed dislike of capital defences.

Nevertheless, he did not decline the Barney brief, and this without doubt was artistically fitting. Here at last for the sophisticated advocate was a murder case that had at least grown out of his own world.

7

Any murder trial at any time tends to attract spectators if only because the stake is human life. A sensational Victorian trial like Mrs Bartlett's or a sensational Edwardian trial like Robert Wood's was not only sure of a continuously packed court, but also—as has already been remarked—would draw and hold great multitudes in the adjoining streets. More recently this latter phenomenon had been rarely seen. It reappeared, however, at the trial of Mrs Barney, which, on 4th July and the two succeeding days, made the Central Criminal Court like a fortress under siege.

The military metaphor is far from inappropriate. For in one respect, at least, the crowds on this occasion easily surpassed all their predecessors. They were less demonstrative than some, partly because of the changed bent of the time, partly because at no point was there anything approaching unanimity of view upon the case's merits. But they were surely unique in ferocity and resolve. The waiting crowds of earlier years may have envied those within; they did not themselves seek entry by violence and brute force. But many of those who stood and stared at the walls of the Old Bailey, hour after hour while Mrs Barney was being tried, only accepted this second-best sensation after a pitched battle in which they were repelled.

The queue had begun to form on Sunday afternoon, more than twenty hours before the court was due to sit. Well before midnight it had grown so long and deep that the police decided it ought to be dispersed. Those who had already waited nearly half a day did not receive this decision with good humour. There were loud cries of protest; heated disputes developed; one poor old lady burst into bitter tears —she had been there since two o'clock and now her last train had gone.

The police, however, insisted on their orders being obeyed, and reluctantly the crowds withdrew from their vantage-ground. Some gave up altogether and went home. Some took refuge in the all-night cafés, where they debated plans for making a fresh attempt. But the majority merely split up into groups of two or three, who walked and stood and squatted in the neighbourhood all night and took up posts next morning within sight of the court door like so many beasts of prey around a water-hole.

These omens were not lost upon the police, and a strong protective cordon was established before giving the signal that the queue might be re-formed. Strong, but not strong enough to seize immediate control. From all directions men and women flew towards the spot with an impetus as if they had been shot from catapults. The cordon swayed, retreated and at one point finally broke; the mob hurled themselves madly at the gap; and that first afternoon the newspapers had pictures of police and civilians struggling on the ground.

Only a handful of these warriors gained admission to the court, where most of the space had been allotted in advance by tickets bearing the full name of the successful applicant. But there, too, disorder threatened, though of a different kind. Many of the tickets had somehow been obtained by young, well-dressed and frivolous-minded women who regarded the trial as a theatrical first night and proceeded to behave like the audience at one. They giggled and chattered with indecent zest as they waited, all agog, for the performance to begin.

At any intimation of weakness on the Bench this animated bevy might have got right out of hand. There was no such intimation. 'If there is any more of this,' remarked his lordship coolly, when the female babble broke out for the first time in his presence, 'the whole court shall be cleared.'

Thenceforward silence reigned. Even the silliest could see that Mr Justice Travers Humphreys was a man who meant exactly what he said.

8

Hastings had come into court just before the appointed hour. After one contemptuous glance at the gay parade of fashion, he took his place without ostentatious fuss and sat there very straight and very quiet and very still. Those present who had witnessed Marshall Hall's volcanic entries on similar occasions, and the indisputable gallery play that followed them, could hardly fail to be struck by the sharp contrast. One thing only the two men had in common—a personality magnetic and commanding. Without the slightest effort—almost as though it were contrary to his wish—from the very moment when he first appeared Hastings dominated the entire Old Bailey scene. Long before he had said a single word, even during the opening statement for the Crown, the eyes of the jury were straying constantly to him. . . .

A practised observer can usually detect when a prosecutor feels full confidence in his case. If he harbours any serious doubt himself, being imbued by his training with the salutary doctrine that the prisoner must receive the benefit of a doubt, this is almost sure to be reflected in his speech. He will pitch his argument in a lower key, sprinkle it with exceptions and provisos, leave the issue conspicuously open. In short, he becomes more narrator than accuser.

Nothing of this kind occurred at the trial of Mrs Barney. Percival Clarke, leading counsel for the Crown, gave the jury at the outset a strong and clear lead. His manifest integrity—befitting a son of Mrs Bartlett's great defender—lent his comments additional effect. Some of these consisted of direct denunciation. Of the prisoner's hysteria on the arrival of the doctor he said: 'Perhaps she realised then what she had done.' Of her assault upon the police: 'You see what sort of temper this woman gives way to on slight provocation.' And of the actual shooting he spoke in these uncompromising terms: 'The medical evidence can definitely establish the direction in which the revolver was held when fired. You will learn from that that it is practically impossible for the man to have caused this injury to himself. If he did not, who did? There was only one other person there. If you are forced to the conclusion that she shot him, you will have to consider whether she did it by accident or design. In that connection you will bear in mind her admission of the quarrel. You will bear in mind what she shouted before the gun was fired. You will bear in mind that she had fired the gun during another quarrel on a previous occasion. Members of the jury, is there any explanation consistent with common sense which will enable you to understand how that man met his death unless this woman *deliberately* fired?'

To the lawyers in court—and there were a great number, some even disposing themselves upon the floor—it became more apparent as each minute passed that the prosecution were not pulling any punches. Obviously they believed in their case and they were both seeking and expecting a conviction.

9

The chief witnesses called on the first day of the trial were Mrs Barney's much-enduring neighbours from the mews.

There were three altogether; but the last, a chauffeur, was of little consequence. It was the two women who mattered—the women, each of them a decent chauffeur's wife, who had had their lives made wretched by Mrs Barney's escapades. The defence could not hope to find them favourably inclined, and their cross-examination needed infinite finesse.

One important gain, though, Hastings made without

exertion; simply by watchfulness and tactical restraint. The first chauffeur's wife was being examined by the Crown. She had given her account of the earlier incident in the mews, describing how Mrs Barney leaned out of the window; how she was holding 'something bright' in her *left* hand; how there was a report and witness saw 'a puff of smoke.' Now she had come to the night of Michael's death, and to the one real point at which she might have thrown some light upon it.

'So you heard the sounds of their quarrelling,' Clarke said. 'Were there any words—any *important* words—you could pick out?'

'Yes,' she replied. 'Just before the shot I heard Mrs Barney say, "Get out. I'll shoot. I'll shoot."'

Now 'I'll shoot' is not at all the same thing as 'I'll shoot *you*,' which was what the woman had originally told the police; otherwise Clarke would not in turn have told the jury. 'I'll shoot' is as consistent with a threat to commit suicide as a threat to commit murder. If the evidence stood thus—and no other witness claimed to have overheard this passage—it need no longer conflict with the prisoner's own story.

'You heard her say "I'll shoot"?' Clarke repeated interrogatively.

The rules of British procedure do not permit counsel to put leading questions on matters in dispute to any witness that he himself has called. A leading question, one should point out, is not—as common usage would suggest—a question peculiarly probing or embarrassing; it is one so framed as to indicate the answer that the questioner desires or expects. It is not 'leading' to ask 'Where were you yesterday?'; it is 'leading' to ask 'Did you go yesterday to Brighton?' It would certainly have been 'leading' had Clarke at this juncture asked the witness 'Did you hear the prisoner call out, "I'll shoot *you*,"' and Hastings, though he sat with folded arms, looking straight ahead, was poised to intervene with an immediate objection. But it did not prove necessary. Clarke bowed to the inevitable and passed to something else.

Hastings carefully refrained from mentioning the matter in cross-examination. Any attempt at that stage to emphasise the witness's cardinal omission ('So, after all, you only heard the prisoner say "I'll shoot"?') might prompt her to reconsideration and retraction ('She *first* said "I'll shoot," and then after, "I'll shoot *you*" '). There would be a later and a safer chance to enlarge on this discrepancy. Meanwhile prudence prescribed leaving well alone.

But there was still of course the earlier shooting to be dealt with, and the court now got its first glimpse of Hastings in full action.

10

He began in a tone so soft, so conversational, that spectators in the gallery held their breath for fear of missing a single word.

'This incident in the mews—it happened late one night?'

'Yes.'

'About eleven o'clock next morning did you see the young man again?'

'Yes.'

'Was he then leaving the cottage?'

'Yes.'

'Was Mrs Barney with him?'

'Yes.'

'Did they seem friendly?'

'Yes.'

'On the best possible terms?'

'Yes.'

Marshall Hall would have paused there and stared hard at the jury. Hastings would no more emphasise a point in such a fashion than Noel Coward would wink at the stalls to stress a witty line.

The questions continued; terse, pithy—and exact. They left no room for evasion or misunderstanding.

'You saw this earlier incident while standing at your window?'

'Yes.'

'And the young man was below you in the mews?'

'Yes.'

'Did you give evidence at the police court?'

'Yes.'

'Did you say there that immediately after the shot was fired the young man spoke to you?'

'Yes.'

'And in the police court there the matter ended?'

'Yes.'

'But now,' said Hastings, 'I want you to tell us what he said.'

That he had touched a highly sensitive spot was attested by the quickness of the Crown's reaction.

'My lord, I object.' Percival Clarke had at once sprung to his feet. 'I submit that what this witness and the young man may have said outside Mrs Barney's hearing cannot be admissible. That is why it was not tendered at the police court. And if it cannot be evidence for the Crown, equally it cannot be evidence for the defence.'*

He sat down. The judge cast an inquiring look at Hastings.

'In all my experience at the Bar,' declared the latter, 'I have never heard such an objection made before. The prosecution ask a question in the lower court and then they don't allow it to be answered.' It was a perfect example of his gift for deadly ridicule, for deflating opposition in one swift, colloquial phrase. The jury, unversed in procedural technicalities, must have rejoiced in this attractive simplification—well calculated to excite their sympathy if the evidence should be ultimately excluded.

But the defence was very anxious that the evidence should be heard, and this depended not upon the jury but the judge.

Travers Humphreys listened attentively, impassively, as Hastings made his submission on the law. 'Here the prosecution have proved a fact. They have proved there was the firing of a revolver from a window and that the deceased

* Clarke was pleading the same rule, but for Crown instead of prisoner, as Marshall Hall had done concerning the barmaid from The Eagle. (See p. 128.)

man *at that moment* made a statement to a witness. I submit it is always admissible to give evidence of any statement accompanying such an incident.'

It was in fact a question involving much more doubt than might have been deduced from the defender's confident air. The judge, although an unsurpassed authority in this field, reflected deeply before giving a decision. 'The matter is not free from difficulty,' he said. 'I think the objection was quite properly taken. But'—and the lawyers knew then the defence would get their way—'but . . . I do not think this evidence ought to be excluded.'

The reason why both sides had treated this as a prime issue soon became apparent when Hastings, armed with sanction from the Bench, resumed.

'What conversation passed,' he asked, 'between you and the young man?'

'I told him to clear off,' said the first chauffeur's wife, 'as he was a perfect nuisance in the mews.'

'What did he reply?'

'He said he didn't want to leave Mrs Barney because *he was afraid that she might kill herself*.'

To the defence this admission was of immeasurable value. If Michael had previously confided to a stranger that he suspected Mrs Barney of suicidal tendencies, what was more likely than that, prior to going away, he would at least try to dispossess her of the pistol? And if he did, what more likely than that a woman of her temperament, whether genuinely contemplating suicide or not, should struggle fiercely to defeat him in this purpose lest her expressed intentions should appear frustrated?

It was the beginning, this—the beginning of a long series of scores by Mrs Barney's advocate that gradually cemented what had seemed a flimsy case.

11

One such score was to be added before this witness left the box.

The defence were not going to disavow the earlier shooting, when Mrs Barney was upstairs and Michael in the mews. But they were going to deny that she had fired *out* of the window, maintaining she had fired, for effect, *inside* the room.

Others had seen Michael; others had heard the shot; but only this lady spoke of seeing Mrs Barney with the pistol in her hand at the moment it was fired.

There was ground for supposing an imaginative faculty occasionally influenced her powers of observation. Hastings brought this out into the light.

'When the shot was fired,' he said, 'you say you saw a puff of smoke?'

'I did.'

'How big was it?'

The witness knitted her brows.

'Well——'

'As big as that?'

Counsel extended his hands about a foot apart.

'Oh no; not as big as that.'

'How big, then?' Hastings asked encouragingly.

The witness spread her hands in turn.

'As big as that?'

'Yes.'

Hastings nodded slightly. His next two questions seemed to come as afterthoughts.

'I suppose you didn't know that Mrs Barney's revolver contained cordite cartridges?'

'No.' The witness answered with indifference.

'And I suppose you don't know either,' Hastings added casually, 'that cordite cartridges don't make any smoke?'

The ten men and two women on the jury may have known nothing of the properties of cordite; but they did know, by applying ordinary sense, that so shrewd a counsel would not make such an assertion if it were open to subsequent disproof by the Crown. The puff of smoke disappeared into thin air. . . .

The second chauffeur's wife seemed to have seen a good deal less, but heard a good deal more. It was she who thought that on the night of Michael's death more than one shot had been fired, and that they came in quick succession. If the jury thought so too, the outlook for Mrs Barney would be bleak indeed.

Once again Hastings sought his ends without direct attack. Keenly aware of psychological resistances, he made no suggestion that the lady had been wrong. Instead of pressing her to cut down the number of the shots, he almost appeared to help her run them up. In no time at all she had sworn to hearing *five*.

'Quite a fusillade,' observed defending counsel, absently fingering the barrel of the pistol, from which only two bullets had been fired in all. . . .

Few yet realised exactly what had happened. They felt instinctively that this sardonic advocate, restrained but masterful, was having his own way and getting what he wanted; they did not at once perceive how much he had wanted nor how far he had gone. There had been none of the orthodox phenomena associated with a crisis in a murder trial; the rising voices, the deepening gravity, the open conflict between witnesses and Bar. All they had heard were some crisp and simple questions asked in the most natural and unpretentious style. But where now was the mews evidence—the shouting and the shots?

It was like a conjuring trick—but a conjuring trick performed without any drum rolls or spotlights or hey prestos. Nor did the conjurer bother to take a formal bow.

12

The witnesses from the mews, for all essential purposes, constituted the whole of the Crown's evidence of *fact*. But in a trial the emphasis may be more upon *opinion*—the opinion of experts formed after the event.

Many have gone to the gallows in consequence of these. Would Norman Thorne have been hanged but for Spilsbury's opinion that no cord was ever passed round Elsie Cameron's neck? Would Seddon have been hanged but for Willcox's opinion that Eliza Barrow died from acute, not chronic, poisoning? Would Rouse have been hanged but for Colonel Buckle's opinion that the nut in his carburettor pipe was purposely made loose?

This is not written in disparagement of experts—none will deny that Seddon and Rouse, at least, were rightly hanged—but simply to recall again their influence and power. A famous name, an authoritative style, the mystique of science and the glamour of detection—these may combine to produce such an effect that juries on occasion find it almost irresistible.

Unless, of course, the glamour can be stripped off and the mystique penetrated.

13

The experts in the Barney trial were called on the second morning, and Spilsbury was the first to go into the box. He made his usual excellent impression: suave, sure of himself, with every detail at his finger ends, he took great pains to make the jury understand that Michael could not possibly have committed suicide. He made play with the pistol. He explained the nature and direction of the wound. He told of experiments he had made upon a skeleton. It was all immensely neat and competent; it bore on every word and movement the authentic Spilsbury stamp.

As the pathologist went through this demonstration Hastings preserved an appearance of detachment. 'A most interesting performance,' his expression said; 'remarkably learned, extraordinarily instructive; but, as the defence is not and never has been one of suicide, it has nothing whatever to do with Mrs Barney or with me.' None the less, he was following most intently—waiting for any attempt on Spilsbury's part to dismiss as impossible the real defence of accident.

Although the point might not have struck the ordinary observer, no such attempt was ever made in positive terms. Whatever may have been the general tenor of his evidence, Spilsbury did not rule out accident in so many words. The omission, it seems certain, was one of policy. Both the

Crown and their star witness doubtless expected events to trace a long familiar pattern; they thought defending counsel in cross-examination would try his utmost to get Spilsbury's blessing for his client's story. Better to hold direct comment on that story till then. Better leave the accident defence till it was raised.

But Hastings was a subtle and unorthodox tactician; he did not mind forgoing the slight chance of Spilsbury's blessing, provided he had not incurred his express condemnation.

The crowd was waiting eagerly for a titanic struggle between two such masters in their respective spheres. When Spilsbury's interrogation by the Crown was over, and Hastings was seen to be rising in his place, heads craned forward and hearts beat faster. People felt on the brink of an historical event.

Spilsbury watched Hastings narrowly as the first question was put.

'To qualify yourself to show how the bullet was fired into the body, you had to examine the skeleton of someone else?'

'I had to *confirm* it on the skelton of someone else,' said Spilsbury

'Does each human body differ in formation?'

'Yes, in the formation of the bones.'

'And the best way to see how a bullet is fired into a body . . is to look at it, I suppose?'

'Yes,' Spilsbury admitted.

They had quickly got to grips. The spectators resettled themselves for a long and thrilling tussle.

The next thing they knew was that, incredibly, unaccountably, Hastings had sat down.

'Sir Bernard Spilsbury,' he observed later to the jury, 'gave no shred of evidence to suggest that the young man's death could not have been caused in the way that Mrs Barney has always said it was. . . . He did not affect my case. I had no questions to ask him.'

This neutralising of the country's crack professional witness was ultimately justified by the strictest of all tests. Meanwhile those in court received a shock of non-fulfilment, the kind of shock you get when you put your foot on a step that isn't there.

14

A more spectacular battle, however, was to come—a battle fought out toe to toe with every move in view, a battle in which the art and flair of Hastings were displayed so that laymen no less than lawyers could admire.

Robert Churchill, who followed Spilsbury, was also a leading expert and a seasoned witness who had figured prominently in numerous murder trials. Whenever in a shooting case anything seemed to turn upon the bullets that were fired or the weapon that was used, more likely than not Churchill would be called on by the Crown. Level-headed, matter-of-fact, a savant in his sphere, he shared with Spilsbury an enviable legend of impregnability in cross-examination.

Upon that legend a chill wind was now about to blow.

Churchill had examined Mrs Barney's pistol and gave his views about it with definite conciseness. It was one of the safest revolvers ever made. It could only be fired by the exercise of considerable strength. Therefore the idea of it going off accidentally when no one wished to fire certainly did not commend itself to him.

The defence could not skirt gracefully round such evidence as this. It struck at the essentials of Mrs Barney's story. This time when Hastings rose it was no false alarm.

He placed the revolver on the flat of his hand and held it out before the witness and the jury.

'Do you seriously say,' he asked, 'that this is one of the safest weapons made?'

'I do,' Churchill replied.

'Where is the safety device?'

'There isn't one.'

'Isn't there one on most good hammerless revolvers?'

'Yes,' said Churchill. 'What I meant was that it's safer than a revolver with a hammer, safer than an automatic pistol.'

'I see.' Hastings suddenly grasped the pistol and held it up aloft. His finger pressed the trigger. Click-click, click-click, click-click it went continuously, with little more resistance than a child's cheap toy. 'It doesn't seem to require any terrific muscular strength?'

'It would require more,' said Churchill, 'if the weapon were held loosely.'

'Would it?' Hastings promptly changed his grip and held the revolver as the expert had suggested. 'Would it?'

Again he pressed the trigger, quickly and repeatedly, with disdainful ease. And again it was the only sound in the hushed and listening court: click-click, click-click, click-click, click-click, click-click.

'Well,' said Churchill, speaking as best he could in competition with the pistol, 'I still say it's safer than an automatic.'

Hastings kept on pressing the trigger almost languidly. Churchill watched him, a shade uncomfortably. The incessant sound of clicking only ceased when it had imprinted itself on every mind.

The defender laid the pistol on the desk before him.

'You know the sequence of cartridges found in this revolver?'

'I do, yes.'

'Did they go like this—discharged, live, discharged, live, live?'

'Yes.'

'The two discharged cartridges represent shots fired?'

'Yes.'

'Somehow one chamber in between had been passed over?'

'Yes.'

'Have you noticed something peculiar about this revolver—that if you only half pull the trigger the pressure just rotates the cylinder?'

'Yes.'

'Rotates it, without firing?'

'Yes.'

'It looks, doesn't it, as though some time after the first

shot had been fired *something* had happened to press the trigger, but not to the full degree?'

'The cylinder had certainly been moved,' said Churchill guardedly.

Hastings took care not to press the point further, not to involve himself in argument as to what that 'something' was. He relied upon the quicker-witted members of the jury; they would not fail to realise, in present circumstances, that a struggle for the weapon, with fingers clutching at it indiscriminately, was more likely to give rise to a half pull at the trigger than anybody's genuine attempt to fire a shot.

He again picked up the pistol and meditatively pressed the trigger once or twice.

'Supposing a person had got the revolver and another person came and there was a struggle, it is extremely likely that if they continued to struggle and the revolver was loaded it would go off?'

'Yes,' said Churchill.

'And it is quite impossible for anyone who was not there to know exactly how the revolver in these circumstances would go off?'

'Yes,' said Churchill

'And if one person has the revolver in his hand and the other person seizes it and the revolver is pointing towards him, it is certain it will go off if it is pressed hard enough?'

'Yes,' said Churchill.

'And if he happened to be there, opposite the revolver, he would be certain to be killed?'

'Yes,' said Churchill. 'Yes, he would; of course.'

How exactly had they reached this situation? The witness himself might have found it hard to say. He had answered yes to a short series of questions, none of which sounded very deadly in itself and each of which hardly allowed of any other answer. And yet, at the end, he seemed to have agreed that no flaw could be pointed out in Mrs Barney's case. Or hadn't he?

Anyone who shares this slightly puzzled feeling should

study those four questions phrase by phrase and word by word. Their deceptive facility masks perfect craftsmanship.

15

That afternoon Mrs Barney went into the box.

It is highly doubtful whether she had been able to form any clear impression of her trial or any distinct notion about how matters were going. In the first hour or so she had taken copious notes, but mainly with the object of occupying herself, and the effort of concentration soon became too great. Thereafter, most of the time, she had seemed pathetically remote. Now and again a sob, immediately stifled, had shown an awareness of what was being said; she could never hear, without betraying emotion, any direct allusion to her lover's death. For the rest she had sat back in her chair, her grey eyes fixed on some point above the bench, ceaselessly twisting a handkerchief through visibly trembling hands. She had been, as many prisoners mercifully are, partially numb from suffering and anguish.

But now, having taken the oath, as she turned to face the court she beheld her situation in cruelly sharpened outline. The judge, who seemed so frighteningly close; the rows of counsel in their austere black and white; her father's bowed head and her mother's piteous face upturned—all were assembled on her account. She, Elvira Barney, was being tried for murder, and the punishment for murderers was death. Her nerve momentarily snapped, and absolute breakdown threatened just when her life might turn upon her self-command.

Perhaps this challenge, dimly apprehended, lent her strength. Perhaps she drew comfort from her famous counsel, who spoke to her with reassuring informality, putting questions so specific yet so simply framed that she could easily follow them notwithstanding her distress. Perhaps the instincts of a quondam actress stood her in good stead during this critical performance. Certainly she fought and overcame her panic; only the first few answers came in choking whispers; soon she was pouring out the tale of her afflictions in a voice not less audible for being pleasantly low-pitched.

The order of her narrative—imposed, of course, by Hastings—was skilfully judged in its cumulative power. She began by describing the miseries of her marriage and the physical brutality exhibited by her husband; this might reasonably be expected to arouse—in all probability for the first time in the trial—a modest degree of compassion for the prisoner, and go a little way at least towards extenuation of the vicious and discreditable life she had led since. She went on to say that she had sought divorce, but she had been advised of legal difficulties,* and that she had earnestly desired to marry Michael; this put the liaison in a rather better light and made her appear less contemptuous of good morals. She explained her possession of the loaded pistol—not normally a young woman's dressing-table adjunct; it had been given her several years ago by an army friend she named, from whose country house they used to go out rabbit shooting; she had always kept it with her in the cottage, which was easy game for burglars and where she often was alone.

Then Hastings guided her to the first mews episode. She told how she and Michael had quarrelled over money; how she had refused to finance his gambling; how he had walked out of the cottage but would not stay away, returning to create a scene in the middle of the night. 'I was so unhappy,' Mrs Barney said, 'I thought I would make him think I was going to commit suicide. So, when he was outside, I fired the pistol at random in the room. Then I thought if he really believed I'd killed myself he'd go and fetch people, so I looked out of the window.'

'When was the bullet mark made on the bedroom wall?' Hastings asked.

'On that occasion,' answered Mrs Barney.

She maintained the mastery of her rebellious nerves even when asked about the night of Michael's death. Again she

* Viz., that Barney being an American, she was a domiciled American herself.

went through all the agonising details, from the start of the party early in the evening to the finish of it all in the shining summer dawn. Only when she spoke of Michael's last few living moments and of the last few words that she would ever hear him say, her will-power proved insufficient to the task and a storm of weeping broke upon her unrestrained. . . .

She did not give way to the same extent again, but by the day's end, after being searchingly and closely cross-examined, Mrs Barney was not far from emotional exhaustion. But there was one more unexpected test for her to undergo.

'I want the revolver,' said Hastings, 'put on the ledge of the box exactly in front of the witness.'

Everyone watched the usher carry out counsel's direction. Then their eyes moved back to Mrs Barney. She was gazing down wretchedly at the source of all her griefs.

Hastings faced the judge. He seemed about to address him. Suddenly, almost violently, he turned.

'Pick up that revolver, Mrs Barney!'

His voice rang out, deliberately harsh. That it gave Mrs Barney a surprise and shock was manifest to all; it was beyond her meagre acting skill to simulate such a jump. She picked the pistol up at once—picked it up with her right hand.

There was a mighty throb in court as people realised that the first chauffeur's wife had said she fired it with her left.

16

The Crown, though, were neither disconcerted nor deterred. Clarke, it is true, could hardly have foreseen the exact trend of events during the past two crowded days—otherwise so sound an advocate would have modified his opening—but he had patently not wavered in his own view of the case nor in his expectation of its outcome. All along he had shown unabated confidence, and now, winding up at the end of the second afternoon, he sounded like a man merely clinching a decision. He pointed to Mrs Barney's jealousy: 'What was more likely to make her lose control?'

He pointed to the peril in which she knew she stood : 'What stronger motive could there be for colouring her story?' And that story itself? 'It is incredible,' he said. 'If you can believe it—*if* you can believe it—of course, members of the jury, you will be happy to acquit. But'—and here the prosecutor spoke with solemn emphasis—'if you weigh the evidence carefully and dispassionately, I submit that you will find the accusation proved.'

At this stage many, perhaps most, were ready to agree. I personally believe that if the verdict had been taken there and then Mrs Barney would not have been acquitted. The jury must have been keenly aware of the defence successes, so brilliantly accomplished and accented by her counsel, but the relation of these successes to each other and their implication when considered as a whole were as yet almost certainly beyond them. They could only be made plain by a feat of argument—not of eloquence, nor imagery, nor pathos—but sheer hard *argument*, explicit and translucent, which would convince the reason and satisfy the mind.

Such a performance was forthcoming on the morrow when Patrick Hastings made his closing speech.

17

That speech contains no quotable passages of rhetoric. It will never be a feature of collections or anthologies. For perfection of phrase and elegance of form it cannot compare with more sumptuous orations, such as that of J. P. Curran on behalf of Justice Johnson or that of John Inglis on behalf of Madeleine Smith. It was never designed nor intended so to do. It can only be judged within the context of the trial; by its aptness and response to the immediate demand; by its value in advancing the cause of the accused. The test of advocacy, in the last resort, is functional and empiric—and by that test Hastings' speech for the defence of Mrs Barney will hold its own in the most exalted sphere. .

There were no eye-catching preliminaries; no pose adopted, no attitude struck, to mark the imminence of a big occasion. As soon as the court sat next morning he got up and began.

'Members of the jury, I shall not indulge in flights of oratory or dramatic surprises such as are supposed to be the attributes of an advocate. They may be amusing, but we are not in this court to amuse.'

The note had been struck at once. As he stood facing them, almost motionless, hands clasped behind his back, he gave due notice that he meant to launch no emotional appeals. This was a serious matter, to be seriously considered, and not obscured by ill-timed histrionics. It was implied not more by his words than by his manner as he uttered a warning preface to his theme.

'I beg of you not to be unduly influenced by that first simple story that was put before you by the Crown two days ago. We know now that a great deal of it was . . . not absolutely accurate.'

There was a sharp and icy edge to this restrained impeachment. It cut deep into the prosecution's case as Hastings backed it straight away by factual illustration.

'Do you remember how counsel for the Crown described Mrs Barney—took great trouble to describe her—as a lady who lived in an extravagantly furnished flat?' Percival Clarke searched among his notes; he had indeed made use of this expression, and many of the newspapers had found it to their liking. 'An extravagantly furnished flat—I wondered at the time why it was necessary to discuss the furniture. I am still wondering. I also wondered what evidence would be produced to bear out this assertion. That point, at any rate, does not remain in doubt.

'We have now heard that evidence—evidence given by witnesses for the Crown. Downstairs there was a sitting-room with one or two armchairs. Upstairs there was a front room with a divan bed in it and a back room with practically nothing in it at all. That,' remarked Hastings in cool, even tones, 'was the extravagantly furnished flat in which Mrs Barney lived.'

Needless to say, Clarke's blunder had been entirely innocent. He was probably misled at a much earlier stage when he learnt that the cottage had a fitted cocktail bar. This apparatus, though, must have enjoyed priority in the eyes of Mrs Barney and did not typify the rest of the appointments. Hastings was fully justified in emphasising this, even if, as he said himself, the point was secondary.

'But the next thing is rather more dangerous than that.' He recalled Clarke's reference to Mrs Barney's ugly behaviour with the police, and the inference the jury had been desired to draw—that such was the sort of temper she customarily exhibited upon slight provocation. What was this 'slight provocation'? Hastings asked. 'It was this: that she was a young woman, entirely by herself, without the support and comfort of her parents or her friends; that within a few yards of her lay a dead body—the body of the man she obviously loved; that she was surrounded by a group of officers who were proposing to remove her to the station. That, says counsel for the Crown, is "slight" provocation; a "slight" strain upon the temper and the nerves. I wonder,' added Hastings, looking gravely at the jury, 'what provocation he would class as serious.'

The third and final thrust of this introductory phase had long been deferred until the appropriate hour. The Crown knew it was coming; its shadow had hung over them since early in the trial, but there was nothing they could do to parry or prevent it. The prosecution had to sit in silence while the wound was opened with a surgeon's neatness and dispatch. 'Three separate times during the opening for the Crown you were told that Mrs Barney had said "I will shoot *you*." People had heard her; they would say so in the box. A good many people have been into the box, but not a single one has said anything of the kind.'

The prologue was over. The defender had made it clear that the Crown had overcalled their hand. Now he was to bid upon the merits of his own.

'There are cases,' he said, 'in which advocates feel in such despair that they are driven to plead for mercy for their clients and to urge that they are entitled to the benefit of the doubt.'

It was rarely indeed that Patrick Hastings raised his voice. He raised it now, and the effect was all the greater.

'I am going to do nothing of the sort. I am not going to ask you for the benefit of the doubt. I am going to satisfy you that there is no doubt. I am going to show you that there is no evidence at all.'

18

As he set out to implement his pledge he held the jury in the hollow of his hand. Just as the supremely naturalistic actor makes his audience forget that they are looking at a stage, so this supremely naturalistic advocate almost made his audience forget they were in court. They were not conscious of listening to a speech, delivered upon a ceremonial occasion. They were engrossed in what was being said as people are engrossed in private conversation when matters of life and death are being decided. Their absorption was too complete for them to be aware of it.

The whole twelve followed in absolute surrender as Hastings came to deal with the earlier shooting in the mews. He first defined its precise relation to the case. 'The prosecution ask you to believe that Mrs Barney tried to murder on this previous occasion; that she shot at Michael then and that her purpose was to kill.' Three witnesses had said they *heard* the shot on this occasion; only one—the first chauffeur's wife—had said she *saw* it fired. Her evidence alone conflicted with Mrs Barney's description of the incident. And what exactly did her evidence amount to? How much confidence could be reposed in it? 'She says she saw Mrs Barney holding something bright. You can see for yourselves—this is a perfectly black revolver. She says she saw a puff of smoke after hearing the report. This revolver does not make any smoke. She says Mrs Barney held whatever it was in her left hand. You will remember that I asked her to pick up the revolver at the conclusion of her terrible ordeal here in the box. She picked it up—like this—with her right hand.' Displayed in counsel's grasp, the black lustreless pistol told its own tale to the jury. 'It would be very odd indeed,' Hastings quietly commented, 'if the only time that Mrs Barney used her left hand was when it is alleged she tried to commit murder.'

So swiftly and decisively was punctuated the direct, visual evidence relating to this matter—the evidence of what was supposed to have been seen and done. But Hastings had not yet finished with the subject. He turned now to the indirect evidence—the things that were not seen and the things that no one did.

'Supposing *you* had been shot at, what yould you have done? Wouldn't you have taken very quickly to your heels? Michael never budged. We have heard that he still stood about there in the mews, talking up at Mrs Barney in the window—this man who, according to the Crown, stood in great and imminent danger of his life.

'Supposing *you* had been a witness of the scene, and you had believed this woman was trying to murder the man below—what then would you have done? Something, I'll be bound. What did these people do? Nothing whatsoever. They all went back to bed, and—as the police told me when I asked them yesterday—not a living soul ever lodged any complaint. Can you imagine that any of them thought that the revolver had been fired *out* of the window?

'And if it had, wouldn't you expect to find some trace of the bullet in the mews? I asked the police about this too; you'll recollect the answer; they made a thorough search but not a sign of it was found.

'This is not surprising, for the mark of that bullet was on the bedroom wall; it showed that Mrs Barney had fired *inside* the room, to make this man whom she adored think she was so unhappy.'

Any evidence there was against the prisoner on this incident had now been torn to shreds and irremediably scattered. The Crown indeed would have had a stronger-looking case without it. They would at least have been spared the scathing observation with which Hastings finally dismissed this episode. 'If you think,' he said, 'that the prosecution have merely tried to bolster up their case by something of which there is no evidence at all—well, then, it may help you to see with some clarity what is the real position on the charge itself.'

19

The real position on the charge itself—this Hastings now proceeded to size up. He had been speaking for an hour, and the utter silence waiting on his voice was the measure of the grip that he had gained upon the court. 'Not a sound,' said that evening's paper, 'broke the steady stream of words, which seemed to hold everybody in a spell. The jury, it was noted, eagerly leaned forward.'

In calmly level tones, sometimes faintly shot with irony, Hastings anatomised the night of Michael's death, scoring point after point in Mrs Barney's favour. The marks on the revolver had been too blurred for fingerprints to be deciphered, just as one would expect following a struggle; 'if Mrs Barney's fingerprints *had* been detected on it, counsel for the Crown would have said it was conclusive—but is this tremendous artifice of science only to be used when it helps a prosecution?' Within a few hours of the tragedy Mrs Barney had made three separate statements—to the doctor, to the police at home, to the police at the station—but no question had been put to her in cross-examination suggesting that anything she had said in the statements was a lie; 'I don't think counsel for the Crown has mentioned that, so I am venturing to supplement his speech.' Everything denoted that Michael was the object of her passionate devotion; 'in all her distress and anguish, she wanted to kiss the man who was dead.'

Mrs Barney stared up at the high dome of the court. The reference had produced its invariable effect; her mouth trembled, and presently her face was stained with tears.

The compact argument flowed on uninterrupted. 'Put yourself in her position. Put yourself in that box with the wardresses beside you. Suppose yourself under thorough questioning by the Crown, with the thought in your head of what each question might mean; not knowing what you were going to be asked, not knowing what construction might be placed upon your answers. Would you give your evidence like Mrs Barney did if what you were saying wasn't true? Was she caught out anywhere? Was there any discrepancy between what she told you and what she told the doctor and the police? Members of the jury, was that woman lying?'

Was that woman lying? The question was not posed in the traditional Old Bailey style of fierce defiance ('I dare you, I challenge you, to say this woman lies!'), but with the quiet assurance of one who has forged a solid chain of reasoning which will lose rather than gain from declamatory effects.

This was really the climax of the speech. It was the point at which the advocate would gather himself for his touching peroration, if touching peroration there was going to be. But Hastings remained faithful to the undertaking with which he had begun. Both temperament and technique caused him to recoil from anything remotely resembling a harangue. Nor was Mrs Barney's case one where sympathy, as such, could readily be roused; unlike that of Madame Fahmy, which had been heard in the selfsame court nearly nine years before, and was now being frequently recalled and quoted as a parallel. In each a young woman of good breeding and good station was charged with murdering the man whom she had loved. In each a revolver was the instrument of death. In each, oddly enough, Percival Clarke was prosecuting counsel. But Madame Fahmy, a Parisian lady of faultless morals and gentle disposition, had married a rich Egyptian prince whose suave drawing-room manner concealed a savage cruelty and perverted appetites; for several years before the shooting incident—in respect of which her successful plea fused self-defence and mishap—she had patiently borne great suffering at his hands. Mrs Barney, on the other hand, had engaged in an illicit and unsanctified relationship with the young man she was accused of having killed; her general standards of behaviour fell somewhat short of strict; her disposition was volatile if it was not violent; and any suffering there may have been she voluntarily endured, and in all likelihood commensurately repaid. With an English jury the differences were radical.

Notwithstanding, it is of interest to compare Hastings' conclusion to his speech for Mrs Barney with Marshall Hall's conclusion to his speech for Madame Fahmy, if only as an object lesson in contrasting advocates. 'Members of the jury,' Marshall Hall had said, after an address in which he imitated an oriental crouch, pointed the pistol at the faces of the jury, and threw it on the floor with a horrifying crash, 'I want you to open the gates where this western woman can go out, not into the dark night of the desert, but back to her friends, who love her in spite of her weaknesses; back to her friends, who will be glad to receive her; back to her child, who will be waiting for her with open arms. You will open the gate, and'—here Marshall Hall pointed to the skylight—'you will let this woman go back into the light of God's great Western sun.'

It was symbolical, romantic, picturesque—an unashamed and undiluted play upon the feelings. If Hastings had defended Madame Fahmy it is certain that he would have attempted nothing of the kind. It was doubly certain in the less propitious atmosphere of Mrs Barney's trial. Either the jury were won over by his reasoned argument or they would never be won over at all. Hence the simple finish to his magnificent defence. 'I claim that on the evidence that has been put before you Mrs Barney is entitled as a right to a verdict in her favour. I ask of you, as a matter of justice, that you should set her free.'

On the evidence. As a right. As a matter of justice. These —and not references to suns or gates or deserts—were the demands that Hastings formulated for his weeping client.

20

For a brief interval after he sat down there was no sound save that of Mrs Barney's anguish. Then, forthright in phrase and business-like in manner, the judge embarked upon his summing-up. . . .

On Travers Humphreys the public and the legal profession could for once agree. Both rightly considered him the best British criminal judge of his generation. In this place of high regard he was succeeding Horace Avory, whose last years upon the Bench Humphreys overlapped. And, like Avory, Humphreys had assumed judicial office admirably equipped for the rôle he had to fill—equipped not merely with theoretical knowledge of criminal law, but by constant engagement at the Bar in criminal work. As Treasury counsel—an appointment that he held for more than twenty years—Humphreys had taken part on one side or the other in a high proportion of the epoch's best remembered cases. In his twenties he had been concerned with the defence of Oscar Wilde; in his thirties with the defence of Kitty Byron; in his forties with the prosecutions of Crippen, Seddon, Roger Casement and Brides-in-the-Bath Smith; in his fifties with those of Horatio Bottomley and Mrs. Thompson, and with the defences of Colonel Rutherford and the financier Gerard Bevan. A remarkable catalogue of sensational cases, and it is only such cases that stand out, like the visible fragment of an iceberg, above the obliterating waters of remoteness. They act as indicator to several thousand more, now quite forgotten and sunk beneath the surface, that combined to produce the vast experience of the judge who, in his middle sixties, was to try Elvira Barney.

If Humphreys' career bore resemblance to Avory's, the men themselves were of very different mould. Avory was credited with a vein of callousness, a pitiless contempt for human frailty; Humphreys was never lacking in a disciplined compassion. Avory reasoned in the abstract as if all men were alike; Humphreys allied logic with imaginative insight. Avory forced life into the plaster cast of law; Humphreys made law serve the purposes of life. In a word, he had that precious attribute, humanity

He was therefore merciful—but not indulgent; understanding—but not sentimental. He was invariably firm, and could be extremely stern once he had made his mind up that sternness was demanded. And in making up his mind he showed a penetrating shrewdness, bestowed on him by nature and sharpened to perfection by the manifold activities of his busy life.

Humphreys was the first man to appreciate a good point, but he was also the last to be hoodwinked by a bad one. Nor did he deal in compliments unless they were sincere. That being so, the first words he uttered to the jury paid Hastings a tribute that has seldom been surpassed. 'You have just listened,' he said, 'to a great forensic effort. I am not paying compliments,' went on this great veteran of so many famous trials, 'when I say it is one of the finest speeches that I have ever heard delivered at the Bar.'

21

The speech, deliberately aimed not at the heart but at the head, had indeed been of a kind to win the judge's admiration. It was, he went on to impress upon the jury, 'free from anything like an appeal to sentiment and, one should add, of all the more assistance to you because it consisted of careful and accurate analysis.' Moreover, before the summing-up had progressed very far it began to be apparent that in one vital respect Humphreys himself had been convinced by Hastings' argument—or had at least been thinking along very similar lines. He did not try to *impose* any opinion of his own, holding the balance with that scrupulous precision which is the mark of judges who believe in trial by jury. He warned them against shrinking from a disagreeable task. 'If you are satisfied on the evidence as a whole that it is proved that she did intentionally fire the revolver, pointing it at the body of the man, and so caused the bullet wound from which he died, then she is guilty of the crime of murder, and no feeling of pity, no feeling of regret, should deter you from the duty you are called upon to do.' But the judge gave an indication of his personal view in a form that almost echoed Hastings' chief contention. 'What right have we to say her story is untrue?' he asked. 'If it is not inconsistent with the facts that have been proved, a rejection of it would be simply and solely on the ground that it was told by a person under trial.' He was judge, not jury, and took great care not to usurp the function of the latter. None now could doubt, though, that in Humphreys's judgment the prisoner's story was not demonstrably false—and unless that story was demonstrably false a conviction for murder could only be perverse.

There remained, however, another alternative to acquittal which had so far received no mention in the case. 'Counsel,' observed Humphreys, 'have said nothing about manslaughter; on the facts there was nothing that they could have said. It is for me to direct you on the law concerning this. Manslaughter is the *unlawful* killing of another without any *intention* of either killing or of causing serious injury.' Having established the formal definition, he immediately applied it to the case that was before them. 'It amounts to this,' he said. 'If the prisoner threatened to commit suicide—suicide, let me remind you, is a crime—and the deceased man removed the revolver in order to prevent it, and she, in order to carry out her intention, struggled with him and so caused the revolver to go off, she would then be guilty of manslaughter and answerable for that offence at law.'

The sting in this passage was delayed until the end, when it suddenly dawned upon the judge's listeners that his manslaughter example exactly corresponded with Mrs Barney's own account of what had taken place. .

When a judge, in the rightful discharge of his office, presents an assessment of the case for acceptance or rejection, he is sometimes said to be summing-up *for* a particular verdict. The expression is a loose one. But if one did venture to use it in respect of a well-nigh faultless jury charge, one would say that Humphreys summed-up for a manslaughter decision.

22

That the twelve men were not in any way obliged to follow suit had repeatedly been emphasised by the judge himself, and the outcome of the trial still appeared entirely open. No finding could be summarily ruled out. It was possible—some believed it probable—that they would convict the prisoner of murder; public disgust at the background of the case had been crystallised in a justifiable reference by the judge to Mrs Barney and her lover as 'these rather worthless people'—and a jury's natural reluctance to destroy a useful life can sometimes tip level scales in a defendant's favour. It was possible that they would, by voluntary process, arrive at the manslaughter verdict which the judge had mooted. It was possible, after Hastings' great performance in the morning, that they would do neither and instead acquit outright. .

The jury retired at five minutes to three. Judge and counsel also withdrew to their respective rooms. Mrs Barney left the dock like some automaton; it required two pairs of hands to pilot her below. The spectators remained in court, where long-pent-up excitement at last found release in feverish discussion.

The sensation of suspense, greater than any crime reporters present could remember, intensified as the jury's absence was prolonged. Half-past three; quarter to four; four o'clock; a quarter past—they had been conferring now for an hour and a half. Everyone had his own views on the delay. They could not decide between manslaughter and murder; they could not decide whether to add a mercy rider; they could not decide about convicting her at all. Some held that this length of time precluded an acquittal; others that each added minute favoured the defence; yet others that everything presaged a disagreement. Slowly moved the clock and fast the ferment rose.

At a quarter to five the speculative tongues were stilled. The jury had reappeared at the entrance to their box.

Officials hurried in. Counsel came back, the defending side with deeply anxious faces; according to one observer, Hastings was 'almost haggard.' The judge resumed his seat amid the crowded bench; close to him his clerk held the dread black square in readiness. Last of all, the wardresses brought up Mrs Barney; her feet dragged so that the shuffling sounded oddly through the court, and her white, manicured hands clutched the dock ledge for support.

'Do you find the prisoner guilty or not guilty of wilful murder?'

'Not guilty,' said the foreman of the jury.

'Do you find the prisoner guilty or not guilty of manslaughter?'

'Not guilty,' said the foreman of the jury.

The crowd heaved a great sigh; someone laughed hysterically. Mrs Barney cried out, 'Oh!' and put her handkerchief to her mouth. Just beside the dock her mother, who had sat there through the trial, laid her head upon her arms and very quietly fainted.

23

It was a triumph, of course, but what was its especial nature? What were the elements that made Hastings worth every penny of his fee—which was certainly one of the largest ever marked upon a brief to defend a charge of murder?

First, the rare capacity to judge a case's impact on contemporary life, and thus upon the jurors empanelled to decide it. Second, the requisite technique to act upon this judgment in setting the tempo and the key of his performance. Third, the delicate but devastating fashion in which he handled hostile witnesses. Fourth, the cool sense of his realistic plea.

These were the practical contributions of this fascinating advocate to a result that might have easily been different. For the student of forensic style, one point must be added. In the Barney trial the Bar's du Maurier tackled Sir Giles Overreach and, while strictly faithful to his own distinctive method, showed that he could play it as well as any Kean.

Kathleen Ida

NORMAN BIRKETT

CLASSICAL SYMPHONY

Norman Birkett defends Tony Mancini

1

If the Barney case sprang from the putrescence of the rich, the Mancini case sprang from the putrescence of the poor. It embraced the same elements of moral degeneration—drunkenness, violence and sexual laxity—adding drug addiction and blackmail for good measure. But there were none of the smart accessories that gave the earlier case a spurious glamour: no aristocratic names, no wealthy relatives, no fashionable restaurants, no natty cars. The Mancini drama ran its shocking course against a background of unbroken squalor: small-time rogues and *passée* strumpets, dance-hall riff-raff and fun-fair touts, cheap cafés and mean apartment houses in the dark hinterlands of Leicester Square and Brighton Promenade. To the average quiet-living citizen the Baghdad of the Arabian Nights is far more credible. But those who would understand the workings of Mancini's mind must first understand—to quote his illustrious defender—an underworld that makes our own minds reel.

2

In this underworld Tony Mancini (the accused) and Violette Kaye (the corpse) had been familiar figures. Mancini (alias Hyman Gold, alias Jack Notyre) really bore the name of Cecil Lois England. Violette Kaye (alias Joan Watson) really bore the name of Violet Saunders. He was twenty-six, the son of decent parents, who had drifted into crime and was a convicted thief. She was forty-two, a former vaudeville dancer who had drifted on to the streets and was a convicted whore. He—business quite apart—fancied himself with women; the name Mancini was first assumed on the spur of the moment to impress a girl who had disclosed a partiality for Italians. She—business quite apart—had a roving eye for men; there were times when Violette Kaye did not put profit first. .

It was 1933. On the 10th of August Mancini came out from a spell in gaol. He got a job in an eating-place not far from the old Alhambra. Violette Kaye was a customer there; they were soon on friendly terms. Perhaps even more than that; the women of the town are unpredictable, and one would certainly not rule out the possibility that this scarred campaigner of the London pavements actually fell in love with the swaggering waiter and his Italianate façade.

It is as likely an explanation as any of what followed. After a few weeks Mancini's employer shut up shop and left the ex-prisoner without immediate prospects. Violette Kaye had just made plans to move to the seaside. She suggested to Mancini that he should accompany her.

In the middle of September the pair went down to Brighton in amicable bond as prostitute and *souteneur*.

3

Brighton is a curious admixture. It is one of the two most beautiful towns in England. It is one of the three most popular holiday resorts. It is one of the four most favoured retreats on the South Coast for respectable business men who have made money and retired. But it is also—in this regard defying competition—a kind of sink for the residual dregs of London. They are unobserved by most; the eye is held by Brighton's more agreeable aspects—by the Regency curves, by the children on the beach, by the whilom magnates pacing the velvet lawns of Hove. But the dregs are there, and vice consequently flourishes on a scale seldom found outside the capitals. In certain places and at certain times, Brighton could almost pass for a miniature Marseilles.

This did not disconcert Mancini and his consort. Automatically they swelled sub-Brighton's shady ranks. Violette continued to practise her profession, and soon acquired a regular clientele. Out of her earnings she paid the rent, bought food for both, and allowed Mancini pocket-money. The latter's chief duty was to make himself discreetly scarce when Violette brought men home.

Home, one should remark, was not a constant; they were continually on the move. Devonshire Place, Mighell Street, St. George's Terrace, Clarendon Place, Russell Square, Stanley Road, Richmond Gardens, Hampton Place, Grand Parade, White Street, Edward Street, Lansdowne Place, Elm Grove—the succession of furnished rooms and flats became kaleidoscopic; more than a dozen in a period of six months. There was doubtless some reason, possibly more than one. 'It was she,' Mancini afterwards asserted, 'who decided when it was time to find a new address.'

They made their thirteenth change of premises in March. An advertisement put them on the scent; an inspection satisfied them; and so on the 19th they packed their bags once more and took up quarters at 44 Park Crescent.

It lay, prophetically, upon the Lewes Road.

4

They occupied two rooms in the basement of the house. It formed a self-contained flat, with an entrance from the area. The latter was protected by an ordinary railing, the gate of which opened on to the area steps. These steps, which turned off to the left, were old and badly worn—a matter that assumed some importance later on.

The flat was let unfurnished, so Violette bought a few cheap sticks and pieces. 'The furniture,' their landlord noted, 'came in by degrees,' and one may surmise she acquired more as opportunity offered. But they never got far beyond the habitable minimum: a bed, a washstand, a table, a few chairs. Perhaps in due course, if enough time had been granted, Violette would have made the place quite comfortable and trim. For, unlike her other Brighton lodgings, 44 Park Crescent seemed to promise permanence. She remained there continuously for more than seven weeks, and in the end did not depart thence of her own volition. . . .

During those weeks life went on much as before. Violette's patrons, old and new, trod the well-worn steps and paid for her favours in varying amounts; if they were married, and she knew, a pointed reminder often extracted more. Mancini did such housework as appeared to be inevitable; he made the bed, brewed tea and cooked an occasional meal. From time to time they went out together dancing; it was his favourite diversion, but to her had become an inferior substitute for drink, which, like many women of comparable history, she found a transient but effective anodyne.

The rhythm of this existence was eccentric but consistent. It might have gone on for years, repeating its dubious pattern, until the harlot's charms irrevocably faded or the harlot's handyman procured a better place.

These were the obvious, the classical alternatives. But the break in the pattern here was not according to convention.

Mancini took a job.

5

It would be unfair to imply that, throughout his stay with Violette in Brighton, he had excluded the idea of employment from his mind. In February he had actually obtained a post as canvasser, but forsook the work on the day that it began—'I didn't like it and left.' In March he was offered a similar situation, but turned it down, he said, at Violette's insistence—'You won't earn much, and you'll be away from me all day.' But these cannot be considered more than token acts. Since he had cast in his lot with Violette Kaye, Mancini's first real attempt to earn his livelihood dates from the 5th of May, 1934, when he started at the Skylark Café as a kitchen hand.

The Skylark Café faced the sea near the foot of busy West Street; it stood in an archway at beach level, below the promenade, among the small shops immortalised in 'Brighton Rock.' It was open seven days a week for nine or ten hours a day, providing lunches, teas and dinners, and carrying on a subsidiary trade in toffees and ice-cream. Business was good, and the small staff had to be keen and versatile. In Mancini's case the title 'kitchen hand' was not restrictive; he peeled potatoes, certainly, but he also cleaned, cooked, waited at table, wrote out menu cards in a distinctive spelling ('Apple Sause,' 'Fillit of Cod'), and, whenever otherwise unoccupied, touted for custom from the passers-by. He seems to have accepted these duties cheerfully and made himself agreeable to those with whom he worked.

This was not altogether to the liking of his partner. In view of their peculiar and scandalous relationship, one might have expected Violette to shun contact with Mancini in his less unworthy sphere. Instead, she elected to haunt the Skylark Café, calling there daily and ordering a meal. One has no doubt about her underlying purpose. Violette was jealous and she wanted to keep an eye upon him in his new surroundings.

This became apparent on Thursday, 10th of May, when he had been engaged in the job less than a week. That afternoon, between three and four o'clock, Violette made her customary appearance at the café; she ordered some fish, which Mancini cooked and served. It was a slack time of the day, and he was able to sit down for a few minutes at her table—long enough to note that she was rather the worse for drink. Then he was called away to get the staff their tea.

There was a young waitress at the Skylark Café. Her name was Florence Attrell, and she, too, had been recruited only in the last few days. Perhaps not unnaturally, Mancini formed a friendship with the other new arrival. It was nothing more than that and was never to become so—Miss Attrell's respectability is unchallenged—but Violette clearly nursed her own suspicions. She thought his manner with the girl over-familiar; she resented any interchange of banter and the 'Here you are, mate' with which he handed her the tea. When Mancini returned to Violette's table he was surprised to find her trembling with rage.

'What's wrong?' he asked.

'Don't call her "mate",' said Violette; 'I won't have it.'

'All right,' said Mancini, 'but for goodness' sake do pull yourself together.'

'I won't have it,' Violette repeated loudly. 'I don't want you to call her "mate."'

The whole café was silent, those few people present—including, of course, Miss Attrell—listening in astonishment to this ridiculous scene.

'Pull yourself together,' Mancini said again in some embarrassment.

Violette would not, or could not, pull herself together. In the circumstances she did the next best thing. She got up and walked out.

The impulse did not in the first instance take her far—only to a seat a few yards outside the café, where she sat for some time, still in high indignation. Mancini could see her through the door, but decided it was politic to leave her to herself.

Presently, when he glanced in that direction, she had gone.

6

It seems she went straight home, for one Thomas Kerslake, who called at 44 Park Crescent shortly afterwards, found her there and spoke with her for six or seven minutes.

His errand was one of mingled tragedy and farce. A motor driver by profession, he had acted as such for a Brighton bookmaker who had been one of Violette's most constant visitors. Now he had brought her the latest news about this man, who had just been certified insane and confined in an asylum.

He went down the area steps and knocked at the basement door. Violette opened it. Kerslake, at her invitation, stepped into the passage, and they stood talking, only a foot or so apart. He was thus able to observe her closely. She's been drinking, he thought—as Mancini had thought earlier—and something appears to be on her mind as well. Her face keeps twitching; yes, and her hands, too; she's nervous, all on edge, thoroughly distressed. Almost like someone scared she's behaving. Well, it isn't any affair of mine—no more than the voices I can hear in the back room.

He told her what he had to tell; she was not very receptive. Once or twice she asked a perfunctory question, but mostly, Kerslake fancied, her thoughts were quite elsewhere. 'Thanks,' she said when he had finished, and made no move to take the conversation further. Nor had Kerslake wish to do so; he had discharged his mission and prepared himself to go.

She saw him out, and for a second or two stood framed in the doorway, until the closing door blotted her from view. It was a more dramatic moment than Kerslake realised. For many months later, in the course of a murder trial that held the nation in its grip, he found himself presented by prosecuting counsel as the last Crown witness to see Violette Kaye alive.

7

Next morning Mancini turned up as usual at the Skylark. Until half-past seven in the evening he remained there, getting through his work as on any other day. The customary scraps of talk passed between the staff, and somebody happened to refer to Violette Kaye. 'She's left,' Mancini vouchsafed. 'Gone away?' they queried. 'Yes,' he said. 'To Paris.'

It was not only the Skylark that heard on this same day of Violette's continental trip. Her sister-in-law in London, who was due to arrive on Monday at Park Crescent for a holiday, during the morning received a telegram that had been handed in at Brighton at 8.50 a.m. 'GOING ABROAD,' it read. 'GOOD JOB SAIL SUNDAY WILL WRITE.—VI.'

The sister-in-law waited, but Vi never wrote. Hours before the telegram had been dispatched she was already cold and stiffening fast, her half-dressed body crudely wrapped in bedclothes and stowed away in a cupboard like unwanted junk.

8

Outwardly, at any rate, Mancini was unperturbed by Violette's departure. Two nights that week-end he went dancing with Miss Attrell, who did not detect any preoccupation in his manner. On one of these occasions he took her to Park Crescent and gave her some clothes that Violette had left behind. 'She couldn't get them in her case,' Mancini said. 'I promised to send them on, but I don't think I'll bother.'

Miss Attrell surveyed the proffered relics doubtfully.

'You're sure she won't be wanting them again?'

'Sure,' Mancini said. He pressed them upon her: the fawn hat, the black coat, the green costume. 'Come and look round the flat; you might's well see it while you're here.'

He led the way down the little passage to the bedroom.

'Why, there's no bedclothes!' exclaimed Miss Attrell in surprise.

'No, I've given them away,' replied Mancini quickly. 'I'm thinking of moving now that she has gone.'

This was an understatement; Mancini had already acquired a new abode. That afternoon he had agreed to take a room in Kemp Street; he had come to terms with his prospective landlord in the café; he had not even troubled to look at the room first, despite the latter's suggestion that he should. 'That's all right,' Mancini had declared. 'I can see that you're a decent sort of chap. We'll call it on; I'll bring my things round in a day or two. . . .'

On Monday evening, after he left work, Mancini went to

large black trunk, second hand, for which he paid 7s. 6d. cash. The dealer obligingly drove him and the trunk to 44 Park Crescent, and thereafter for some time Mancini stayed in the flat alone, busy with his packing.

That night he asked the landlord, who lived above, to come and see him in his sitting room. By then the trunk had been closed and strapped and moved out of the way.

'Vi has left me, Mr Snuggs,' Mancini said. 'She has gone to France, and I can't afford to run this place myself.'

'All right,' said Mr Snuggs.

'I'll be leaving tomorrow.'

'All right,' said Mr Snuggs.

He thought that Violette was Mancini's wife. Being a good-natured man, he mildly sympathised.

Twelve hours later Mancini with all his belongings had departed. He left no souvenir, except the tray out of a trunk and an unsightly stain inside one of the cupboards—a stain that someone had vainly tried to wash away.

9

The trunk arrived at 52 Kemp Street on a handcart in the charge of Mancini and a friend. It was placed in the room with a blanket on the top, but otherwise entirely unconcealed. The lock was defective; anyhow, there was no key; it could easily be opened by unfastening the strap.

For exactly two months, from the 14th of May to the 14th of July, Mancini occupied that tiny room at Kemp Street. He had little privacy. Acquaintances visited him; the landlady came in; other men also slept there upon occasion. Throughout the trunk remained undisturbed. Sometimes one or other would note fluid oozing from it or complain of an offensive smell. Mancini would explain that it was french polish or that it was because he had his football boots inside. Always he contrived to pass the matter over.

10

It is a fascinating mental exercise to imagine what Mancini would ultimately have done had matters not been extraneously precipitated by an ironically apposite event.

On the 17th of June, when Mancini was already in his fifth week at Kemp Street, the police made a gruesome and sensational discovery at Brighton railway station, two hundred yards away. A trunk, deposited ten days earlier in the cloakroom, had given rise to some concern and finally been opened. Inside lay a woman's corpse, minus the head and legs.

Public interest and police activity were alike intense. While every inn in Brighton became a forum for ventilating theories, spiced with recollections—usually imperfect—of the Charing Cross case several years before, detectives laboured hard but fruitlessly in search of clues to victim and to crime. None was forthcoming, and as days and weeks went by the scope of the investigations steadily grew wider. Gardens were dug up, local gossip was explored, and every scrap of information sought about women recently missing from the town.

It was this last path, of course, that led them to Mancini. They knew Violette Kaye because of her profession. They knew Mancini had lived with her, if not on her. They knew that she had not been seen in Brighton for some weeks. In such circumstances every possibility must be reckoned with, so on Saturday morning, the 14th of July, a constable caused a stir in the Skylark Café by requesting Mancini to come to the Town Hall. There the latter was questioned at length by an inspector and signed a statement ('I arrived home one night and found Violette had left') before the officers permitted him to go.

He had indeed no connection whatsoever with the matter into which they were then enquiring, and he fully convinced them of this fact. They were still as far as ever from finding the solution to what was being generally styled the Brighton Trunk Crime, but which, under the pressure of subsequent events, had to be rechristened Brighton Trunk Crime Number One.

11

Despite what seemed a satisfactory outcome of the interview, its immediate effect was to destroy Mancini's nerve. He could clear himself—had cleared himself—with regard to the headless body in the trunk at Brighton station. That was not Violette—but Violette was still missing; he felt sure that they were keeping him under a constant watch; who could foretell with certainty what their next move might be?

The more Mancini thought of this, the more his panic grew. He decided to bolt and leave his trunk behind. .

That evening, after finishing work, he went straight to a dance hall. (He had been out dancing just as much since Violette disappeared.) Shortly before one o'clock, with two male acquaintances whom he had encountered, he went to an all-night restaurant, where all three had a meal. Mancini remarked, in the course of casual talk, that he was tired of Brighton and intended going to London by the early morning train.

The two acquaintances were most unselfish and considerate. They returned with him to Kemp Street, where he washed and shaved ('Do you keep rabbits?' one enquired, noting a singular smell), called with him at the railway station, where they ascertained the first departure time, returned with him to the all-night restaurant at five o'clock, and finally walked with him to Preston Park, the first stop out of Brighton on the main London line. 'It's so as nobody'll see me,' Mancini said. The others appear to have been content with this odd explanation. . . .

At 7.28 the train slid out of Preston Park with Mancini on board. His fears had not deceived him; he eluded his pursuers by only a few hours. At noon that day the police descended upon Kemp Street. They entered the front basement of Number 52 and opened the trunk that the fugitive had abandoned.

A nauseous stench at once assailed their nostrils; a hideous spectacle at once assailed their eyes. The appalling truth was out at last. For weeks Mancini had been sharing this same room with the decomposing body of his former mistress.

12

They caught up with him in the early hours of Tuesday as he trudged along the London-Maidstone road.

All Sunday and most of Monday he had spent in the East End, sleeping at a Salvation Army Hostel and eating at cafés in Cable Street and West India Dock Road. He got rid of some old garments and acquired some new ones, selling a labourer his suit for a few shillings and buying a pair of overalls for sixpence. At the hostel he registered by the name of 'Swintey,' and in general took what steps he could to wipe out his identity. It was, presumably, his initial plan to be swallowed up and lost among the teeming back streets that cling like a monster cobweb to the London docks.

But on Monday he learnt, with an overwhelming shock, that no time was to be granted for this purpose. The newspapers were full of the discovery at Kemp Street. They reported that the body was that of Violette Kaye, that she had apparently been killed by a blow on the head after a fierce fight, and that police throughout the land were on the look-out for Mancini, as it was believed—most ominous of phrases—'he could render them great service in their investigations.' All ports were being watched, it was announced, and inquiries made even on the French side of the Channel.

Taking all into account, London still remained Mancini's safest hiding-place. But a hunted man seldom finds inaction tolerable; he is for ever hearing the footsteps of the hunters; wherever he may be, he longs to get away. So on Monday night, instead of going back to the hostel, Mancini began to walk without specific aim; out of the East End, out into the suburbs, out into the country—anywhere so long as he could keep upon the move.

The black car drew suddenly alongside. One of the officers got out.

'Where are you going?' he asked.

'I'm on the road,' Mancini said. He spoke wearily; he was short of sleep and food. 'I'm going to Maidstone.'

'H'm.' By the light of his torch the officer looked him over closely. 'So you're going to Maidstone? Well, I think you answer the description of a man who's wanted by the police at Brighton in connection with the murder of Miss Kaye. Better get in the back there. We'll take you to the station.'

Mancini submitted without protest.

'Yes, I'm the man,' he said to them as the car drove away. 'I didn't murder her, though. I wouldn't cut off her hand. She's been keeping me for months.'

13

But has ever a case against anyone looked blacker? Has any man, whether innocent or guilty, ever seemed to have the rope more firmly tied about his neck? He had a criminal record; he had lived upon the dead woman's immoral earnings; he had concealed her body, even moving it from one place to another; he had told countless lies to explain her disappearance; finally he had fled. To these undoubted facts were added wicked fictions by one over-enthusiastic section of the press: as that Mancini had taken part in many Soho brawls and had lately been involved in the stabbing of a woman.

These falsehoods in the long run operated in his favour, adding force and plausibility to his main defence. At the moment, however, they added to the prejudice sufficiently excited by his admitted conduct. There remains strong faith that what appears in print must necessarily be true, and millions read these unscrupulous inventions—including, no doubt, some at least of his prospective jurors. One is apt to think of jurymen as a class apart, immune to that which influences the public as a whole; but they are, of course, the public's representatives in court, and cannot forget—however hard they try—all that they saw and thought as private citizens. And the private citizen soon made up his mind about Mancini. A. E. Bowker, for many years clerk to Marshall Hall and Norman Birkett and a notable figure of the law in his own right, describes in his fascinating book *Behind the Bar* the scenes when Mancini was before the Brighton Bench. 'It was during the height of the summer season. . Mobs of pyjama-clad girls, and others wearing only swim-suits, swarmed round the entrance to hiss and hoot the Black Maria which conveyed him to and from the court.' The only possible deduction to be drawn is that they were prompted by assumption of his guilt.

A trial begotten in such an atmosphere naturally places the prisoner's cause under heavy handicap. It is one indeed that requires to be sustained by the skill and power of a master advocate. But Mancini himself was penniless, and though his family rallied gallantly to help, they could only raise a fee that was—relatively—modest. The brief, so marked, they boldly offered to one of the greatest counsel in forensic history.

It was their good fortune that the greatness of this advocate is more accurately reflected in the fees he could command than in the fees he would occasionally accept when his strong sense of duty so dictated.

14

Norman Birkett was the spiritual heir of Erskine. Because great counsel do not figure in scholastic history books to one half the same extent as warriors and statesmen, Thomas Erskine is far less known today than his contemporaries, Wellington and Pitt. And yet few men have deserved better of posterity than that mighty paladin of the Bar who so often, at financial disadvantage to himself, put aside his large and lucrative civil practice in order to battle on behalf of one whose life or liberty was gravely threatened.

To Erskine's pattern Birkett in a later age conformed. For a legal generation he was the *vis-à-vis* of Hastings, as Isaacs was of Carson, as Russell was of Clarke; opposed to one another time and time again, they shared the pick of fashionable work. A few—a very few—academic lawyers specialising in Chancery or appeals might compete with them on the mere parade of fee books; but so, for that matter, might stockbrokers or bookies. The fact remains that, in their contemporaneous prime, these two men were the glamour and the glory of the English civil Bar, and rarely was there a material inducement sufficient to tempt either into the criminal courts. In those courts, however, Norman Birkett was often to be found.

Erskine once wrote to those who sought his help: 'The situation of the prisoners entitles them to enjoy every degree of tenderness and attention, and their inability to render any professional compensation does not remove them at any great distance from me.' Birkett might easily have written such a letter. Accustomed to the highest rewards of the profession, like Erskine he would sacrifice them without hesitation. He mostly defended cases of a different type from Erskine's, due to the different nature of their times, but the underlying impulse was the same—a passionate desire for justice and fair play. If the one man had his Horne Tooke and Thomas Hardy, his Admiral Keppel and his Lord George Gordon, so had the other his William Frederick Oakley and his Willows Crescent sisters, his Mrs Beatrice Pace and his Mrs.

Sarah Hearn. All were human beings who stood in direst peril and were saved only by a great defender's art.

That Birkett's record of remarkable acquittals has never been surpassed I have very little doubt. That Mancini was the most remarkable of these I have no doubt at all.

15

In the first week of December 1934, Birkett was at Birmingham in a heavy libel action which reached a timely finish late on Friday night. The whole of the third week he spent in the Divorce Court in a suit involving a number of Society notabilities. He was also at this time concerned on behalf of the brewers in seeking an extension of licensing hours in Paddington, and advising on a point of defamation one of the most prominent members of the Government. All these, however, were temporarily put from mind and much other work inevitably rejected so that he could devote the second week completely to the fight at Lewes for Mancini's life.

There have been perhaps a score of murder trials this century that have won a place for themselves in British folklore. Of these Lewes has had an ample share. Field and Gray, Norman Thorne, Patrick Mahon, John George Haigh—each in turn has made that little court the focal point of a whole nation's interest. In this respect Mancini bears comparison with any. Day after day outside the court queues waited patiently; there was always a chance that someone might faint and so vacate a seat. Inside, star reporters, specially sent down, sat in close phalanx and rubbed elbows as they wrote. Fifty miles away in London the evening newspapers stood by with cleared decks, and their readers grabbed eagerly for each succeeding issue. There was hardly a man or a woman in the land who did not learn the details in the Brighton trunk case almost as soon as the jurors did themselves.

Mancini's answer to the charge had been foreshadowed in a statement he made on the night he was detained, and which was to be put in evidence by the Crown. It described how one evening he had returned alone from work to the basement flat at 44 Park Crescent. 'I went into the bedroom and she was laying on the bed with a handkerchief tied around her neck and there was blood all over the sheets and everywhere. Well, I got frightened. I knew they would blame me and I couldn't prove I hadn't done it, so I just went out and tried to think things over, what to do. . . . I hadn't got the courage to go and tell the police what I had found, so I decided to take it with me. For the purpose I bought a trunk on the following Tuesday. You see, she was a prostitute, you see; that was the unfortunate part about it. There was always men coming to the house. . . . I don't know who killed her; as God is my judge, I don't know. . . . I am quite innocent, except for the fact that I kept the body.'

In a word, his defence was Panic—panic that made him hide the body in a cupboard; panic that made him take it with him to his new abode; panic that prompted his multitude of lies; panic that steeled him to the grisly nights in the mortuary of Kemp Street; panic that unmanned him and drove him into flight.

Truth is one thing, credibility another, and that which is true is by no means always credible. At first impact such a story excited, in the minds of most, derisive disbelief. It was Birkett's feat to clothe it in the garb of plausibility—a feat which still seems almost outside human compass as one watches the curtain rise upon Mancini's trial.

16

'How say you, are you guilty or not guilty?'

In nine hundred and ninety-nine trials out of a thousand this is a wholly formalistic rite; blunt denials are instantly recorded by innocent and guilty prisoners alike. But Mancini proved to be one of the exceptions; the words of denial stuck strangely in his throat.

'I am not .' he mumbled; and then stopped.

The crowd sat waiting in embarrassed silence.

'Are you guilty or not guilty?' asked the Clerk again.

Mancini licked his lips. He made a visible effort.

'I am . . . not guilty,' he faltered.

This unexpected and unfortunate scene was doubtless rooted in his agony of nerves—an agony which does not confine itself to those afflicted by the pangs of conscience. It seizes as often and as violently on those who, though they need not fear the Bar of Heaven, sense the almost overwhelming odds disposed against them in an earthly court.

If Mancini was indeed a prey to dark despair, there was nothing from which he could draw comfort in the opening statement for the Crown. It was not in the least flamboyant or inflated. Quite simply and without a wasted word, J. D. Cassels, the prosecution leader, presented the material on which the Crown relied. But the case acquired an added force from his studious moderation. The quarrel in the café, the purchase of the trunk, the abrupt decampment, the hideous discovery—they followed one another in his coldly factual narrative with deadly and seemingly unanswerable effect. Nor did Cassels lack, at this stage of the case, additional items of incriminating evidence. The original message telegraphed to Violette's sister-in-law had been brought to light and carefully examined; in expert opinion, the writing was Mancini's. From rubbish in the cellar at 44 Park Crescent there had been extracted a dull-coloured hammer head which, in expert opinion, looked as though at some time it had been passed through a fire; the immediate cause of Violette's death was a fracture of the skull and—in expert opinion once again—that could have been caused by this very hammer head. Stains had been detected on Mancini's clothes; expert tests had shown them to be blood. And, to crown all, three men had come forward with reports of conversations they had had with Mancini, during June, in an amusement arcade called 'Aladdin's Cave.' These, suggested Cassels, were of very great importance. Mancini, it was said, had talked of 'giving his missus a good hiding,' and had also vouchsafed this astonishing remark: 'What is the good of knocking a woman about with your fists? You should hit them with a hammer, the same as I did.' . . .

In barely forty minutes the whole story had been told, and

Cassels was winding up his succinct exposition. 'The evidence,' he said, 'points, I submit, irresistibly to the conclusion that Mancini murdered this woman and is therefore answerable for that crime in law.'

One wonders if there were a dozen people in that court—one wonders if there were a dozen in all England—who would not, at that moment, have been ready to agree.

17

The tall, spare figure rose for the first time. The long arms were stretched out with an actor's grace and ease; the wig was lifted and replaced upon the tawny head; the vibrant voice fell on the ear like music. As he spoke he lightly waved a silver pencil; it was like one conducting the introductory bars of a symphony he had himself composed.

'You prepared this plan of the basement flat at 44 Park Crescent?'

'Yes,' said the Inspector.

'Did you observe the steps from the street level to the area?'

'Yes, sir.'

'Were they very worn?'

'Yes, sir.'

'Were they steep?'

'Fairly so.'

'Were they narrow?'

'Yes, sir.'

'Did they call for care?'

'A little.'

'And the area floor; had that a hard, stone surface?'

'Yes.'

It was short; hardly a foretaste of the great things that were to come. Nor did most perceive at once to what end it was leading. And yet, such is the magic wielded by great counsel, even in those few moments something changed. Norman Birkett had begun, and the first faint breezes of a different wind blew gently through the court.

18

More followed as the opening day wore on.

The landlord from Park Crescent was in the witness-box. He had been called mainly to furnish formal proof that Mancini and Violette Kaye were the 'Mr and Mrs Watson' who had occupied his basement flat from mid-March to mid-May. The tale he told was true, and the defence accepted it, but Birkett had some questions ready when the Crown was done.

'Whenever you saw Mancini and the woman, did they appear not merely friendly but affectionate?'

'Yes,' said the landlord.

'I want to get this plainly before the jury.' Birkett spoke with emphasis. 'At no time, from start to finish, did you ever see anything, of any kind, to the contrary?'

'No, sir.'

An important point had been established—and from a source that was patently unbiased and reliable.

'Did you ever see any men going down to the basement flat with this woman?'

'Once.'

'You saw her going there with a man?'

'Yes.'

'Did she go down first and the man follow afterwards?'

'Yes.'

'Do you know who he was?'

'No,' said the landlord. 'He was a tall man; that's all I can say.'

'How long did he stay?'

'About half an hour.'

'What time of day was this?' Birkett asked evenly.

'It was at night,' replied the landlord, 'between ten and eleven.'

The defender was skilfully sketching in the background against which to project the substance of his case—the case that Mancini had outlined to the police. 'I went into the bedroom and she was laying on the bed. . You see, she was a prostitute, you see; that was the unfortunate part about it. There was always men coming to the house.'

The first swift strokes were promptly supplemented.

'In addition to this man, did you see a man come whom you knew to be a bookmaker?'

'Yes,' said the landlord. 'I only saw him once myself, but I know he came two or three times.'

'For all you know he may have come more frequently?'

'Yes.'

'Is it within your knowledge that this man did certain things for the dead woman?'

'Yes.'

'Did she tell you he was giving her a wireless set?'

'Yes.'

'Was electric current put into the basement?'

'Yes. They asked my permission.'

'Were you told it was to work the wireless?'

'Yes.'

'Did the bookmaker give the order for it?'

'Yes.'

Birkett slightly altered course.

'Have you heard of a man called Darkie?'

'No.'

'Of a man called Hoppy?'

'No.'

Counsel was not put out.

'You tell the jury, do you not, that your opportunities for observing the number of men who came to the basement flat were limited?'

'Oh yes.'

The implication was apparent to the dullest. If the landlord, with limited opportunities, knew so much, must there not have been a great deal more to know? . . .

Still further light was thrown on Violette's mode of living when Thomas Kerslake gave his evidence—Kerslake, who had talked with her at 44 Park Crescent on the very afternoon when she must have met her end. He told the jury how she had seemed 'shaky' and 'excited.'

'Are you familiar with the effects of drugs on people?' Birkett asked.

'Yes,' Kerslake said.

'Would you say that the appearance of this woman was like that of someone under the influence of drugs?'

'Yes—drugs and drink.'

'Was she agitated and twitching?'

'Yes.'

'Did she seem extremely frightened?'

'Yes.'

'Her condition was really remarkable, was it not?'

'Yes, sir, it was.'

The dead woman momentarily came alive again; the unlovely pattern of her days stood manifest—the men who trailed after her like libidinous shadows, the sombre carnality in the basement room, the drink, perhaps the drugs, the named and nameless fears, the solitary return home when no custom had been won, the erratic descent of the area steps, worn and steep and narrow, towards the hard stone surface of the area floor. . . .

Through most of that first day Birkett worked at the same task: re-interpreting the characters in the drama, re-setting the stage on which the battle must be fought. Connoisseurs of advocacy—and there were many present—loudly sang his praises after the court adjourned. 'Excellently done,' they said to one another. 'Never been a man who could defend a murder better. But even Norman Birkett can't work miracles. It's hopeless, of course; absolutely hopeless.'

19

The Crown had an unusually large number of witnesses; exactly fifty had been called before the Bench and now, consequently, figured on the depositions. The evidence of some of these was undisputed, and Birkett did not challenge them in cross-examination. (One such was the handwriting expert, Mr Gurrin, and this implicit admission that Mancini had indeed sent the telegram signed 'Vi' caused a kind of puzzled shock to the spectators; it seemed to make the prisoner's fate now more than ever certain.) Other witnesses, of course, had to be questioned and engaged; for instance, the previous tenant of the basement at Park Crescent, who said that when he went away he left behind a hammer. Cassels showed him the salvaged hammer head.

'When you left it,' he asked, 'had the hammer head the appearance it has now?'

'No,' said the witness. 'It was shining bright steel.'

Behind this apparently innocuous assertion lay the expert theory that the hammer head in court had been dimmed or dulled by fire. Behind that theory, in its turn, lay the broadest of broad hints that the fire had been used to deal with tell-tale stains. It was therefore highly important to Mancini that the hammer head, now being passed from hand to hand, should not be proved to have been 'shining bright steel' only a few months before it was discovered.

This was accomplished in the minimum of time.

'Isn't it a common type of hammer?' Birkett asked.

'Yes, I suppose it is.'

'A standard type, used everywhere by shoemakers?'

'It's rather old-fashioned,' said the witness.

'There are plenty of old-fashioned things remaining, are there not?'

'There are.'

'Look at that hammer head. Look at the state it is in. Can you really say that *that* is the hammer head you left?'

The witness looked from counsel to the hammer head, then back again from the hammer head to counsel. From Birkett's bearing and expression he had borne in upon him all the gravity and stress of the occasion.

'Well, no,' he said. 'It isn't possible to say.'

This passage occurred on Monday, in the first hours of a trial destined to last the week. But it was not till Tuesday that the real clash came—on the second day, when a Brighton woman pledged her Bible oath that Mancini had told her he and Violette quarrelled bitterly; when the genii from Aladdin's Cave materialised, each with his own account of Mancini's observations; when Dr Roche Lynch, the famous scientist, spoke of the human bloodstains on Mancini's clothes.

20

She was a decent-looking woman, quietly dressed and quietly spoken. Asked her occupation, she called herself a waitress. She knew both Mancini and Violette Kaye, she said, and inquired after the latter whenever she met the former. One day at 'Aladdin's Cave' he considerably surprised her by saying that Violette had gone away to France.

'What did you say?' Cassels asked her

'I asked him if he missed her, but he said, oh no; they'd been quarrelling, and now she'd gone there'd be no more following him about and calling him names in the street.'

Now this was very serious indeed for the defence. Mancini's credibility depended in large measure on the absence of motive or of predisposing atmosphere. What reason was there for him to do violence to the woman? What sign of that hostility in which crimes of violence breed? Yesterday the landlord spoke of seeing neither—but then it wasn't often that he had a chance to see. In fact, it now appeared that there were both—and, more than that, upon Mancini's own admission, if this waitress could be trusted and believed.

That small proportion of the eager waiting crowd which filled up every space in court upon the second day, even the jury that had followed every word, may not have grasped the situation in its full significance; they may not have realised until later on just how much hinged upon the woman's credit. In retrospect, however, Birkett's cross-examination of this minor witness stands out as a major crisis of the trial.

Issue was joined the moment that he rose.

'I have some serious questions to put to you,' he began. 'Where are you a waitress now?'

'I am not working now,' the woman answered.

Birkett gazed at her intently.

'I am sorry to have to do this,' he said, and his voice betokened that compassionate spirit which made him pity all the derelict and outcast. 'I am very sorry indeed. But you haven't been a waitress, in any sense of the term, for years. Have you?'

There was a tiny pause, and then a husky 'No.'

'I suggest you were at "Aladdin's Cave" on other business.'

'I was there on no business.'

'How did you live?' Birkett asked simply.

A longer pause this time; then the witness spoke almost in a whisper.

'On the streets,' she said.

So quietly, so pathetically, her status disappeared.

'You had known Mancini well for five or six years?'

'Pretty well.'

'In London?'

'Yes.'

'I suppose you read a great deal in the papers about this case?'

'No,' she replied. 'I didn't read much about it.'

'Look at the jury.' Birkett was peremptory. 'Look at the jury and tell them: did you not read every single word about the man Tony you had known?'

'No,' said the witness, with a stubborn pretence of indifference. 'I wasn't interested that much.'

'Interested, madam!' exclaimed Birkett sharply. 'You had known him all those years. Do you mean to say that you did not read with eagerness every word?'

The mumbled rejoinder hardly mattered now; this woman's evidence had lost its power to persuade. Not merely because her last denials sounded unconvincing; not merely because of her debased profession, although it could have been argued with considerable force that harlots as a class are not too scrupulous of truth. But there might be a still stronger point, in these circumstances, which Birkett did not choose to carry further at the time. He himself, as things turned out, had no need to reinforce it; his client was to do that under cross-examination.

'Why should that woman say you told her,' he was asked, 'what you say you did not?'

'I have a good idea,' Mancini said. 'Being a prostitute in

Brighton, she's been asked to make damaging statements against me. If she did not, she'd be liable to arrest every night that she showed up on the front.'

It may well have been an utterly unfounded imputation, made as it was against the Brighton police. But no man, nor woman either, with experience of the world, would deny that pressure of this kind has been applied elsewhere. And men and women with experience of the world are occasionally found on the most ordinary of juries.

21

Birkett handled the 'Aladdin's Cave' affair with great restraint. Nothing could have been easier than to launch a punishing attack on these three men: the proprietor of a skittles stall, one of his attendants, and a third individual, all of whom declared that Mancini had admitted doing violence to his 'wife.' Each of them in some respects was clearly vulnerable, and would have tempted many counsel to a fireworks display.

But it was precisely the attribute of restraint that made Birkett this century's greatest criminal defender. He had Marshall Hall's virtues without any of his failings. He was as colourful, but less quarrelsome; as tenacious, but less touchy; as eloquent and persuasive, but vastly more discreet.

In his cross-examination of the 'Aladdin's Cave' triad, Birkett did not miss a single valid point. He brought out the fact that the assistant (who came first) had put Mancini down merely as a 'boasting boy.' He brought out the fact that the proprietor (who came second) had since discharged the assistant for a theft. He brought out the fact that, although all three men were supposed to have been present at the selfsame conversation, two only said Mancini had made reference to a hammer. But he did not press them just for the sake of pressing. He had his own plans for dealing with their evidence and would blow it sky-high when the right moment came.

It was otherwise in the case of Dr Lynch, whom Birkett proceeded to blow sky-high there and then.

22

The anonymous author of *Forensic Fables* wrote many witty satires upon law and advocates. One of these concerns an action in which the plaintiff was a man who had served a term of penal servitude. The defendant briefed a Silk 'whose fame as a cross-examiner was world-wide.' Before the case came on a conference was held, at which the defendant's advisers discussed among themselves how best to establish the plaintiff's bad character in court. Junior counsel suggested it would be sufficient to produce the certificate of conviction. The Silk, however, pooh-poohed this idea and 'gave other directions.' The fable goes on to detail his cross-examination as he conducted it before an expectant crowd. 'The Silk First Asked the Plaintiff whether he was in Good Health. Having Learned that the Plaintiff's Physical Condition was All that Could be Desired, the Silk Enquired where the Plaintiff Lived. After ascertaining that he Resided in Tooting, the Silk Begged to be Informed Whether he ever Went to the Country or the Seaside? If so, Which Place did he Like Best? The Silk then Took the Plaintiff Through a Long List of Inland and Marine Health-Resorts and Gathered that he Usually Spent his Holidays at Margate. Did the Plaintiff Care, by any Chance, for Devonshire? What did he Think of the Moors of Devonshire? Did he Know them Well? Had he Found them Salubrious? Had he Found them So Salubrious that he had Lived on them for Seven Years? Did he Know the Stout Gentleman Standing Up at the Back of the Court? Was the Stout Gentleman a Warder at the Dartmoor Convict Establishment? Did he Know the Gentleman with a Broken Nose Standing Up in the Gallery? Was he a Fellow-Convict with the Plaintiff at the Said Convict Establishment? Were the Plaintiff and the Gentleman with the Broken Nose Employed in the Quarries at the Same Time? When the Plaintiff had Given Satisfactory Answers to these Various Queries, the Silk Resumed his Seat. Was his Reputation as a Cross-Examiner Enhanced? It was. The Daily Journals Reported his Masterly

Performance Word for Word, and the Public Wondered Once More at the Amazing Skill with which the Silk Managed to Worm the Truth out of a Cunning Scoundrel.'

And the moral to be derived from this instructive anecdote? 'Do It in Style.'

One laughs, of course, at the overdrawn example, but the maxim itself is not to be despised. There are times when it is only by Doing It in Style that counsel can make a full impression on the jury, so that they can *sense* as well as *apprehend* his point. But Doing It in Style with discretion and success has always been the enviable talent of the few. It is admirably illustrated in its highest form by Birkett's cross-examination of Roche Lynch.

The latter was a witness of distinction and importance. As senior Official Analyst to the Home Office he enjoyed both professional respect and public fame (in this capacity, of course, he had often measured strength with Birkett). At Mancini's trial he spoke of finding traces of morphine in the corpse, but the primary part—and the danger—of his evidence concerned the stains upon Mancini's clothes.

They were handed about from witness to counsel, from counsel to the jury: the shirt, the flannel trousers, one or two other articles of masculine attire. They had belonged to Mancini, that was undisputed; and now Dr Lynch gave his scientific verdict—that all were spotted or smeared with human blood. He drew particular attention to the shirt. 'One of the spots on it is pear-shaped,' he observed. 'That shows the drop of blood was deposited from a distance. It might have spurted from a small artery.'

Birkett rose to cross-examine with an air of utmost gravity, to be reinforced at once by the pitch of that magnificent voice. It made the moment almost irresistibly evocative—and not only of his own past struggles with Roche Lynch. Edward Clarke questioning Stevenson about chloroform, Marshall Hall questioning Willcox about arsenic, Roland Oliver questioning MacFall about *rigor mortis*—all were now recalled to the minds of many present, together with other life-and-death encounters between great advocate and famous expert on the latter's ground. For here, surely, was another such encounter in the making, another scientific duel that would become historic.

Birkett's first few queries were thoroughly in keeping with these anticipations. They concerned the witness's discovery of morphine. Had Dr Roche Lynch found it difficult, due to putrefaction, to tell what quantity of morphine that there was? Dr Roche Lynch knew the difficulties and had made no estimate. Was it impossible to tell, then, what quantity he found? In terms of giving a numerical figure, yes, it was. Did he know that, in the past, morphine had been commonly used by prostitutes? He did. Might this have been a fatal dose? He was not prepared to say.

This subordinate matter satisfactorily disposed of, Birkett turned at once to the major issue.

'Tell us,' he said, 'tell us, if you will, what is the importance of distinguishing blood groups?'

'Here we go,' whispered the connoisseurs; 'this is it. This is where they're bound to go all out. Birkett might just as well throw in his hand today if he can't shake Roche Lynch about those stains of blood.'

Certainly the defender appeared to have equipped himself for a laboratory battle. A microscope now stood before him on the table, and from time to time he gazed through it at the marks upon the clothes.

Dr Roche Lynch told the jury, as invited, that every human being belongs to one of four blood groups. Its value in criminal work, he said, was this: if an alleged murderer has blood upon his clothing of a group the same as the victim's and different from his own—why, then, he naturally has to make an explanation.

'In the case of these articles,' Birkett said, pointing to the clothing, 'is the blood group impossible to distinguish?'

'Yes, and more than that. Owing to the decomposed condition of the body, we were unable to discover the group of the dead woman.'

Birkett, his brows knit, pored over the shirt.

'You say these marks indicate that the blood was *splashed* upon it?'

'Yes,' said Roche Lynch firmly.

'How long after death would blood splash from a dead person?'

'It might a few hours after, if there had been extensive bleeding.'

He's going to follow this up, the connoisseurs felt sure; it's not much in itself, but it does present a chance. Birkett, though, had dropped the shirt and picked up the flannel trousers and was peering through his microscope at those.

'It's a very minute spot of blood, this, isn't it?' he said.

'It *is* small,' said Dr Lynch. He was finding this cross-examination easier than expected. It was forceful, of course Birkett was never otherwise—but he hadn't found himself conceding vital points as he well remembered doing in the case of Mrs Hearn.

'Could it have been caused by a finger on the lining of the pocket?' Birkett still had his eye glued to the microscope.

'Yes, it could,' said Dr Lynch, with a sceptical inflection.

Birkett straightened up and pushed the microscope away.

'Do you know when this shirt was bought?' he asked.

'I do not.'

'Or when these trousers were?'

'No.'

'If,' Birkett said, even more solemn than before, *'if I were to establish that they were not in the accused's possession during the woman's life, would it be clear, do you think, that the blood could not be hers?'*

An uncontrollable burst of laughter swept the court. The witness looked surprised, even a little hurt. The judge mildly observed, with an indulgent smile, that it didn't require an expert just to tell you that. And the jury, suddenly freed from the toils of esoteric science, thankfully returned to the world of plain horse sense—the world in which sight is the touchstone of belief, and Dr Johnson, merely by kicking a large stone, can triumphantly refute all Bishop Berkeley's metaphysics. . . .

That second evening the connoisseurs agreed that, though of course he hadn't more than one chance in a hundred, Norman Birkett certainly was Doing It in Style.

23

'My lord,' said Cassels, shortly after the court resumed next morning, 'this witness is in a very nervous and distressed condition. Perhaps she may be allowed to sit?'

'Yes,' said the judge, and a seventeen-year-old girl with the face of a frightened child sank into the seat and glanced timidly around.

Doris Saville was a luckless waif, one of those to whom society gives nothing and yet is pained when it gets nothing in return. She had lost her mother when she was only four; had been passed on to an aunt, and then an orphanage; had left the latter for domestic service when she was fifteen; and ever since, if out of a situation, had slept at Salvation Army hostels and places less commendable.

Last July, she told the court, she was staying at a women's lodging house in Flower and Dean Street, Stepney. On Sunday, the 15th (the day Mancini bolted), she and a fellow-lodger went out for a walk; in the street they saw four men, one of whom she knew; he introduced her to another in the group.

'Is this the man?' asked Cassels, pointing to Mancini.

Yes, that was the man. He had asked her to go for a walk, and she had not refused; they went by bus to a park, and through it to a field; there they sat on the grass and Mancini went to sleep. After he woke they got some tea nearby, and then, on the homeward bus, Mancini suddenly asked her if she could keep a secret. 'Yes,' she said. 'Are you sure?' he demanded. 'Yes,' she said again. 'Well,' Mancini said, 'it's about a murder, and if I'm caught you're to dictate this story to the police.'

'What was the story?' enquired Cassels.

The girl related it in one tremulous rush. 'He said that I was supposed to have met him on the sea front at Brighton at the end of May, and he told me we were supposed to have gone to tea with a woman at 44 Park Crescent, and while there she told us she was expecting three men to come and see her about some business, so we left her alone with the three men and went for a walk, and when we came back we found the woman dead.'

The torrent stopped abruptly, and the court seemed deathly quiet.

'What did you say to that?'

'I agreed at the time because I was a little afraid of him.'

'Did he tell you why he wanted you to give that story?'

'He said he wanted someone to stand by him in court, and I could save him.'

'When you got off the bus, what did he do?'

There came another burst of words.

'He went in and changed some money and he gave me one and six and told me to go to the pictures to pass the time away, and that I was to meet him at half-past eleven that night at the other end of Flower and Dean Street.'

'Did you keep the appointment?'

'I went up there,' Doris Saville said. 'I didn't see him, so I came away.'

24

Cassels sat down. Birkett got up. He fastened straight away upon that last reply.

'You said in the course of your evidence that you had agreed to do what he asked because you were afraid of him?'

'Yes.'

'Is that true?'

'Yes.'

'Then why did you go to meet him at half-past eleven that same night?'

'*Because* I was afraid.' Birkett waited, his eyes steadily upon her. She gulped wretchedly. 'Well, I was frightened something might happen if I did *not* turn up.'

'You have stayed at the Salvation Army Hostel, haven't you?'

'Yes.'

'And they've proved good friends to you, haven't they?'

'Oh yes.'

'Weren't there plenty of people you could have asked to protect you if you were afraid?'

'I didn't think of it,' she answered, in confusion.

'Yet you, a girl of seventeen, went at half-past eleven at night to the street corner to meet him, *though you were afraid*?'

'Yes.' It was a whisper.

'And you say that is the truth?'

'Yes.' One had to read it from the movement of her lips.

Thus, in the first minute, Birkett raised strong doubts whether Doris Saville could be looked on as reliable. His next step was wholly characteristic of the man. Nothing damped his sympathy with the unloved and forlorn; if he had felt sorry yesterday for the self-styled waitress, he felt doubly so now for this bewildered prey of an unequal and uncharitable world.

'Miss Saville,' he said, 'I hope I shall be understood. I want to deal with you as kindly and as gently as I can but you know I have my duty to do about this matter.' He returned to the unwelcome but necessary task. 'You are very different in appearance today, are you not, from what you were on Sunday, the 15th of July?'

The white face puckered piteously. Everyone strained to hear the barely audible reply.

'Yes.'

'On that Sunday were you dressed to appear like a woman—much older than a girl of seventeen?'

'Yes.'

'And were you with a woman about forty years of age?'

'No.' Doris Saville shook her head obstinately, like a child in fear of punishment for playing with bigger children.

'Were you with a woman named Sally?'

'Yes.'

'What age do you say that Sally was?'

'I should think she was in her twenties.'

'Had you ever seen her before?'

'Yes. On the Friday.'

'Had you ever seen her before the Friday?'

'No.'

'Did you ever see her again?'

'No.'

'Do you know where she lives?'

'No.'

'Do you know how she made her living?'

'No.'

'Who put it into your head that you should appear like a woman and go out and see men?'

'Nobody.'

'Yourself?'

The girl seemed about to cry.

'I didn't do it with the intention of going to meet men' she said. 'I just went out to have my dinner.'

'Do not misunderstand me.' There was no mistaking the note of genuine regret in Birkett's voice. 'Believe me, it is very painful to have to do this. You say nobody suggested to you that you should make yourself look older. It was just your own idea, was it?'

'I didn't do it with the intention of making myself look older.'

'Very well.' Birkett had now got sufficient for his purpose. Exactly what that purpose was he very soon disclosed.

'That was on the Sunday. You were seen by detective officers, weren't you, on the Monday night?'

'Yes.'

'Were you taken from that lodging house?'

'Yes.'

'Where did you go?'

'I'm not sure of the name.'

'How long did you stay there?'

'A decent while.'

'About how long?'

No answer.

'What do you call a decent while?'

No answer.

'Have you any idea?'

The girl simply stared at him. On her lashes were huge tears.

'Tell me, Miss Saville,' Birkett said with patient courtesy, 'weren't you trying to excuse your conduct to the police as I suggest you are now trying to excuse it to the jury?'

Nobody could ever have expected her to agree—least of all if the suggestion was well founded. No importance attached, therefore, to her negative reply. It did not remove, it may even have enhanced, the possibility that had been implanted in the jurors' minds—the possibility that this poor girl, scared and fearful of the police, might have told them what she thought they would like to hear about Mancini in the vague hope of winning favour for herself.

Presently Birkett was to carry this still further.

'Did you know,' he asked, 'before you saw the detectives, that they wished to see you because Mancini was wanted for murder?'

'Yes,' said Doris Saville.

'And since you were interviewed by the police you have not done any work?'

'No.'

'You have been—I don't suggest there is the smallest impropriety—you have simply been kept by the police in various homes?'

To this Doris Saville once again said yes.

It was different, however, when Birkett put to her Mancini's version of their brief encounter: that it was *she* who had invited *him* to take her out; that he had unenthusiastically agreed; that the conversation about murder had begun only when she had asked him from what place he came; that he had said 'Brighton' and she had said 'Oh, I know—where the trunk murder was'; that she had insisted on talking of the murder and had jokingly asked Mancini if he was the man; that she had also asked where Mancini lived in Brighton and that 44 Park Crescent had only been mentioned then. All this she categorically denied.

'Now,' Birkett continued, 'I want to ask you about what you said before the justices. You remember when you gave your evidence there?' Doris Saville nodded. 'Did you say these words?' He read aloud from the depositions. ' "On the way back to the bus he talked about the murder, he did not say what murder; he said that the murder was done and that *he was innocent of it* and that I was supposed to have met him on the front." Did you say that?'

Again Doris Saville nodded.

'He was saying then: "There has been a murder, and I am innocent of it, and I want you to help me." Is that what it was?'

'Yes.'

'Do you know what an alibi is?' asked Birkett unexpectedly.

The girl said nothing.

'Have you heard the word before?'

'I've read it in the paper.'

'Do you know what it means?'

'No.'

'According to your story, Mancini never gave you the date when you were supposed to have met on Brighton front?'

'He told me to say "at the end of May." '

'You are clear about that, are you?'

'Yes.'

'Quite clear?'

'Yes.'

Sobbing bitterly, she was led out of the court. None can be sure about the workings of her mind, and it may be she caught fresh fright from a dim realisation that she hadn't greatly helped the side by whom she had been called.

25

'I want you to tell the court of the prisoner's convictions.'

The Chief Inspector, an old hand from Scotland Yard, looked quizzically at Birkett and slightly raised his eyebrows. In his experience this was a novel invitation.

He began to read from a single sheet of paper.

'There are three convictions. On September 4th, 1929, at West London Police Court, prisoner was convicted of stealing a quantity of silver. That was his first conviction, and he was bound over. On 24th July, 1931, at Birmingham, he received three months imprisonment for loitering with intent to commit a felony. In March 1933, at Thames Police Court, he received six months imprisonment for stealing clothing from a dwelling-house.'

The Chief Inspector put the paper down and showed himself again at the advocate's disposal.

'Those are the only convictions?' asked the latter.

'Yes, sir, they are.'

'Then there has been no conviction for any crime of violence?'

'No, sir.' . . .

Counsel usually fight to keep a client's bad record out. Birkett had deliberately worked to get it in. It was an inspiration on which was to be founded Mancini's most effective moment in the box.

26

Sir Bernard Spilsbury wound up the prosecution's evidence during the last hours of Wednesday afternoon. That remarkable witness was in his finest form. Mancini's trial gave birn far more scope than Mrs Barney's. He had placed beside him in the box a human skull upon which to demonstrate the nature of the injuries, all these virtually being upon the head. He created a grim and unmistakable sensation by suddenly holding up a scrap of bone and announcing it was the fractured piece from the head of Violette Kaye. He gave his decided and unqualified opinion that the fracture had been produced by some blunt object—possibly by the hammer head discovered in the cellar. Was the fracture received during life or not? asked Cassels. Unquestionably during life, Spilsbury replied; it was in fact the cause of death.

That Violette Kaye had had a fractured skull was common ground. That it had caused her death was at least formally in dispute. That the hammer head had been involved was vigorously contested. Some sort of Birkett-Spilsbury clash was therefore indicated.

Birkett began by bringing Spilsbury down a few degrees from the pedestal to which the British public—rather than he himself—automatically raised him whenever he appeared.

'Your views,' Birkett said, 'are rightly described as theories, are they not?'

There is nothing that jurors distrust more than theories—once they are nailed down by their rightful name. The success of an expert witness generally depends upon his reconstructions taking rank as fact. Strictly, however, they are not facts at all. A fracture in a skull may be a fact; the way that it was caused, deduced from subsequent inspection, is at very best a well-reasoned hypothesis.

Spilsbury, shrewd as he was honest, saw both the force and danger of the question.

'I am not quite sure that that is right,' he said, 'when my opinion is based upon experience.'

'They are the results of your experience but are mere theories without question?'

'They are,' admitted Spilsbury, 'in the sense that they are not facts.'

It is cold in the sense that it is not hot. It is dry in the sense that it is not wet. This was a large and liberal concession—more perhaps than counsel had expected. He promptly transferred the angle of attack, suggesting that in one respect Spilsbury had failed to maintain his own high standards of equity and fairness.

'How long have you been in possession of the small piece of bone, which has been produced here for the first time on the third day of the trial?'

'Since my first examination.'

'Your first examination—on the 15th of July?'

'Yes.'

'Five months ago?'

'Yes.'

'Did it not seem to you that the defence might have been

informed that that small piece of bone was in your possession?'

Spilsbury came as near to an appearance of discomfiture as that imperturbable man was ever known to do.

'I am afraid it did not occur to me,' he said.

'You appreciate that there was no doctor for the defence present at the post-mortem?'

'No, I don't think there was.'

For Cassels, sitting watchfully by, this must have stirred up memories. Almost ten years ago, in this very court, he had been conducting the defence of Norman Thorne, and had protested against Crown evidence of technical experiments performed without the prisoner being told or represented

What had been established now, from a jury's point of view? That Spilsbury was a theorist, and that he did not invariably give others every chance of testing his theories and putting them to proof.

This made a powerful prelude and a useful taking-off point for the main attack which Birkett was now about to launch. The success of it must be considered all the more outstanding because he was not buttressed by experts of his own. There were no defence pathologists, prompting, advising, waiting to be called. It was a single-handed effort, and though any fledgling barrister may recognise its delicacy and tactfulness of phrase, only those who have themselves cross-examined Spilsbury can adequately value this little masterpiece.

'You will concede at once that there are many other possible theories available to account for the death of this woman?'

That was the opening shot. Spilsbury did not seek to resist it.

'Take morphine. Dr Roche Lynch has said that he could not be sure whether a fatal dose had not been taken. Assume it *was* a fatal dose. Does not that account for death?'

The form of the question could not have been bettered. On the face of it, what other meaning has a 'fatal' dose than one that causes death? Spilsbury, however, disentangled himself neatly.

'Why, certainly,' he said. '*If nothing else were done.*'

Birkett had prepared himself for this.

'A person can get severe injuries to the head, be unconscious, and recover?'

'Yes.'

'A person can get injuries akin to the injuries here, and recover?'

'Akin, yes,' said Spilsbury cautiously.

Disaster might have followed any attempt to obtain more. Instead came a lesson in how to make the most of what you have.

'Postulating *these injuries from which you say a person may recover*, and a dose of morphine which is *described as a fatal dose*, death may be due to morphine, though the injuries to the head are apparent?'

Spilsbury looked all round it. The wording was exact; there was no ambiguity, no flaw.

'Yes,' he said.

The theory of death through morphine had been sketched, however lightly, into the general picture. It was a theory that stretched coincidence, as Norman Birkett knew; doubtless that was why he took it first, where it could not act as anti-climax to the stronger card he was to play.

'In many cases of injuries,' he asked, 'does not controversy arise as to whether they are caused by a blow or by a fall?'

'That's so.'

'If a person five feet two inches in height and slightly drunk were standing on a platform seven feet from the ground, and fell, it would mean a fall of something like twelve feet, wouldn't it?'

'It would.'

'The possibility of a fatal fall in that case is apparent?'

'Quite apparent.'

'Will you please look at this plan and at this photograph.'

Spilsbury did not need to look for long at either. They

15

depicted a familiar spot—the entrance to the basement flat at 44 Park Crescent.

'Do you see the stone stairway that leads down to the flat?'

'Yes.'

'Does the plan show a stone brace at the top of the steps?'

'It does.'

'A person slightly drunk, or under the influence of a drug, might trip over the brace?'

'It is quite conceivable,' said Spilsbury.

'At the foot of the steps there is the projecting stone ledge of a window?'

'Yes.'

Nobody could fail to see what was coming next, and certainly the lawyers present realised how far Spilsbury had been drawn along the path towards agreement. He refused, however, to travel the full distance. When Birkett suggested that a fall from the top step could have produced the depressed fracture in the skull of Violette Kaye, Spilsbury curtly replied 'Impossible.'

'Could it have produced any depressed fracture?' Birkett asked.

'I do not think it would, because the ledge would be too long.'

Spilsbury rarely overreached. He had been tempted to do so now. Birkett seized the advantage.

'Sir Bernard,' he said, holding up the photograph to view, 'are you telling the jury that if someone fell down *that* flight and came on *that* stone ledge he could not get a depressed fracture?'

'He could not get *this* fracture,' said Spilsbury—in effect withdrawing his previous answer.

'This fracture being depressed one-eighth of an inch?'

'Yes.'

'Could you get a depressed fracture of one-eighth of an inch by such a fall as I have been describing?'

Put in that limited form—no overreaching there—the question duly gathered its affirmative reply.

'So the only thing in your mind is the shape?'

Spilsbury agreed, and Birkett chose to leave the position thus—with nothing opposed to his purely tentative theory of a fall except another theorist's view about the fracture's shape. . . .

There were other theories, outside Spilsbury's sphere, to be advanced; further facts to be elicited or explained. There was still much to be done, much headway to be made, before the prisoner's friends could indulge in optimism. But at last the connoisseurs were deeply pondering the question: Is it conceivable Mancini may get off?

27

Birkett himself, for the first time in the trial, was seeing glimmers of light among the clouds. . . .

It is commonly supposed to be part and parcel of a great defender's make-up that he believes implicitly in the innocence of his client. That is a matter open to debate. It certainly does not mean that he necessarily believes in the likelihood or even in the possibility of persuading any given jury to acquit.

Over Mancini's case Birkett had been greatly exercised. Whatever the strength of his own faith in the accused, he could not be other than acutely sensible of the enormous obstacles standing in his path. From the start he had fought with all his usual fervency, and his confidence had never for a moment seemed impaired. None the less, his misgivings were justified and deep.

They persisted almost unrelieved throughout those first three days. He had gained some ground, of course, a piece here and a piece there; he had demolished certain witnesses and circumvented others; on any reckoning of forensic points the trial already was a Birkett triumph. But counsel's triumph avails a prisoner nought unless it wins for him the verdict that he seeks.

It was on the Wednesday evening, when he was able to review the whole Crown case, that Birkett first thought success might be within his grasp. His hopes were modest and cautiously conceived; he knew that an almost superhuman effort was required, and that even then defeat might very likely be his portion. But the stimulus of hope, however faint, produced effect. It caused the advocate to redouble his exertions just when such a feat appeared impossible; heightened the power and grip of a performance that had seemed already to have touched the topmost heights; and consequently brought about a prodigious storming finish without parallel in any murder trial of our time.

28

When he rose on Thursday morning to open the defence 'there was tense silence' (wrote a press reporter) 'and women sitting in the public gallery craned forward to make sure of catching every word.' They could have saved themselves the trouble. As he scored a whole series of points in quick succession, each syllable carried to the corners of the court.

He began with a reference in the most scathing terms to the lies that had been published about Mancini's previous history. (The worst of these had appeared in a London daily paper, and one marvels that those responsible escaped legal proceedings. At the time of the Haigh case, in circumstances not dissimilar, the editor of another journal was less fortunate.) Birkett turned these libels to his purpose. 'I cannot find words,' he said, 'to describe this kind of conduct—that when a man is under suspicion, when he is obviously in jeopardy, when for him it is literally a matter of life or death, there should be published stories that are lying and false, as we know from the police these wicked stories were. It is not merely unjust and un-English; it is a crime. And, in consequence, we who represent the prisoner had to take grave decisions, and we decided that you should know the true history and the true record of the man you are trying, even down to his criminal convictions. It is far better, when a man is being tried for murder, that there should be no feeling in the minds of the jury, "I wonder what kind of record this man's really got?" You know it; you had it from the Chief Inspector's lips. And this is the whole of it. But when so much has been written that is false you will forgive me if, right at the outset, I warn you not to allow anything other than evidence proved before you in this court to influence by one hair's breadth the decision that is yours.'

He spoke next about the character of certain witnesses. 'It gives me no pleasure to say this—you have eyes to see and ears to hear—but they were drawn from a particular class. Your emotions may have been of disgust. I know not. Or they may have been of pity. I know not. But these witnesses had read—of a surety had read—these things alleged against him that were false, and subsequently they were asked to cast back their minds to events and conversations in the past. You will watch every single word of such evidence with a vigilant eye.'

He now broadened the scope of his plea with the submission that the Crown had failed to prove the charge beyond a reasonable doubt. He pointed to Spilsbury's evidence about the hammer head. 'If it leaves you, as I suggest it should, in the gravest possible doubt, then the burden that rests upon the Crown is plainly not discharged.' He pointed to Roche Lynch's evidence about the blood that was supposed to have 'spurted from a distance' on to the clothes. 'If I prove to you beyond all question that Mancini did not have these clothes when that woman died, what are you to think? If parts of the evidence are of such a nature, how can you trust it when the issue is so momentous and so grave? Our common speech says: Give a man the benefit of the doubt. That is a misnomer,' Birkett earnestly declared. 'It is not a gift. It is a man's right under our law.'

Prejudice, doubt; doubt, prejudice; these twin elements had so far composed his theme. But there was at least one item in the prosecution case that could be disposed of outright here and now. A delayed-action fuse, most carefully prepared, went off under the three deponents from 'Aladdin's Cave.' 'You know what the prisoner is supposed to have said there—that he had given his wife the biggest hiding of her life, that he had bashed her about from pillar to post. And yet Sir Bernard Spilsbury said that *there wasn't a sign of bruising on the body. . . .* Here was this man,' Birkett continued, with contemptuous irony, 'concealing this dreadful thing in his room, mopping up the blood, explaining where the woman had gone, trying to deal with it day in and day out, week in and week out—and yet he is supposed to have told these virtual strangers, "You should hit them with a hammer, the same as I did." '

The logic of this argument was irresistible. The 'Aladdin's Cave' evidence simply ceased to count. 'On this part of the case,' the judge was to say later, 'my own view is in the prisoner's favour.'

Birkett touched only lightly at this stage on the alternative explanations of the woman's death. She had taken morphine; she may have fallen down the steps; she was visited by men and may have died by another hand. There would be opportunity later to dilate on these. For the moment his main concern was not with theory, but with fact, with what could be established, not with what might be surmised.

'There is a feature of this case that has never been in dispute—the concealment of the body and the lies told to explain it. But concealment and lies, remember, are not murder. Consider the position in which this man found himself. When he went home that night from work and found the woman dead, his immediate reaction was one of sheer terror. "I shall be blamed," he thought, "and I cannot prove my innocence." So he went out; he walked about; he turned over this dreadful situation in his mind; and when he returned he put the body in the cupboard and nailed the door upon its hideous secret. Members of the jury, *once that is done, all the rest follows.*' Birkett paused slightly to stress this cardinal point—the very heart and core of the defence. 'All the rest follows. Once you have started on the road of lies, you are compelled to keep on telling lies. There is no turning back.'

Vividly he recounted the story of the trunk, of the move to Kemp Street, of the flight to London. Vividly he charted Mancini's mental progress through these harrowing events, with many a phrase that touched the nerves like an ice-cold finger ('There, as he sits alone in the basement room, behind the panelling of the cupboard is that *hunched-up* body'). And subtly he effected the requisite transition. 'I can tell you what he did. I can tell you how he did it. But he himself can best tell you what he thought and felt—of the strain, the anxiety, the overwhelming fear.

'I call Cecil Lois England.'

Clutching his black rosary, the prisoner climbed into the witness-box and took the oath.

29

'Were you in any way responsible for the death of Violette Kaye?'

'I was not, sir.'

'Did you ever use that hammer in any way at all?'

'I have never even seen it.'

'Did you live with Violette Kaye at Brighton?'

'I did, sir.'

'Where did she get money?'

'She was a loose woman and I knew it.'

'Did she appear to be in fear?'

'Yes. That's why we were always on the move.'

'Was she often intoxicated?'

'Often.'

'How did you get on together?'

For the first time Mancini hesitated. When at last he poke his voice was very low.

'Strange as it is,' he said, 'I used to love her.'

'Had you any quarrels?'

'None.'

'Does that cover the whole time you were together?'

'Every second she was alive.'

'How did she behave when she came to the Skylark Café on Thursday, the 10th of May?'

'She was staggering a little. She wasn't herself. She was affected by something. All that week she had been rather strange.'

'What time did you get home that night?'

'About half-past seven.'

'What did you do when you saw her lying on the bed?'

'At first glance I thought she was asleep. I caught hold of her shoulder and I said, "Wake up." Then I saw blood on the pillow and on the floor.'

'When you found she was dead, why didn't you fetch the police?'

It was the key question of the whole examination. Mancini's answer, set off by Birkett's imaginative strategy, created an immense impression in the court.

'I?' he said. 'I fetch the police? With my record?' He drew himself up and took a long breath. 'Where the police are concerned, a man who's got convictions never gets a square deal.'

30

The pace of a trial, like that of dramas more contrived, depends only in part upon the relationship between events and time. It is equally affected by factors that are primarily psychological: the force of personalities, the intensity of conflict, the degree of uncertainty felt about the outcome.

The last two days of the Mancini trial certainly appeared to move along at breakneck speed. The onlookers—and here it is worth bearing in mind that the jury are not far removed from onlookers themselves—experienced the sort of sensation one derives from a violently exciting episodic film. Sharply contrasting figures flickered on and off the screen: Mancini himself, quick-witted and alert, gathering confidence as he went along ('I knew that some day this matter would come out, but I trusted in God; I trust in Him now'); Cassels, shrewd, efficient, purposeful, closely cross-examining the prisoner or marshalling the points that most strongly told against him ('Isn't such conduct—the concealment of the body—contrary to human instincts and to human nature unless there is the overwhelming stimulus of guilt?'); Mancini's mother, a wistful little lady dressed in black, telling how Violette Kaye had once stayed at her house and had behaved like one under the influence of drugs; the tailor who sold Mancini the pair of flannel trousers, swearing the sale was made three weeks after Violette Kaye had died; the judge—Mr Justice Branson—summing-up, reviewing the evidence in his own unvarnished style and asking the jury, in a less leading form, the vital question Cassels had already posed ('Can you imagine an innocent man dealing in this way with a woman whom he says he loved?'). Each had his hour or his moment in the limelight, but—corresponding with cinema convention—one star performance dominated all.

Birkett's initial speech had made the issue really open; for the first time the connoisseurs came round to thinking that this was a case which might go either way. The witnesses for the defence, including the accused, had not fallen short of counsel's expectations; the ground gained had been at any rate maintained. His closing speech now became the pivot of decision.

His was not the last, nor even next to the last, word. But in that single hour on Friday before noon, beyond all dispute the verdict was determined.

31

At the very outset he commented adversely on the procedural rule that compelled him to speak first. 'I do not know,' he observed, 'what Mr Cassels will be saying in reply. You may think one reform that might usefully be made is that counsel for the defence should always speak last, so that he can deal with everything that is said.' It echoed Edward Clarke's protest in the Bartlett trial—Clarke, who had tendered no evidence at all, but had been deprived of the last word none the less because he was opposed by a law officer of the Crown, whereas Birkett was deprived of the last word because he had called witnesses other than his client. 'I want very much to emphasise this: I must speak to you now, and I shall not be allowed to speak to you again.'

Viewing these two complaints from the academic standpoint, that of the earlier advocate would seem more firmly based. The law officers' prerogative should long have been abolished, and indeed in practice is occasionally waived. On the other hand, Crown counsel's right to speak last in such circumstances as obtained in the Mancini trial is, upon the face of it, a less glaring anomaly, because it derives from the state of the case and not even remotely from the status of the speaker. Nevertheless, English lawyers, who are justifiably proud of the protection their system affords to an accused, might reconsider this rule regarding speeches that has been impugned by one of the greatest of them all. Abstract logic is not the only test to be applied. Jurors are not reasoning machines but human beings, creatures of short memory and variable mood; unless exceptional factors supervene, what they have most lately heard will influence them most. And if the argument they have most lately heard is one against the prisoner, and not on his behalf, that tends to place him at a disadvantage—precisely what our system is intended to avoid.

All experienced defenders are constantly and painfully conscious of this fact; hence The Last Word is their professional obsession. Sometimes they deliberately refrain from bringing evidence, provided its nature is not absolutely vital, because they believe The Last Word will prove of greater value. On many occasions their judgment may be right, but is it a choice defenders should be called upon to make?

In this instance Birkett was at least spared the dilemma. He might, at a pinch, have done without Mancini's mother; he could not have done without the man who sold Mancini clothes. And therefore, 'I must speak to you now, and I shall not be allowed to speak to you again.'

But for Birkett at his best this handicap was hardly more than nominal. His sway over a court was not only powerful, but enduring. It could be said of him, as it could be said of few counsel in history, that whenever he spoke he was having The Last Word.

In the Lewes courtroom there was not a movement, not a sound, as all his resources were committed to the fight.

'When the prisoner was in the box,' he said, 'I waited to hear—no doubt you waited to hear—some suggestion as to *why* he should murder this poor woman. Mr Cassels asked him no question on this matter. All the evidence—mark this, and mark it well—is that before the death of Violette Kaye they were friendly and affectionate; they had no quarrels, no rows, no words of bitterness, no malice; there were none of those things that are concomitant of cruelty or injury. *Why should he do it?* . . Members of the jury'—Birkett placed his hands upon his hips and faced them squarely—'it was surely the business of counsel for the Crown to put to the prisoner what the suggestion was. But no question, no word, no hint of any kind. Only complete and impenetrable silence.

'This case is simply riddled with doubt,' he continued. 'There is the morphine, for instance. Is it not a most astounding thing that there was morphine in the body, and —you heard the reply of Dr Lynch—it may have been a fatal dose; he was not prepared to say.

'Is it not an even more astounding thing that Mancini was not asked about it when he was in the box? What part does morphine play in the theory of the Crown? Where she got it, from whom, and why she took it—that is beyond my power to divine. But certainly no inference should be or can be drawn in that respect against the prisoner on trial.'

The morphine had never been more than a subordinate motif; an additional strand in the tangled skein of mystery. But the next blow was aimed at, and landed on, the centre of the target. 'It is the Crown's theory that Mancini killed the woman with that hammer—the hammer that was found weeks and months afterwards lying in the cellar of the flat where they had lived. Does this seem to you a convincing supposition? If he had really murdered the woman with that hammer, it would have been the simplest matter in the world for him to take it to the end of Brighton pier and drop it out of sight in the depths of the sea.'

Here was a strong appeal to ordinary sense. It is natural when reviewing the behaviour of another to imagine what, in his place, would have been one's own. That's what *I'd* have done if I'd been guilty—got rid of that hammer, I would, and no mistake; more than one juror, it is safe to surmise, found that his thoughts were being directed on those lines. And if that's what I'd have done, and what Mancini didn't do—why, doesn't that make his guilt less likely than before? . . .

Birkett passed to the scientific evidence, and again those who had given it were raked with deadly fire. 'Men may have names and reputations,' he observed, 'they may have experience, distinction and degrees, but all of them—high and low, famous and obscure, known and unknown—all men are human and all are fallible.' With the tailor's testimony now before the jury he stressed Dr Lynch's discomfiture afresh. 'We have the firm fact, clearly proved, that these garments, which we were informed with greatest emphasis had had blood deposited upon them from a distance, were neither worn by Mancini nor even in his possession until after Violette Kaye had died. Do you wonder,' Birkett slowly said, 'that I say: the Crown case is simply riddled with doubt?'

But if Mancini did not kill her, then how did she die?

It was not incumbent on the defence to provide hypotheses. The question, however, could not be absent from anybody's mind and could not be safely left without potential answer. Birkett therefore pressed hard now a theory of his own that he had adumbrated in his earlier speech. While asking the jury not to dismiss outright the possibility that Violette Kaye had fallen down the steps, he laid much greater stress upon 'a second view, because the evidence is very, very strong.' Did *someone else* kill that woman, if killed she was?

'Violette Kaye,' he said gravely, 'was a prostitute. That man'—with voice suddenly raised and arm suddenly outstretched he pointed at Mancini sitting in the dock—'that man lived upon her earnings, and I have no word to say in extenuation—none. But you must consider the world in which such people live and the dangers to which they are continually exposed.' He evoked the former ('the background from which these events have sprung') in a single striking sentence: 'We are dealing with a class of men who pay eightpence for a shirt and with women who pay a shilling for a place in which to sleep.' He evoked the latter by reference to the prisoner's testimony: 'Mancini has said that they went everywhere in fear. Isn't it reasonably probable that in that woman's life—an unhappy, a dreadful, an unspeakable life—blackmail may have played a considerable part?' Birkett linked this suggestion with a concrete piece of evidence that the court had heard on Monday and that most had since forgotten. Its reintroduction was admirably timed. 'Somewhere in this world,' he said, 'are the people whom Kerslake heard speaking in the flat when he went there on the 10th of May. The finding of this body was proclaimed from the housetops. Those who were in the flat that day—they had a tale to tell. But not a word; never a word.'

He had been speaking now for fifty-seven minutes—speaking without any note of any kind. His communion with the jury had thus been uninterrupted; it had grown more intense as every minute passed, and reached its highest pitch as he made his final effort.

'Defending counsel,' he declared, 'have a most solemn task, as my colleagues and myself know only too well. We have endeavoured, doubtless with many imperfections, to perform that task to the best of our ability. The ultimate responsibility—that rests upon you, and never let it be said, never let it be thought, that any word of mine shall seek to deter you from doing that which you feel to be your duty. But now that the whole of the case is laid before you, I think I am entitled to claim for this man a verdict of not guilty. And, members of the jury, in returning that verdict you will vindicate a principle of law—that people are not tried by newspapers, not tried by rumour, not tried by statements born of a love of notoriety, but tried by British juries, called to do justice and decide upon the evidence.' The great guns of his advocacy flashed and pounded. 'I ask you for, I appeal to you for, and I claim from you, a verdict of not guilty.' He stopped—and then his voice rang out in exhortation. 'Stand firm!'

32

They stood firm. Their discussion was prolonged—nearly two and a half hours—but when the jury at last returned to court they brought with them the verdict that set the prisoner free.

Mancini was half dazed. 'Not guilty, Mr Birkett; not guilty, Mr Birkett'—those were the only words at his immediate command when he attempted to signify his thanks. He was a sharp fellow, though, and under no illusion; none had known better how perilous was his plight, nor realised more keenly now his debt to his defender.

AFTERWORD

WHAT happens to the players in these tragic melodramas? What is the latter history, not only of the acquitted prisoners themselves, but also of those lesser figures caught up in the plot and temporarily floodlit in a blaze of notoriety? Where is Doris Saville? What became of the ship's cook? Did Dr Leach return to the routine of general practice, treating coughs and colds without a thought of chloroform? Did the chauffeurs and their wives settle down again to peaceful life in William Mews, where Mrs Barney and her lover were unremembered wraiths?

Few there are who know. Mercifully for them, these nine-day celebrities soon fade from public view, and are allowed to live and die in tranquil privacy. Even the accused, unless an exceptional and vivid character, declines to a mere case label as the years roll by.

Only the master advocates remain; the unsurpassable champions of defence. They are the bodyguards of human liberty; theirs is the acme and the miracle of art.

Printed in Great Britain
by Amazon